BETWEEN THE SHADOWS

Adrian O'Donnell

Copyright © 2021 Adrian O'Donnell

All rights reserved

The characters and events portrayed in this book are fictitious. Any similarity to real persons, living or dead, is coincidental and not intended by the author.

No part of this book may be reproduced, or stored in a retrieval system, or transmitted in any form or by any means, electronic, mechanical, photocopying, recording, or otherwise, without express written permission of the publisher.

Cover design by: thegreyghost www.fiverr.com

For my wife Jo and all my friends, in particular Jaye Taylor

CHAPTER ONE

The thud of a heavy fist crashed once more into the face of Stephen Byfield as a broken tooth fell onto the metal floor of the ship's engine room. Tied to a chair unable to move, he had no choice other than take the beating. Blood dripped down his once pristine white T-shirt and onto the black filthy floor. "I will ask you one more time Byfield, why are you working with British Intelligence? What use would they have for you? Tell me and this all stops now."

"I don't know what you are talking about, I'm here on holiday and I wish I could help you," Stephen replied as a stream of blood ran down his chin.

"Why would you come to Tunisia without your family?" The educated English accent seemed so out of place in the dark end of this foreboding port. Tunis had seemed a throwback to another era, one in which an accent such as this may have been common place but at this particular time, surrounded by container ships and danger, it stood out. Its owner remained in the shadows, unseen by Stephen.

"I just needed time away, that's all. I know nothing about what you are telling me," he repeated, his tone verging on desperation. Even as the words tumbled from his sore and bloody mouth, he could hear the high pitch signs coming from his own voice that a trained ear listened for. His lie was as clear as the tone floating from a lonely lighthouse crying out it's warning to drifting sailors. The heel of a dirty, oil-stained boot came from nowhere and crashed into the side of his jaw, knocking him sideways, down onto the stinking floor. A blanket of stars flashed around inside his head and the ropes bit into his wrists as he was hauled back into a seated position.

"Stephen, maybe I have got it all wrong, or then again maybe you are just giving me a pack of bullshit. You stay here and have a think and I will be back in a while. I am sure that my friends will take good care of you." The owner of the voice left the room.

Sitting in the gloom of this fuel-stinking hell hole was certainly not in the Byfield plan, a plan that in hindsight, could never have been as simple as when first explained. He had to fly over to Tunisia for a series of meetings in comfortable hotel rooms, meet local intelligence sources and then offer substantial amounts of foreign aid to a tribal arms dealer in the hope of sharing information. But the real prize would be having access to his hidden book of contacts, which was, according to Whitehall sources, 'The Holy Grail.' The stench of desperation behind the hunt for information had begun to stink out the oak clad government offices of Westminster. The very same scent which had led Stephen to Tunis.

He looked around, there had to be some options for getting out of here. Two men sat by the only obvious doorway leading out of the room, but restraints securing his wrists and a head that felt split in two prevented any heroics. Not that he would be in any condition to carry out an escape plan, particularly with an AK47 leaning against the wall next to the guy who nearly took his ear off with his boot. The stink of stale alcohol and tobacco that seemed to leak from every pore of his jailers invaded his nostrils and increased his feeling of nausea.

The English guy however, was a different entity. Perhaps early thirty's, he smelt freshly showered and the suit he wore was immaculately pressed. His shoes were obviously unused to the environment they found themselves in being highly polished, soft brown leather. Educated, toned and classy, he didn't belong here. He was certainly British intelligence, and his manner indicated the distinct feeling that Stephen was an expendable asset for Her Majesty. His lie had been exposed which left two options, tell the truth or die. In fact, if he told the truth he would still die, just hopefully a better death.

Thirty minutes passed, a distant chiming bell from the town clock tower seemed to give a running countdown to what was left of his life. A rap on the thick door brought both guards to their feet as the Englishman returned, this time holding a long devilish looking knife, the light glinting on the blade as he held it up theatrically.

"Mr Byfield, I guess by now you know that I know you are lying to me. Let me give you a starter and you can finish the story for me. You are working with a government team trying to uncover corruption in government offices." He stopped. "Right so far Stephen?" Stephen nodded his aching head.

"So, all I need to know is why you are here and what have you done with my little parcel?" He walked towards Stephen, stepping out of the shadow and showing his face, exposing its hidden evil. Byfield had miscalculated this character; his early Englishman abroad impression was wiped away by the sight of the cruel scar that crossed his face. A warrior, well-educated and classy for sure, but an absolute cold-hearted killer as well. A man who served his country fiercely, able to look an enemy fully in the eyes and smell their dying breath as he pressed the blade deep into his opponents exposed throat.

"Talk to me, tell me what I need to know."

"I honestly don't have any parcel," Stephen insisted shrugging his shoulders. "What happens next if I can't give you what I don't have? Can't you just let me leave? I will not tell anyone anything about what has happened here."

"My employers say no, I say perhaps, it really does depend on you. You see where we are going with this?" Without warning, the lights flickered before failing completely. Stephen heard the shuffle of the guard's feet trying to ready themselves for action before something eased past him, the flick of a jacket sleeve brushed his cheek and the smell of expensive aftershave cut through the putrid atmosphere before the door burst open. A flash light and the burst of flame from a gun barrel illuminated the room as cordite filled the atmosphere, catching the back of Stephen's throat. The initial crack of the automatic weapon ended, leaving his ears ringing but still straining for what was coming next. The lights flicked back on and a stocky figure stood in the doorway, eyes scouring the room. "Where is he?"

"I don't know, someone passed by me, over there somewhere," Stephen indicated to the back of the room with his head. The man sprang forward, barging past Stephen, nearly upending the chair as he hurried towards the back of the room. He stopped just as quickly, and bending down behind the chair he untied the ropes holding Stephen captive.

"He's gone, don't worry about him, just follow me and don't fuck up." The draft coming from the previously unseen door at the rear of the engine room was the only clue to where the Englishman had gone. They didn't follow but instead dashed up the metal stairs and into the chill of the Tunisian night. A black Range Rover parked in the darkness spun into life and glided to a halt beside them where Stephen received another order.

"In the back, head down and do not move." He climbed onto the leather back seat, laying down facing the rear of the driver's seat as the car sped off. The man spoke again. "We are taking you to the Embassy, say fuck all and don't look at us, understand?"

"Yep and thanks."

"Save it Mr Byfield, we aren't there yet."

After another few minutes of back street driving in almost total darkness, the car once more hit the main road, street lights illuminating the inside of the car with an eerie orange glow. Both men scanned the pavements on either side of the streets, looking for danger before bringing the car to a brisk halt. Stephen rolled forward almost slipping from the seat into the footwell behind the driver's seat. He composed himself and sat up, squinting in the bright lights to find they were in a pretty, open square in front of a magnificent white building. Balconies jutting out from the first three floors and light blue window shutters gave it a mediterranean feel from a hundred years ago. A blue arched door stood at the corner with a British Embassy sign on the wall beside it.

"Get out and ring on the bell, the rest is up to you. Goodbye Mr

Byfield."

He stepped out as the car sped off, not completely understanding what had happened or what was coming. His head thumped and the pain from his broken teeth was catching the night time chill. Ringing on the bell Stephen heard a distant echo of the chime. Shivering and immediately regretted taking in another large gulp of cool air, he looked down and was surprised by the covering of blood over his new shirt. His mind briefly flickered back to the brutal conflict he'd had with Martin Heard the serial killer, who had come within an inch of taking his life, and the Broods, a ferocious criminal gang who had come just as close to taking his family and reputation. All in all, the past two years had been hell and he felt a surge of desperation rush over him before the door swung open. So lost in his thoughts, he hadn't heard the key turn in the lock.

A short, slightly built man in his forties with thick black hair, stood in the light of an imposing hallway. He wore a crumpled suit that looked like it had been worn for too long and a blue tie, slightly offset, completed the image of a very tired consular official. Large paintings hung from the walls behind him, overseeing the proceedings as they would have done for the past hundred years, whilst the obligatory photograph of the Queen watched all below. "Mr Byfield?" he stood waiting for a response. Stephen nodded, unwilling to open his mouth again and expose his broken teeth to the air.

"You'd better come in, we have been expecting you. My name is Trevor Hinton, Embassy official. I am the duty official this evening, it has been a very long day so forgive my somewhat dishevelled appearance." The door closed behind them with a comforting clunk, the sound of safety.

"I will show you up to your room where we have clean clothes waiting for you. I have taken the liberty of calling in the doctor, although it looks like you may need a dentist as well. They haven't spared you any mercy, bloody savages." He showed Stephen into a small bedroom, possibly used for on-call staff. He couldn't help but wonder if this would have been the Embassy official's own room for the night. A small pile of clean clothes lay on the bed and a fresh white towel and shower gel were on the plain wooden chair. Everything looked government issue, a real contradiction to the elegance of the rest of the building.

He stripped off his dirty, blood-stained clothes, tossing them into the grey, steel bin sitting by the sink and glanced at himself in the mirror. Red eyes and a face caked in blood and dirt stared back at him as he inspected the insides of his mouth and saw the broken stumps where white teeth once stood. Carefully cleaning his remaining teeth, he waited while the shower warmed up before climbing into the cubicle. The hot water cascaded over his filthy hair and ran down his body, every cut crying out in protest. With the adrenaline dissipating, his body began to stiffen up and he could hardly raise his hands high enough to wash the soap from his hair. All he wanted to do was sleep but he felt that this wasn't going to be allowed to happen anytime soon. Dry blood and engine oil disappeared down the plug hole with the suds as he turned the shower off and dried himself. The radiators boomed in the room making it pleasantly warm and adding to his fatigue. A polite tap at the door was followed seconds later by a quizzical face popping around it. A white middle-aged man entered the room carrying a brown leather bag. Stephen guessed who he was.

"Hello Mr Byfield, I am the duty doctor," he introduced himself, staring at Stephen's battered face. "What's been going on with you? You look as though the other guy might have won the round. Lie down on the bed and let's have a look." After a thorough examination, the doctor closed his bag. "Seen worse. A couple of broken teeth and a nasty swelling to your cheek, your jaw will be stiff for a couple of weeks. The good news is nothing is broken. I am going to give you these pain killers and once back in the UK, you must see a dentist or infection will set in. I suggest you take a couple of tablets now because the guys downstairs need to chat to you about this evening's events. Don't eat anything too substantial as it will hurt your mouth, but you can have a little soup and maybe some soft food."

Stephen took a couple of the tablets as the doctor headed towards the bedroom door. He stopped, and turning around to Stephen said, "You may as well follow me, they are only going to come up and get you anyway."

They both walked down the tiled stairs and into the hallway where a door to the left was ajar with a light shining through the gap. The scent of food drifted across and made Stephen feel nauseous. The shock was kicking in and the last thing he needed was food. The doctor stopped outside the room and turned to him.

"I think that they are in there. Have a good evening, stay safe and give my love to Blighty on your return." They shook hands and Stephen walked through the open door. He stopped and looked around in awe as he found himself on a beautiful terrace where five white tables stood on a blue and white tiled floor. Ornate tiles of the same colour also covered every wall leading up to an elegantly painted ceiling. Three golden chandeliers hung down, illuminating the whole area in a warm glow, while white Greek pillars stood guard over a manicured lawn. The previous notion of cold air had evaporated as he realized it was cool, but not cold, a typical February evening in Tunis.

"Take a seat Stephen, we will be over in a minute." The voice caught him by surprise as it seemed to come from another room. He looked over as Trevor and another man of similar age walked through an interconnecting door. They joined Stephen at one of the white tables, each sitting on a wrought iron chair covered with a luxurious padded cushion.

"Can I get you a drink, tea, coffee or something stronger?" Trevor asked him. "Just a water please," Stephen replied and he slipped back through the door and returned with a small glass and a plastic water bottle.

"We have a little food prepared but firstly we need to complete some paperwork and fill in the details," Trevor continued. "You know it's not every day we deal with a senior Prison Governor turning up here after torture and a firefight. Bit strange don't you think?" Stephen looked at him.

"Who mentioned that I am a member of the Prison Service?"

Trevor moved in his seat a little awkwardly. His colleague tossed him a glance before interjecting.

"We know a lot about you Stephen, including why you are here. What we are unsure about is why you were taken captive and questioned. It doesn't make sense to me. You are a minor cog in the wheel, over here to ask a few questions. If the people who took you wanted you out of the way they would have killed you in the street. No, they wanted something from you." He sat studying Stephen for a short while before divulging some more information.

"The English guy who took you is known to us, we have followed him around the world. He is a member of a privately run security team and acts as a consultant to Security Services for any government where dirty tasks need doing. He is a deniable asset, as we say, and he doesn't make mistakes." Again, he stopped and stared at Stephen. "What did he want?"

"I don't know, he kept asking me about a parcel that he wanted. I don't have one. I don't know what he was talking about."

"I don't believe you Stephen, as I said he doesn't make mistakes. What is in the parcel?"

"Like I said, I don't have a parcel. Thanks for arranging the Calvary to get me out but I honestly have nothing to give you." Stephen took a cautious sip of his water, waiting for the pain to hit from his teeth. Thinking deeply about Stephens's response, the man looked out over the lawn, as if calculating the conversation against what he already knew. He shrugged and looked briefly at Trevor.

"No problem Mr Byfield, it is a dangerous world that you chose to enter, be cautious." He pushed his chair back with a harsh scrape and got up and left without a backward glance, leaving Stephen and Trevor together. They heard the familiar noise of the front door closing before absolute silence descended. "Who was that guy Trevor?"

"I am not at liberty to disclose that Mr Byfield. Can I interest you in some soup?"

CHAPTER TWO

H.M.P. Northway

The Governor, Mark Skinner, sat at his desk. He had worked for the prison service since leaving the Navy sixteen years before. More used to the Victorian local prisons in London, he decided to head north to try his hand at a new project, a brand-new state of the art prison. He felt that the government were demanding a far softer approach, one in which prisoners made the decisions which affected them. Tempted by the promise of a blank canvas and fresh beginnings, he took a promotion and waved goodbye to the city.

H.M.P. Northway sat in the middle of a large brown-field site just outside Manchester, another desperate solution from a struggling government who had long ago run out of ideas and prison places. Being tough on crime took its toll as those in charge had to be seen to address society's problems of rising violence. And this High Security prison, holding twelve hundred prisoners was seen as part of that solution. The other headache the British Government had inherited from twenty years at war, was the rising problems extremist prisoners could cause. The public feared an epidemic of I.S. fighters taking to the streets and they were not far from the truth.

Grabbing his notepad, Mark made his way across a large tarmacked area overlooked by cell windows and security cameras, as he headed to a small isolation unit sitting in the middle of the establishment, the classic prison within a prison. Security was extra tight here and no one could work within the confines of this unit without the express permission of the Director of

High Security Estate. Even then, the prison control room had to authenticate a reason for entry and it could be a royal pain in the ass if you were already late for a meeting. Having just experienced exactly this form of delay, Mark entered the meeting room.

"Sorry I am late everyone, let's get straight on with business. Top of the agenda is the visit next week from the Home Secretary, and Mr Sadiq's visit tomorrow afternoon. Can I please have an update about where we are with the discussions with the Home Sec's office?" Deputy Governor, Lisa Burton picked up her briefing notes.

"Thank you Mark. Susan Whitfield, Home Secretary, will be arriving at the prison in her official car at 14.00. She will have her own unarmed security staff with her at all times. All weapons normally carried will be left outside the prison in the car supervised by the driver. She will meet five selected prisoners from the unit who are taking part in a group work session with the Imam. She will then meet some unit staff before leaving the Prison at 16.00. We will have a Control and Restraint team available in the unit but out of sight in case of any dramas. I do not expect anything to go wrong as the prisoners chosen are near to release and are considered lower risk if that actually exists. Whitehall and the Met Police are responsible for security en route, we just have to get things right here and look after the publicity." She glanced down at her notes before continuing.

"All journalists are security cleared and will be briefed by our Head of Operations while outside the prison in the visitor's waiting room, all domestic visits are cancelled on that day. They will all go through enhanced security checks as they enter the prison as normal.

We'll have a police helicopter overhead and the normal no fly zone is in operation. Should we have an issue while in the unit, we have staff assigned to take the journalists directly to the gate. The Control and Restraint team along with her bodyguards will ensure that the Home Secretary is safe and removed from the prison once the press have been escorted away. The

Home Secretary does not want a lunch or buffet and needs to be back at Westminster for a debate at 20.00 regarding Brexit." She looked around the room at the management team, "Can anyone think of anything that I may have missed?"

"Sounds very thorough Lisa," Mark confirmed. "How about you Matt, where are we with tomorrow's visit?"

Matt Phillips was a young Governor on an accelerated promotion scheme. At thirty-two, he had taken on the responsibility for the running of the isolation unit. He had volunteered for the role after having extensive knowledge of Afghanistan and Iraq while serving as a Captain in the Rifles.

He left the Army feeling disillusioned after seeing two Afghan interpreters thrown out of Camp Bastion after an argument over money. They had helped the Regiment for six months and walked out on family ties in order to help the British. As a result of a petty squabble with a civilian manager they had been asked to leave. The following day both men were found bound, tortured and beheaded. They had been badly let down and it stuck in Captain Phillips' throat. He threw himself into learning as much about Islam as he could in the hope of making sense of the chaos he found himself in. He secretly donated two month's wages to the families of the dead men after inviting them into the base. Their dignity in the meeting struck a chord with him and he made the decision that the UK had no right to be at war with these peaceful people. He was invited to leave the Army after questioning the role he was asked to perform, and gladly accepted the offer of redundancy. Matt then thrust himself into Islam, converting to becoming a Muslim within a year of discharge. He also spoke at mosques about the horrors he had witnessed and the peace that his religion had given him. Within a few months he was approached by fellow Muslims expressing extremist views and Matt found himself drawn towards these thoughts and quickly became an active member.

When the idea of an isolation centre opening on his doorstep was raised in the local papers, the group were very quick to suggest that Matt should apply for a job inside the Prison Service. With the help of some senior prison service managers who also shared these views, they assisted him with the application process and once successfully enrolled onto the promotion scheme, they manipulated him into the unit. The fit was perfect for the upcoming operation. In truth he had become a ticking time bomb for the Government.

Matt looked up at Mark. "The plan for the Home Sec sounds really good and I will make sure that my guys are all playing ball. It should be a great visit and good publicity for the unit and for the Home Secretary. Mr Sadiq's visit is still as we planned with no issues at all."

"Fantastic! Okay everyone, we will get together again on Monday just to run through things once more and I will chat to the five prisoners as well, Matt. Let them know please."

"No probs."

Mark packed his things up, he was proud of the way the unit had been set up. After year of chaos in the prison service and the thought that Muslim gangs were taking control over many prisons, with poison being preached to vulnerable people in order to convert them to extremist thinking, the Justice Secretary had taken the brave decision to make separate units for the most disruptive extremist prisoners. The units were to hold twenty-eight prisoners, working closely with religious leaders, probation and psychologists in the hope of changing behaviour. It was one answer to the issue but others however, thought that these places encouraged extremist views. What was unknown to Mark and most others was that a small group of influential people had concocted the very idea of these units with the sole intention of the promotion of violence and terror.

Blissfully unaware of the danger in his own camp, Mark left the unit to visit the other areas of the prison for his daily inspection. Unlike the isolation unit, this brand-new dream was quickly descending into a nightmare. Opened one year before, it had rapidly lost the promise of hand-picking prisoners to take part in constructive group work. Prison cells with phones and computers installed along with flat screen televisions, were supposed to encourage prisoners to behave or risk losing their luxuries. Staff would have to knock on cell doors before being invited to enter and prisoners were to be called 'Mister' as a sign of respect.

This brave new world lasted around four months before becoming openly hostile with prisoners hating staff, staff hating prisoners, and everyone hating the management. The phones were abused and organised crime was conducted from within the prison walls with prisoners becoming rich by arranging large shipments of drugs on a regular basis. Corrupt members of staff living and mixing with these same people outside the prison quickly found wealth from smuggling contraband into their place of work. Staff had lost control and due to the shortage of numbers, had become punch bags for prisoners who knew that there were no repercussions and management who were looking for someone to blame. It was a bubbling pot of hatred that simmered away from the public eye.

Every prison in the country had emptied their segregation blocks of the most disruptive prisoners, and these were all sent to Northway. Mark mused on these issues as he walked. At least in the London prisons they still had a number of staff with experience of how a prison should work. The staff here had no clue and prisoners ruled every wing, it was a mess and no one cared so long as the prisoners were happy.

That very evening, a young lad from Liverpool was admitted back into custody. He had only been released two days before and he had been given an offer too good to miss, a thousand pounds into his bank and the promise that his family home would not be burnt to the ground. His instructions were to fill his stomach with packages of heroin and breach his licence so that he would come back into Northway. He sat on the wooden bench trying to ignore the stares from those around him. All he had to do was get through reception, get the drugs out of his aching gut and do the twenty-eight days before gaining release again.

"You packed up scouse?" the prisoner sitting next to him

demanded.

"No man, just fucked up with probation, bitch didn't give me a chance. Missed an appointment and straight back." The fact that he had thrown her computer screen through the window and was arrested the same day wasn't mentioned.

"Bollocks, you are packed with gear you cunt. You better cut me in."

"Sweet mate. Drop by later." He didn't want to draw any attention and to agree was the easy way out.

"Flynn!" That was music to his ears, he jumped up and swaggered through the recently unlocked door into reception. "Fuck me Flynn, back already?" the officer looked at him, shaking his head.

"Love it boss. Can I go back onto House Block 2?"

"I think your old cell is still empty," the officer scanned his computer, "yeah it is. Grab your stuff, you can go straight up there." Fifteen minutes later, David Flynn was sitting on the same bed which he had left barely forty-eight hours earlier.

House Block 2 held one hundred and fifty prisoners. This evening there were only three members of staff on duty and every prisoner was unlocked. All three staff sat in the office, it was much easier for them as they saw nothing and didn't get in the way of anything the prisoners wanted to do. In return the prisoners promised staff an easy time, and at 21.00 they would all return to their cells without any issue. In truth, the wing was drug filled and a horrendous experience for some prisoners who got bullied to within an inch of their lives.

The Office door opened. James - known to all as Jimmy - Sullivan stood at six feet four, a travelling man who dined out on the fact that he was Tyson Fury's sparring partner, a tough bare-knuckle fighter who feared no one.

"Boss." All three staff looked up. "Stay in the office for the next thirty minutes, you understand me?" The officers knew the score as one replied, "Yeah Jimmy, don't cause us a problem though." He turned and walked towards David Flynn's cell, en route calling over another three prisoners to join him. Flynn was expecting a visit tonight, just not this type of welcome committee. His door was pushed open with Jimmy blocking the view outside.

"Where are my drugs you little scouse cunt? If there is even half a gram missing, I am going to cut you into little bits." With that, the other three men piled in and grabbed Flynn, pulling down his track suit bottoms and tearing his prison boxer shorts off.

"Ey Ey lads, easy!" Flynn protested. "I've swallowed, they aren't up my arse for fucks sake!" Throwing him down onto the bed, they grabbed a plastic spoon and rammed it straight into his anus, digging around, searching for drug packages.

"I've swallowed Jimmy; there's nowt up my arse," he continued to insist, but the attack didn't stop. A hand was forced up as far as it could go, the pain excruciating, before the shit and blood was wiped onto the back of his shirt. Now sobbing with pain, he curled up onto his bed trying to protect himself as the blood flowed down the back of his legs. Jimmy stepped back into the cell. "Hold the bitch down," he ordered. They grabbed his arms and forced him into a kneeling position. Pulling his shorts down, Jimmy parted the bleeding arse cheeks and raped him before pulling his shorts back up.

"You've got twenty-four hours to get that package to me bitch. Don't make me come back for you again." He turned around and walked out. Still held down by two of the men Flynn realised that the third had filmed the entire scene on a phone.

"One fucking word Scouse and everyone out there will see you getting your arse fucked, you want that to happen?"

"Course I don't, you bastards, fuck off and I'll get your package for you." They laughed as they left the cell, shouting, "You've just got arse-fucked for a grand!" Left alone he climbed painfully under his sheets, *fucking bastards* he sobbed to himself.

The sun shone through Flynn's window waking him from a restless sleep, he was still in agony as he tried to walk to the toilet but the pain was too great. He had less than twelve hours to get these drugs from his stomach. He limped down to the queue of prisoners waiting to see the nurse.

"I can't go to the toilet miss," he told her when his turn came. "I need something to help me crap."

"I will put you down for the doctor, he will see you tomorrow."

"I need to shit today Miss, my stomach is killing me."

"Tomorrow," she insisted, "I can't give you anything without a prescription."

"Fucking bitch," he spat in the nurse's face. She pushed the alarm bell and staff came running from everywhere before Jimmy appeared and stepped in.

"What's going on? No one is touching my boy. Call all the staff off and I will deal with it." A member of staff stood waving others away from the scene.

"Okay everyone, it's all dealt with." The wing manager cancelled the alarm bell and sent the staff away. He turned to the nurse, "Give him what he needs, I don't want trouble." Feeling absolutely alone, she handed over the medication and walked away from the incident. Jimmy turned to the manager. "There's a good boy. Now go back and read your paper."

From the landing above, the six Muslim prisoners watched and waited. In one week they would be the ones running this jail.

CHAPTER THREE

Sitting in a meeting room in central London, three men discussed and exchanged progress from establishments around the country. Mr Uden, Deputy Director of the National Security Group, Mr Sadiq, Executive Director of Public Service Prisons and Mr Khan, Governor of Wood Hill Prison, Milton Keynes. Imran Uden spoke first, and clicking the mouse on his laptop, he displayed a number of graphs.

"Okay, firstly as you can see, our profit margin for the movement of items into and out of the prison estate is looking very healthy. We have five high security establishments with unlimited access to class A and class B drugs and steroid shipments. The cancellation of all drug testing within the high security setting has masked the problems created and the media will be, and will remain to be, unaware. After we have taken into account our costs, we are showing a return of 1.5 million," he looked at the other two, "each."

"Each?" Mr Sadiq questioned. "That is unreal."

"The quantities going into our establishments are unreal," Uden explained, "and we have a steady market place. However, in Milton Keynes we are also flooding the local areas through prisoners working on outside projects."

"Brilliant work," added Amir Sadiq. "Anything else to report from the security front? We must move quickly as I am expected at Northway this afternoon."

"We also have access to a number of weapons intended for operations still in the planning, we must include specific weapon training within the isolation units. When we move, we need to hit the ground running," Uden concluded his report. Amir Sadiq took over the briefing.

"Okay, from the public prison front I am delighted that we

are operating so well with the new units almost fully delivered. I am visiting the isolation unit at Northway to host some questions and answers with selected staff, followed by a private meeting with the prisoners on the unit. This will be very beneficial to all. The units in Woodhill and Kent will be opened later this year and we have invited the Home Secretary to officially open Northway. We have a unique opportunity provided for us and our cooperation with our Muslim brothers will make us both rich and powerful. Once the work is complete, we will disappear from this stinking cesspit of a country." He turned to Mr Khan.

"How is your unit coming along Mo?"

"It is progressing nicely, we have selected the staffing groups and the management is in place. I am pleased to report that we have some sympathetic people on board already. We are, as we speak, selecting the candidates for the unit. We will only hold twelve prisoners in the unit so not as large as the Northway one which I understand is housing twenty-eight?"

"That's correct Mo," Sadiq confirmed. "We need to formulate our training plan for the units as it is imperative that all of our soldiers operate as one in order for us to succeed."

As the meeting drew to a close, the three men left the room and melted back into the London traffic. Amir Sadiq climbed into the back of his chauffeur driven car and spent the journey reading his official papers as they headed towards the newly built Northway.

Arriving at the gate, he took a deep breath. He hated brand new prisons. The militant tendencies established in the London prisons during the past few decades were history, however all the staff here were new and inexperienced. They were keen, but their hands were tied with the new Prison Service Policy of appeasement. The down side was that old staff were lazy but new, fresh eyes were more likely to see suspicious activity and uncover a plot.

The Governor bounded out and shook Sadiq's hand. He detested this, hated the feel of the sweaty white flesh grasping his own hand. He could tolerate it, only because he knew that in the next few days it would all come to an end. An explosive end that would shake the Prison Service to its stinking white roots.

"Hello Mr Skinner, thank you for your time today. I need to return to London sooner than I thought so I wondered if I could shorten the meeting with staff before I assess the unit?"

"No problem Mr Sadiq, we can do thirty minutes with the staff and I have arranged a meeting with the prisoners requested. Are you sure that you don't want staff present in the meeting room?"

"No, they can stay outside. I need to hear what is really going on and the men will only tell me the truth if they think that staff will not be vindictive. Let's get this started, shall we?" He followed the Governor into his boardroom. A number of staff were sitting at the rectangular table, a mix of races, ages and experience and it looked like a promising group. The time flew past, he had enjoyed the questions asked and staff seemed to have bought into these dedicated units. The fools believed that they could make a difference and in truth they would be making a big difference, just not in the manner in which they anticipated. He drew the meeting to a close and turned to Mark Skinner.

"Right, I need to get to the isolation unit Governor, would someone be so kind as to show me the way?" Sadiq passed through the security process to enter the unit and was quickly shown into a small classroom. The atmosphere was heavy with twelve sweaty bodies all sitting on blue plastic school chairs, surrounded by flip chart paper stuck to walls promising confidentiality, honesty and all the other bullshit that went into pre-course agreements composed by psychologists. The young officer who had accompanied him to the unit stopped at the door. "Mr Sadiq, I understand you wish to interview the group alone so I will be outside if you need me." Sadiq gave him a brief smile. "Thank you very much, I'm sure that I will be fine." The door closed and they had peace. He took his jacket off and placed it on the back of his chair before looking around at the faces and smiling as he addressed them.

"Well done my brothers, our plans are coming together but we still have work to do. We are at war and there will be casualties along the way but we will crush these people. Show me what you have learnt." A large prisoner stood and spoke directly to Sadiq.

"We have studied the plans for this prison and we have memorised the staffing routines. We have the weapons and could take this place whenever and however we want to. I was due for release in four weeks' time but I have my targets, I have my orders, I have the weapons and I have the training. At the right time you will see what we are capable of."

"Excellent, and the rest of you?" A much smaller, older Indian man spoke next.

"The training is of a good standard and the links to the Pakistan training facilities are fully in place. On a local level, we are able to control large areas of the prison from this unit and almost everything is in our hands but we need the staff to stop searching our cells. It is getting to an important time where an officer may get lucky and uncover a vital part of the plan. Sadiq nodded and made a note.

"Okay, I will deal with that as nothing must happen before the visit, we cannot put that plan in jeopardy. Our friends outside are testing our resources and abilities, it is imperative we get this one right and after that, we can progress to our next goal. That will not happen in Northway, but you must be trained as two of you will be moving to London later this year and you must be ready." The group nodded. "Anything else that we need to take care of?" The large prisoner replied.

"Nothing at all Mr Sadiq, just make sure that you are also ready." Sadiq stood and placed his jacket back on.

"I have been ready for years, I have made my way through this vile organisation for this ultimate sacrifice so I am prepared, you can be assured of that." He knocked on the door and the same young officer escorted him to the gate. Sadiq kept his face expressionless as thoughts of what this guileless young man would face before the end of next week passed through his mind, along with the irony of the fact he would be murdered and beheaded in the same classroom that he had just been protecting.

CHAPTER FOUR

The 15.50 from Tunis touched down at Heathrow and Stephen was exhausted after hardly any sleep at the Embassy. He was still wearing the clothes given to him by Trevor and they were starting to have a life of their own because, for all of the organisation that goes into running a foreign embassy, they couldn't find any deodorant. He passed through customs and was greeted by a miserable looking woman holding a sign stating that she was there to meet Stephen Byfield. It looked as though it had been written in a hurry he thought as he approached her.

"Hi, I am Stephen Byfield, where are we going to?"

"Whitehall sir. That's all I know I am afraid."

"Sounds about right."

"Do you have any bags sir?"

"No, I'm travelling light today." He followed her out of the terminal, stopping by the pay machine as she fumbled around in her bag looking for a bank card. Mumbling to herself she tapped in her number and took the ticket before she led him on a brisk walk to the waiting car.

"You don't look as though you want to be here," Stephen observed, making idle chat to cut through the silence.

"No, I was supposed to be picking my son up from school but apparently there was no one else in the office able to come and get you and the taxi companies were busy with school runs." Stephen immediately felt guilty and apologized.

"Oh, I am sorry, I hope you managed to make arrangements?" There was no answer, just the type of silence that told him to shut up and continue the journey in peace. Nosing out into traffic, the car headed towards central London before pulling up in Whitehall where she produced a pass to a waiting policeman and drove him into a courtyard.

"Thanks for the lift," he said to the now disappearing car and entering the building, he showed his identification before walking through the body scanner. He looked across to the reception area where he recognised the familiar face of the beautiful Irish lady sitting tapping away at the computer. Although he had visited a number of times, he realised he still didn't know her name as she looked up and smiled before standing to welcome him.

"Good afternoon Mr Byfield, do you have an appointment?"

"Yes, I am expected, shall I take myself up today?" She nodded, "Yes, I am sure you can find it by yourself, have a good meeting."

He walked to the lift and pushed the button for the second floor, his mind still trying to make sense of the whole trip, his body still aching from the beating and his teeth reminding him of the dentist visit still awaiting him. The lift jolted to a stop before the steel door slid open and he exited, turning left and walking along the hallway to room twelve. The door was open and a man was working at the imposing desk. Knocking, he waited to be acknowledged as James Childs, British Security Services and former Special Forces looked up and waved him in.

"Come in and close the door Stephen. Take a seat," he invited, pointing to one in front of his desk.

Slumping back into the cosy leather chair Stephen relaxed, suddenly feeling safe, as though the horrors of Tunis were a world away from his own civilised country. The stress of the last twenty-four hours swept over him in a rush of fatigue as Childs informed him as to why he was there.

"Thanks for coming in Stephen, I know that you must want to be at home right now, but we do, however, have to make some sense of what has happened. Take your time and run through the events." Stephen explained everything in detail, the interviews, the ambush and the rescue. James seemed almost accepting that these things were a normal process. However, when describing the meeting with the man in the British Embassy, a different atmosphere crept into the room as Childs began to quiz him.

"What was his name?"

"He didn't say."

"Can you describe him to me?"

"A bit non-descript to be honest, sorry I didn't really take it all in. I suppose he was in his forties, in good shape, was definitely in charge, around five foot ten, well dressed, dark hair, nothing much more to say. The embassy guy Trevor didn't want me to know his name I seem to recall." Childs looked thoughtful.

"Okay, I am aware of Trevor, but don't know the other man which is a worry given the questions he has asked you. Stay alert Stephen, I fear we may have rattled some cages. In the meantime, I have taken the liberty of arranging for a dentist to sort your teeth out before you go home and scare the family." He handed over a card with the appointment details. "See him immediately, then go home, a car will be waiting outside. Do not discuss anything with anyone. I will need to meet you here again tomorrow at noon, is that okay?" Stephen nodded as he examined the card before leaving the office, heading for his much needed dental appointment.

James continued to work at his desk for another ten minutes before he heard another knock on the oak door. He looked up and smiled. "Come in Ernie, take the weight off your feet."

Ernie Stocken, twenty-eight-year-old former SAS soldier, sat in the same chair that Stephen had just vacated. He looked quizzically at James.

"So, what's the deal? You have got me bang to rights on arms dealing but you don't have me arrested. You fly me out to Tunis to follow a guy who knows precisely fuck all about working covertly and then I have to save his arse and babysit him back to the embassy. Now you want me in London. What the fuck is going on?"

"Ernie, if we turned you over to the law you would be serving thirty years in jail right now. We are facing one of the biggest potential terror attacks on British soil since 1066 and we need you on the right side. You have made your money, keep that. Help us and you will have full immunity from prosecution." He handed over a typed Government letter which Ernie studied.

"No jail time, life of luxury and just a few weeks of work is what we're offering." He gave Ernie a few minutes to read it through.

"Okay, deal, no problem. What's the plan?" Childs handed an envelope over the desk, Ernie stood to take it and opening it, read the contents before tossing it back.

"So, they are my opening instructions, just so that you can get out of the shit that you have created? Just to clarify, my get out of jail free card applies to this as well?" Childs nodded, "Just don't get caught. Get this little job done first and we can meet up next week to discuss our future plans."

Beverly McCullock sat in the Belfast bar she had used for most of her life, the one which her uncle introduced her to when she was fifteen years old as he conducted IRA business without the landlord's knowledge. McEnaneys sat on the Glen Road, its old pub style exterior hiding the fact that this was an excellent place to drop into, good food, great beer and a real Belfast atmosphere. The fact that decades of bombings and shootings had been authorised from the brown leather bench seats sitting below a stunning old wood ceiling was not the fault of the owners, it was just business done quietly and out of sight.

She laughed as another joke spilled out of the group of seven people, three of Beverley's most loyal female friends who had grown up in the same area as she had, and three of her uncle's old friends, still plying the same business of terror. A young barman in his early twenties came to the table with a large tray and cleared the numerous empty Guinness glasses. "Same again ladies?"

"Go on then Dominic, bring 'em over, be a darling." Beverley could charm the birds from the trees when she wanted, and she wanted to now as she passed a roll of ten-pound notes over to him.

"Keep them coming and tell me when you need more," she instructed. He nodded and headed back behind the bar. Today was a slow day and apart from this crowd, there were only three other people in the bar sitting on the far tables, studying the horse racing form over a few whiskeys before wasting their unemployment money on the 3.50 at Newbury.

The next round of drinks arrived and the empty glasses started to reform. The door swung open but nobody seemed to notice apart from Dominic, who swiftly headed into the back room and silently locked the door. Three men walked in wearing hoods, the first man carrying a shotgun across his chest and the other two pointing pistols towards the occupied table at the far end.

One of the men on Beverly's table saw what was happening first and stood, throwing his half full glass straight at the man with the shotgun. He was met with a blast from the weapon and slumped back onto the table, knocked the drinks onto the floor before rolling over with his feet on the seat and his head under the table. He gasped, blowing blood from his mouth, and looked up almost pitifully at the others before closing his eyes for the last time.

A swift burst of pistol fire cut down the other two men before they could fully stand up, the frosted window behind them shattering onto the busy street outside. They both thudded back into the seat before dropping onto the floor. One climbed back onto his knees trying to pull out a pistol from his hidden holster but the shotgun destroyed his chest in an instant and he died still unable to produce his own weapon.

Beverly twisted her head to find an escape route just at the wrong time as a bullet caught her in the right ear exiting her head from the left eye, her cheek bone exploding onto the three friends now cowering under the table. She was dead before her body slumped back into the seat, the smell of cordite drifting across the bar as the gamblers ran for the exit.

Dominic reappeared holding a baseball bat, a futile gesture

but he realised that if he let these people leave the bar without a fight, he was a dead man anyway. He rushed towards them screaming, and as the first shot hit him in the right shoulder spinning him around exposing his back, the shotgun exploded severing his spine and sending him gasping onto the floor. He lay there for what seemed minutes, the pain he had felt from the first shot had gone, replaced by a numb sensation spreading throughout his body. Trying to get back to his feet, he flopped hopelessly back into his own pool of blood, a pistol appearing in his eye line. "Quick or slow son?" The back of his head exploded with the exit wound of the bullet before he could answer.

The three remaining women, appearing from under the table covered in blood, brain, Guinness and broken glass, looked around the bar before standing defiantly in front of the gunmen. One looked straight at them, fury in her eyes "Don't get too comfy, wherever you fuckers try to hide, we will be coming to find you." The two men with the pistols held them out and fired, only to hear two clicks from the empty magazines. "You lucky bitches!" one muttered before turning away. The door swung shut as the men left, a scene of devastation remaining as distant police sirens wailed. The three girls stood for a moment looking at each other in disbelief before the one who had threatened the men headed for the door.

"Come on ladies, it's time we left," and stepping over the bodies of the dead, they never gave a second glance back into the bar. Cut from the same granite as Beverly Mc Cullock, they had one thing and one thing only on their minds - vengeance.

The phone in James Childs' pocket vibrated as he left Westminster tube station, he didn't speak but listened to the voice on the other end.

"You can get rid of the envelope on your desk, I have delivered the message in person."

CHAPTER FIVE

Susan Whitfield arrived at the main gates of Northway prison. This visit was a longstanding commitment, but in truth had come at a terrible time for a government torn apart by Brexit negotiations. The house had sat until late the previous evening and she was still exhausted by the ongoing cabinet meetings that seemed to last for hours without any real productivity.

The opening of the isolation unit was, however, a distraction and fitted in with the country's feeling towards terror suspects and returning ISIS fighters. The press coverage would be a vote winner should a snap election be called, plus she had her eyes on the top job.

The Deputy Governor waited patiently in the gate area while the security checks were carried out on the government team. She held out a hand. "Home Secretary, I am Lisa Burton the Deputy Governor. I will be your host today so any questions that you may have, or places you may want to visit, please let me know. I understand that you are on a tight deadline today so shall we get on with it?"

"Excellent idea Lisa, will the Governor be joining us?"

"He has asked if he can catch up with us in the isolation unit as he is on a conference call at the moment with the Justice Secretary. He will be free in around ten minutes and sends his apologies in the meantime." She led Susan Whitfield away from the reception area and towards the isolation unit, explaining along the way, who they would meet when they got there. Susan wanted to ensure she got good publicity from the visit as she questioned the deputy governor.

"What are the plans for the press? I understand we have extensive media coverage of the visit."

"They are already in place in the unit and we have arranged a short press conference before you leave. They will broadcast this tonight I believe," Lisa reassured her. The team walked briskly across the open area towards the isolation unit. The smell of fresh paint stuck in the nostrils as they approached the single-story building surrounded by two high wire fences topped with razor wire, and a fifteen-foot wall inside this perimeter area with an anti-climb device attached to the top. It was an imposing sight even to the trained staff who worked there. A single sign stood by the first gate announcing 'Authorised Access Only.' Matt Phillips stood in between the two gates separating the wire fences and holding out his hand, he introduced himself to the Home Secretary as the Governor in charge of this specialist unit.

Once inside, the buzz of anticipation grew and the hum of whispered conversations between media teams was incessant as the harsh lighting systems were set up, and on cue, the cameras rolled. Susan Whitfield, without pause, entered another mode of working as years of media training kicked in, moving around effortlessly, always with a sound bite. Through the thick glass walls of a classroom, five men sat looking at the Imam as he ran through some preset work, all seeming very engaged in the process. Matt Phillips tapped gently on the door and spoke quietly to the Imam, he nodded and all five faces looked up in anticipation of seeing their visitor. She walked silently into the classroom with Matt and a young officer who worked on the unit, he smiled and nodded at the men who seemed to have a good relationship with him.

There was a very peaceful atmosphere throughout the unit, the sort that can't help but put you at ease and as Susan Whitfield addressed the men, they hung on every word she said with cameras rolling from the open door and through the classroom window. She ended her talk with an acknowledgement of the hard work and dedication from staff and prisoners alike, all text book stuff which the viewers on TV this evening would love and know that all the boxes had been ticked, showing her to be hard on crime and hard on extremists, a true vote winner.

Matt Phillips then brushed past her, knocking her onto her heels. His manner seemed a little rude and she made a mental note to speak with the Governor whenever he appeared. A thump behind made her jump and although controlling herself in front of the cameras, she looked around to see the classroom door had been closed and locked with Matt standing in front of it staring directly at her.

The prisoners stood in unison and pushed a heavy bookcase that they had insisted be provided to the room, directly in front of the door, ensuring she was trapped. The glare of lights and cameras filled the room from the long window as the area outside bustled with media, and staff seemed to explode into activity. Frantic calls on the prison radio net were screeching out as panic took over and wide, staring, disbelieving eyes looked on. A host of mouths opened and closed and although Susan Whitfield couldn't hear a word they were saying through the thick glass, she felt the panic grow inside and suddenly realised the predicament she found herself in.

A large prisoner jumped onto a table, and punching through a roof panel into the space above, produced a long deadly looking sword. The other four prisoners grabbed her and tied her hands and feet before placing her on a chair in the middle of the room. The muscular man pushed her head down and rested the sword on the back of her neck. She tried to speak but no words came out. A gag was forced harshly into her mouth to prevent any pleading for mercy.

Then silence, as anticipation spilled into every corner of the unit. Matt Phillips and the Imam moved to the window. They were unsmiling and focused. Matt spoke, slowly but loudly enough to be heard through the thick glass.

"This Government has overseen the killing of thousands of our Muslim people around the world, illegal acts by this Government and its allies. They have ensured that our men, women and children have been slaughtered without justification. When we respond with our own actions, we are deemed terrorists and placed in cages such as these. But we are soldiers and we will fight to the death to destroy your immoral beliefs." He let these words sink in while looking at the audience in front of him before continuing.

"Today we are striking back at the heart of Government and you will watch our strength." From within the class room a blur of movement caught his eye stopping his speech. The young officer, Darren Pollard had drawn his baton and had struck one of the prisoners across the head, the prisoner falling onto the floor at the feet of Susan Whitfield. Moving to the door, Darren tried to push the bookcase out of the way as he fumbled for his keys but it was too heavy to move on his own and he turned, looking for help. A swish of the sword blade filled the air and the blood splatters hit the wall and ceiling as Darren's head rolled under a table and his body crumpled onto the floor where he had stood. Susan Whitfield sat in stupefied horror as the bloodied blade was wiped clean on her white cotton jacket. Matt Phillips turned back towards the disbelieving faces through the glass, "Okay, that was not planned, but unavoidable. It is a shame, I liked him." He sighed but continued.

"If you don't want the Home Secretary to suffer the same fate, we have a simple request. Release every prisoner presently held in Isolation Units around the country and return them to Afghanistan. Once they are in place and safe, I will release the hostage." He looked down at the dead officer.

"I will be the last person to leave and I will bring her with me, dead or alive." With that, Phillips took a seat next to the now sobbing Home Secretary.

The Governor, Mark Skinner's phone rang again in the command suite. He had been en route to the unit when he heard the commotion on the radio net. He now sat with the Chief Inspector of Lancashire Police and the Senior Tactical Support Advisor from the prison service. This was a doomsday scenario. There was another call on the radio.

"Hello Mike Two Papa Oscar, urgent message." This was a call from a member of staff notifying him that something else was going wrong. "We have lost control of Houseblocks one and two. There are large numbers of prisoners rioting and causing damage." There was a brief silence before it was followed with, "We are withdrawing from the scene."

Houseblock Two was in chaos. The staff retreated from the unit and had moved to a secure area, the staff from Houseblock One doing the same. The southern end of the prison was effectively out of control and three hundred prisoners were loose and able to do as they pleased. The Muslim contingent were directing operations, this had been months in the planning and was designed to divert staff from the hostage area. It had started well, however a quick-thinking staff member had prevented a full-scale riot by securing corridor gates along the route preventing other areas from being overrun by the rioters.

Prisoner Jimmy Sullivan sat in his cell listening to the volcanic noise escalating around the building. For him, this was the worst news he could have heard as it risked interrupting his own drugs business, along with the free ride he was having on the wing. He left his cell and looking along the landing, shouted out to a man who was in the process of throwing a screaming prisoner over the railings.

"Jon, put him down, we need to get a fucking grip of this. Get the boys together and get them in here quick." He went back into his cell and tossed his mattress up against the wall exposing a large metal bar. He tucked this into his waistband while he paced the floor. A short time later, ten prisoners crushed into the cell, with Jimmy standing on the bed like Montgomery addressing the troops in Africa.

"These cunts are fucking up our little business so we need to shut them down now. Let's get out there and show them who's boss." Tumbling out of the cell they raced down to the bottom landing where Jimmy stood in the staff office, staff long gone, looking around him at the pandemonium. Walking towards a large man trying to kick in an office door, he drew the bar out and caved his head in. The man dropped unmoving. He looked around expecting a response but there were too many people involved and his action had gone unnoticed.

"Let them have it boys," he shouted to his own gang and in they waded, fists and boots smashing bones and teeth until eventually silence descended. His men stood, panting with their efforts and staring at Jimmy as he announced that Houseblock Two was back under control.

"Now fuck off back to your cells and shut your doors. Anyone got a problem with that?" he demanded to the rapidly dispersing rioters. A flurry of activity and door slamming suggested not. One of his boys soon returned.

"The Muslim guys are missing, about ten of them." Jimmy raised his iron bar again signalling to his men. "Let's go find the cunts, I want this over." The men left Houseblock Two and headed over to Houseblock One. Jimmy turned around and saw the staff watching from a safe area. He grinned at them and shouted, "Oy Oy, I'm winning your prison back for you, join in when you feel like it." He gathered the others together and went into the second riot.

The Governor was was in the middle of a briefing from the police in regard to rescue attempts and the only solution which they seemed to keep returning too was an explosive entry. The Home Secretary was at risk of death and all they could do was watch. The Chief Constable putting down his radio announced, "I have handed over the incident to the military, Special Forces are at the front gate." Five minutes later his phone rang, it was a man calling himself Bronze One, the commander of the SF intervention team. Mark listened to a briefing from the Isolation Unit. He said nothing at first before instructing, "Wait for me to get clearance; I will speak to you once I have it. Good luck." Hanging up the phone he said to a full command suite, "Fingers firmly crossed."

Jimmy and his team moved onto the first landing of the Houseblock. It seemed to be a little more chaotic than Houseblock Two with a large Indian guy from Jimmy's wing standing on the pool table and the remaining nine Muslims listening to him commanding dozens of prisoners to cause damage.

Racing in, Jimmy smashed the guys knees away with the bar and he collapsed screaming onto the floor, begging for no more.

"Fuck you. You are going to get plenty unless you call your boys off," Jimmy promised.

"I can't, I am under orders." Jimmy kicked him in the mouth knocking out several teeth, "Now you are under my fucking orders." Staggering back onto the pool table, he dragged his shattered left knee into position. The pain was intense as he spoke through his remaining gritted teeth.

"Okay brothers, enough. Go back, we have done our job." He fell back crying out with the pain. The Muslim gang seeing that the fight was over threw their weapons to one side, before retreating back to the remains of their own wing. The thump of cell doors closing marked the end of the trouble and the sight of Jimmy in full flight was enough to persuade any others wanting a fight to down tools and return to their cells. Hoisting himself onto the bars of the gate, Jimmy shouted down to the waiting staff.

"All yours again boys," and the sound of his laughter echoed down the corridor as he made his way back to the comfort of his cell.

Susan Whitfield sat on her chair, head bowed. She was a strong woman and anger had taken over her fear. Anger that her security had allowed this to happen, anger that she knew the cameras had captured the moment, anger with the prison, but more than anything anger with herself. Her security team had advised her against the visit, Phillips and the Imam had betrayed their country, she had indirectly caused the death of a young officer and now she would face the same fate, all because she had craved a good publicity opportunity. There had been a threat sent to the Security Services that a prominent cabinet minister was targeted for assignation. The signs were clear but ignored as she had thought that there were political points to be won. She had considered that it was worth the risk but now she would leave a husband and two teenage sons behind. Silently, she prayed.

An eerie calm had descended over the unit, the media had been moved out of the establishment, along with all nonessential people and the only talk was conducted between prison service hostage negotiators and Phillips. It was a bizarre situation for the staff involved to be negotiating with one of their own Governors. The other hostage takers were losing patience, openly questioning Phillips and the Imam about their release to Afghanistan and the atmosphere was starting to ramp up further. A deadline was set by the man with the sword, one hour and their hostage would get hurt. Matt looked around the scene, aware that it was beginning to fall to pieces with the prisoners questioning his authority and no plans in place for negotiation. His head started to spin with the stress.

Another man entered the unit dressed in casual clothing, holding an expensive camera and wearing a press badge. Matt recognised his body language as he took pictures, he was certainly military, possibly Special Forces. This was the first inkling that they were being thrown to the wolves. Previously discussed plans with the three senior plotters were now worth nothing, he had been promised by them that he wouldn't be left alone, but the true reality was looking different, and he could guess what was coming. He would be left high and dry and he knew it, but the other poor bastards with him didn't have a clue.

Mark Skinner's phone rang again, the command suite falling into silence before he relayed the message. "We have the prison back under control," immediately reporting this to head office Gold Command before relaying it to the waiting Special Forces team leader.

"Bronze one, you have authority." Silent saws cut through brick and steel ten feet above the classroom, not a sound was made and every grain of dust was suctioned silently up before suspicious eyes could see it. Five men crouched out of sight on the rooftop while inside the classroom, tensions were rising as the time slipped way.

"You have five minutes left...." The guy raised the sword bringing it down towards the Home Secretary's unprotected neck, stopping inches away. He laughed at the negotiator.

"Your face, you shit yourself. Next time it's for real."

A silent '*go*' was whispered into an unseen headset and the ceiling exploded into fine powder and brick dust. Stun grenades detonated simultaneously leaving everyone, including the negotiator dazed as five men fast-roped down holding automatic weapons. The man with the sword was killed instantly with a shot to the head, his weapon clanging onto the floor. The other prisoners dropped onto the floor including the Imam, pleading for mercy. Phillips also sank to his knees but he remained silent.

The team leader untied Susan and helped her up.

"Follow me Home Secretary, I think your visit here is at an end."

Phillips sat in the police station interview room in Paddington Green, London. Stephen Byfield sat watching and listening, unseen behind the two-way mirror. He was perplexed as to how this man who had served his country and become a good Prison Service Governor could have turned traitor. Phillips had refused all calls for legal representation but he had a statement to give. He fully accepted his part in the hostage taking of Susan Whitfield and the plot to behead her. He did however feel betrayed and he had something he wanted to share.

The interview began with an overview of his actions and intentions and he expressed no regrets for his part in the crime. He did not act alone and had been promised a new life in Afghanistan once he had committed the act. The interviewer pushed Phillips for more information.

"Tell us who you were working with. If you help us now, then it may help keep you safe later." Phillips continued to stare ahead.

"They have left you to take the rap and you are all alone now Mr Phillips. How does that make you feel?" Phillips stared at his interrogator before coming to a decision.

"I have told you what I planned and the part that I played in it and I am proud of that. You want the organisers? Find them yourself, I did. The answers are under your nose." His hand thrust to his mouth as he swallowed an unseen tablet, struggling with staff as they tried to stop him before he dropped to the floor. Frantic police officers tried to give resuscitation but death was declared five minutes later when it became apparent that he was gone.

Stephen watched the drama unfold, the frustration boiling within his body. Phillips had taken the secret of who else was involved to his grave. He phoned James in Whitehall.

"He committed suicide before naming anyone James. I am no closer to the truth."

"Come in, we need to talk. I've just found out your English friend from Tunisia is in town, so be cautious."

Arriving at Whitehall, Stephen made his way quickly to room number 12 where James was waiting for him.

"What is going on James?" he greeted him before sitting down.

"I have just had a confidential debrief. It looks as though we have a leak within MI6 and high-level corruption within senior Prison Service managers. We are to trust no one."

"You said that the Englishman is here. Why?"

"He has some unfinished business is my best guess and it may be with you."

"For God's sake, I am a no one. Why would he want me?"

"That's the big question and the one we need answering," replied James thoughtfully.

CHAPTER SIX

It was the following Saturday and spending a much-needed day with the family, Stephen and Tanya rounded the children up and into the car. Stephen's father stood at the door of the annex watching the action take place.

"Have a great day you lot. See you later." They all waved as the car crunched over the drive before disappearing onto the country roads. Harry and Ellie bubbled with excitement at the thought of a day by the seaside and it was the first time the twins had visited Brighton. Hector who had just reached fourteen months old, sat quietly, his eyelids growing heavy as the soft purr of the engine lulled him to sleep.

The motorways seemed to blur into one another until they reached the end of the M23. Brighton was only eleven miles away and the sun was shining in a bright blue sky. The songs on the radio chirped away as Tanya looked into the back of the car. The twins were fast asleep and Hector, now awake, was busy playing with a toy car. After the battles the family had been through over the past two years, it seemed appropriate to name their son after the greatest warrior Troy had ever seen.

Brighton seafront was in fine form, stretching out along the blue sea, offering a thousand attractions for young children and adults alike. Strolling along the wooden slatted pier, they soon found their way to the amusement rides at the bottom where ghost trains and roller coasters quickly ate up the morning before it was time for lunch, fish and chips, straight out of the bag with lots of salt and vinegar. The children were in paradise eating with their fingers and drinking fizzy drinks that were normally banned at home. Gathering the empty papers, Stephen found a bin to dispose of the waste, and as he returned towards the family, something caught his eye and a distant doubt crept into his head. The woman sitting on the bench around twenty metres from them looked familiar. He thought that he had seen this woman in red shorts and white top on the pier, and also near the car park. It was possibly a coincidence but not one to be overlooked. She had a distinctive mark on the sleeve of her top and this is what first caught his attention. It looked as though a drink had been spilt on her. He shook the feeling of unease off as he helped Tanya clean greasy hands with baby wipes.

"Okay everyone, let's look around some shops for Mummy, and if you're lucky, we might find an ice cream shop. Tanya raised her eyebrows with the *'they will be sick'* look, as the children cheered.

"Let's go," they squealed each grabbing a hand and pulling him along. The woman had disappeared by the time they had got everyone ready for a shopping spree in the famous Lanes, and soon they were up to their necks in jewellery and knick-knack shops. After wandering up and down numerous of the twisting lanes, they found themselves outside a quaint ice cream parlour where the twins wasted no time in slipping onto the plastic seats and ordering bubblegum flavoured ice cream while Stephen and Tanya settled for a coffee. The shop was set slightly back from the street and easily missed unless you were specifically looking for it, so as he sat sipping his drink, watching browsing shoppers walk past, he was surprised to see the same woman again. No longer wearing the red shorts but still in the same white top, Stephen noticed the stain on her right sleeve, which convinced him that it was definitely the same person. This time she wasn't alone but walked with a man, early thirties, well dressed and obviously scouring the street for something or someone. It was clear that they had lost their target as their heads turned from left to right looking into all shops as they passed. Just as these thoughts were going through Stephen's head, the woman looked round and their eyes locked, she had been compromised and knew it. Tugging the man into a nearby shop as though wanting to purchase one of the two hundred flavours of Brighton rock advertised on the window, they vanished. Stephen continued to sip his coffee for another few minutes, until it became obvious that they were not coming back out. Putting down his cup, he got to his feet.

"Back in two seconds, I promised Terry I would bring Tom some rock back," he explained to Tanya pointing at the shop fifteen metres away. He strolled quickly over and entering the shop, saw a couple of families deliberating over the multitude of choices but no one who resembled the couple he had seen minutes before.

"Can I help you sir?" a young lady asked as she came round the counter.

"I have just lost a couple of my friends, I was sure they said that they were coming in here. A man and a woman, no children with them?"

"I'm sorry sir but we've been quite busy this afternoon with various groups so I'm not sure I can be of any help with your search."

"Not to worry, I'm sure I will catch up with them eventually," Stephen replied as he took one last glimpse around the shelves before heading back out into the street. Walking back to Tanya, he knew his initial concerns had been confirmed, he was being followed and his mind drifted back to the conversation he'd had with James. The question was, however, why would anyone want to spy on him? Taking out his phone he quickly found James' number. It rang twice before he answered.

"Hi Stephen, everything okay?"

"I am in Brighton and I have at least two people following me. I have seen a man and women but she spotted me and they've disappeared. She has followed me to three separate locations so I'm sure that I'm not imagining it."

"Okay, don't panic. Go to the seafront where you'll find a taxi rank near the pier. Tell the driver to take you to the station but when you arrive, tell him to turn around and take you to the Grand Hotel, using the rear carpark entrance. There is a door into the hotel there, take it and go to reception where you will be expected. I will meet you there in three hours. Tell nobody else where you are. Do you understand?"

"Yes, it's all clear….and thanks James." Stephen put his phone back in his pocket and hurried back to Tanya and the children. Tanya had been watching him on the phone.

"Who were you chatting to?"

"Whitehall."

"Why?"

"We're being followed and we may be in danger, we've got to move, but don't let the kids know that you are worried." Tanya started throwing Hector's bibs and beakers into her bag, quietly seething.

"You fucking bastard, why do you always bring danger to the children?" she hissed. Stephen had no answer as she was right, this always seemed to be the case these days. He gave her an apologetic hug and turned to the twins.

"Okay kids, who wants an adventure?"

"Me! Me! Me!" came three replies, little Hector copying his brother and sister.

"Follow me then, but we must be secret squirrels, no talking otherwise we lose the game." Silently they made their way down to the taxi rank, where a very patient driver took them to the station before finally arriving at the back of the Grand.

"Are you sure this is where you want this time mate?" he laughed as he spoke. "That will be fifteen quid please." Entering the plush reception area, they were met by a member of staff who knew who they were before Stephen could introduce himself.

"Good afternoon Mr Byfield, if you would like to follow me please." Entering the lift, they were taken to the sixth floor, room twelve. Only Stephen could see the irony in this choice.

"Here we are sir, I hope that you have everything that you need. If you require anything else, contact me directly." She handed Stephen a card. "James will join you shortly." The fact she knew James shocked him slightly. How many people were employed by this agency? It seemed that half of the country worked with the Security Services.

"You are booked in as Mr and Mrs Collins," she continued, "please remain in your room until told otherwise." She left, closing the door behind her. Tanya stood in the middle of the room, staring at him.

"Brilliant Stephen, can our life get any better? I have had enough of this bullshit." There was nothing that he could do or say that would make this better. It was him who had summoned Heard into their lives, it was him who had brought the Broods to their doorstep. Now it was an unknown force hunting them and, in some ways, this felt more dangerous.

After what seemed a silent age, there was a tap at the door. Stephen looked through the fisheyed lens and saw it was James and he was alone. He opened the door allowing him in and warned him quietly, "James, Tanya is furious. She's in the bathroom at the moment and I am not sure what she's planning, but she is very unhappy about the children being at risk." At that moment, Tanya came into the lounge area, phone in hand. James approached her, holding out his hand.

"Hello Tanya, I'm James Childs. I'm sorry that we've had to meet under these circumstances, but we will sort it out I promise." Tanya was unimpressed.

"I have heard it all before." James nodded, "We have a safe house sorted out, you can all go there first thing in the morning."

"No, we can't, she put her hand into her bag and pulled out four passports. The children and I are heading to Cape Town tonight from Gatwick." She turned to Stephen, "We are staying at Sally Cowan's place. Stephen, I am leaving you until you decide what is more important to you, family or thrill seeking. Please get me a cab now." Stephen thought back to how Tanya had visited Sally many years ago while her husband was still flying Concorde, an old friend of her parents who had been part of their family forever.

"Tanya, please!" he pleaded.

"Cab. Now!" Twenty minutes later Stephen was left in the room with James, Tanya and the children long gone. He was not quite sure how they had gone from enjoying a lovely family day out to his wife and children leaving him in so short a time as he tried to focus on what James was saying.

"I have checked out the shop that you say the couple disappeared into. They spoke with an Eastern European accent and told the assistant that a journalist was chasing them. They gave her fifty pounds to let them out of the back and keep quiet about it. I have checked CCTV and found our suspects. They were following you all day, possibly from when you left home. The faces are not known to our team."

"Will my family be safe?"

"One of my men is driving them to Gatwick but once the flight leaves, they are on their own. I doubt that anyone will have a clue where they are so maybe it's for the better that they have left you."

"You really couldn't give a flying fuck could you James, country first, second and third eh?" He looked at him feeling that he could punch him for his uncaring attitude. "Do you have a family?"

"No, Stephen, no family at all. They are long dead. I am expendable, I won't make old bones but I'm not worried about that. Without idiots like me, people like the ones chasing you will win and I can't allow that to happen. As you say, country first every time. Get some rest, we will move out in the early hours." Stephen stood and picked up his jacket. "I can't, I have to get some things from home first and I need to tell Dad what's happening. It'll take me the rest of the day to get there and back."

"That could be a bad mistake Stephen but if you are insistent, at least allow me to drive you there. I'll spot if we're being followed. Deal?" Stephen nodded, "Let's go."

James blasted his sports car towards the West Midlands, they drove in silence, anti-surveillance driving skills practiced throughout the long drive and explanations given to Stephen on how these were the techniques he must use from today. These added some time onto the journey and when they at last arrived, the place was in darkness, Chris's car was not in the driveway and the normal barking of the new dog was missing. Stephen guessed that they were out on a forest walk and should be back soon as the sun had set around half an hour ago. Getting out of the car, he suggested James wait for him there whilst he grabbed a few bits together, and opening the front door, he bounded upstairs, quickly packing some things before coming back down and walking into the kitchen. He found himself sliding on the wet tiled floor by the pantry cupboard and looking down he cursed that no one had bothered to wipe up the water from the floor as he turned the kitchen light on.

He saw that rather than water, the floor by the cupboard was swimming with blood, its source coming from under the pantry door. Heart thumping, he pulled the door open gasping as the interior light flicked on. Hanging from the top shelf was the dog, stomach split open and entrails reaching down to the floor. A kitchen knife wedged in its neck held a bloodied note.

The postman just came calling looking for a package. Unfortunately, your father wasn't available to collect what I had for him so I gave it to the dog. Phone me 07501225788.

A photo of the family playing on the pier sat on the shelf. Stephen vomited onto the floor before kicking the door shut, staggering out of the kitchen and through the front door just as his father pulled up in his car.

"Get in the other car Dad, don't ask questions, just get in." James gunned the engine and they raced off.

"What happened Stephen?" James looked concerned.

"They have been in the house, they killed the dog, only because they couldn't kill Dad as he was out. They are mentioning a package again but I don't know what they are talking about. They want me to phone them."

"Let's wait until we get to London, it's too unsafe to return to Brighton."

"Stephen, what do you mean, they were after me?" Chris piped up from the back seat.

"I don't know Dad, but you're safe now, that's the main

thing."

"Where are Tanya and the children?" Stephen looked at his watch. "A long way away Dad and very safe."

The car pulled into a tarmac driveway of a townhouse somewhere in the North of London. The automatic garage door shut, quickly hiding the car as the three men entered the house from a hidden interior entrance. Sitting in a newly decorated kitchen, James poured three small glasses of whisky.

"Let's make that call Stephen." The phone rang a dozen times before it was answered. He instantly recognised the voice of the Englishman.

"Good evening Stephen, sorry I missed you all today. You still have that package that my employers require returning to them. I had a look around but couldn't find it. Perhaps you could help me?"

"I haven't got your parcel. If I knew what you were talking about, I would be able to help you."

"Okay, have it your way," the voice replied, "You lied to me in the boat and got lucky, you are lying to me now. How about I kill your wife and children in the same way that I killed your barking dog. Will that help you remember what you have done with it?" He didn't wait for an answer before the phone went dead. Stephen dropped it onto the kitchen worktop, his hands shaking and still showing the blood from his dog. He ran the tap and scrubbed as though trying to get rid of the skin itself.

"What the fuck have you let me walk into James? This was supposed to be an investigation, not a spy story."

"You are dealing with corruption at the very highest level Stephen. It is the foundation of every spy film you have seen." James stared at them both. "We either win or lose as one way or another this story will have an ending. The good guys don't always win though." Chris got his own phone out of his pocket and made a call. He had heard enough to know he did not want to be part of yet another drama. Finishing his call, he looked at his son.

"Enough is enough son, I'm heading up to stay with friends

in Scotland, get a bit of golf in and stay out of the way of this bullshit. I am a lot safer up there than sitting here waiting to be hurt and it will be less of a worry for you knowing that I'm out of the way."

Stephen hugged him, "Okay Dad, I understand. It's a good idea. I will phone you if anything changes."

Chris called a cab and disappeared in the direction of Kings Cross Station. Picking up his small sports bag, James headed upstairs to a bedroom. He glanced back at Stephen and said, "Sleep now, tomorrow is another day."

CHAPTER SEVEN

Back in room twelve in Whitehall on Monday, James and Stephen talked through the events of the weekend. Another email pinged onto his computer screen which made James sit back and take note.

"We could have a lead for you," he said nonchalantly.

"Prison Service?"

"Yes, are you aware of a Governor named Barry Shaw? He's in charge of H.M.P. Winchester."

"We've met a few times, high flier, reached the top job in his prison within ten years. He is linked to a senior position within the HQ senior team and earmarked for a director's job at some point. Why?"

"Well, if this information is correct," James tapped the screen, "he may be in a whole heap of trouble. His name has been flagged up in a drug running operation while serving as Deputy Governor at H.M.P. Wood Hill. Initial results from a lifestyle check on him show large quantities of cash available for his use. New car, new house, big amounts into a bank account which he may have thought was secret." Stephen was puzzled, "Why would that information come to security services, that's not how our systems work?"

"Oh, it is when his pay masters are known ISIS leaders." Stephen sat forward in his chair, "You have got to be shitting me!" James printed off some information, and walking over to his printer, handed Stephen a number of pages. He flicked through three sheets of security information, copies of bank accounts and photographs of Shaw meeting two men of Asian appearance in a dark pub saloon bar. He guessed that these were the ring leaders.

"Look at this Stephen," James pushed two other photos over the desk. "These are the same men meeting Abu Bakr al-Baghdadi, an Iraqi national who also met Mr Phillips from Northway while detained in Camp Bucca, Iraq in 2004. His whereabouts are unknown at the moment but he is a key leader of ISIS and we believe he has recruited a number of senior prison service staff."

"Where is Shaw at the moment?"

"At work, he is currently unaware of our interest."

"Okay, let me speak to Julia Matthews, she's my old boss and is now Director of Security, Order and Counter Terrorism. I need high level confidential support if we are to investigate and suspend a Governor."

"Give me a few minutes." James left the office returning ten minutes later.

"She is clean, however she only needs to know the basics. An initial investigation followed by a full police investigation and prosecution. Understood?" Stephen nodded before looking through his phone contacts and dialing his old boss.

"Hi Julia, it's Stephen Byfield. Could I speak with you this morning about a very sensitive security subject?" He listened intently nodding throughout.

"Thank you, Julia, see you at 12.30."

Stephen arrived at the gates of Wandsworth Prison at 12.20. Julia was conducting a visit here and had agreed to see him for ten minutes. He was ushered into the main boardroom, a nondescript plainly painted room with a large table in the centre. He sat sipping on the glass of water provided, until he heard the jangle of keys in the door before Julia walked in alone.

"Hello Stephen, how are you?" she greeted him, "It's been a long time. I see you are on secondment to Whitehall, is that fun?"

"Not a lot of fun Julia, not even sure if it's for me. I'm finding a life in the shadows is a dangerous place to be." She nodded, "I can only imagine. What is it you want to discuss?"

"Barry Shaw at Winchester. We need to suspend and investigate him. This will be a full police prosecution and if he throws his hands up, it will go immediately to Security Services. It's that serious."

"Bloody hell Stephen! Give me ten minutes, I'll wrap this tour up and we will go straight down there. Make sure he is on duty first though so we don't have a wasted journey."

"Done that, he is in a Senior Management Meeting until 4.30. If we leave now, he'll know nothing until our entrance." Fifteen minutes later they were heading towards Winchester. Although Julia prodded for further information, Stephen remained tight lipped. "Julia, if I could tell you I would, it is a serious investigation but I promise that everything will become apparent at the right time. You have been a very good friend, so all I can tell you is to trust no one, even senior colleges." Julia held her hands up, "Okay, I'll quit the questions Stephen, I have always trusted you so no reason I shouldn't do so now."

Arriving at H.M.P. Winchester, they drove through the first barrier which had been left open and turning right, they headed for the main gate entrance before parking the car right by the gate. They climbed out as an officer appeared gesticulating at them.

"Move that car, you can't park there." Julia glared at him, showing him her ID. "Julia Matthews, Director. Let me into the prison immediately and do not inform anyone that I am here." The blood seemed to leave his face as he escorted her through the gate. "Where would you like to go ma'am?"

"Take us to the boardroom straight away please." They entered the courtyard and turned left up a metal staircase where he opened the first door and indicated that they should walk up another set of stairs. They could hear the chatter of a meeting going on and reaching the top of the stairs, they found themselves walking directly into the room where the meeting was taking place. All talk stopped as attendees stared at the unexpected guests. Julia addressed the man sitting at the head of the table.

"Hello, I am Julia Matthews and this is Stephen Byfield. We would like to have a chat with you in your office Mr Shaw."

Papers rustled for an uncomfortable moment before Barry Shaw stood and collected his things.

"Of course, follow me please." They walked back down and across the courtyard to his office. After asking his P.A. to take a break, he shut the door and sat down at his desk. He placed his head into his hands and without waiting for Julia to speak confessed. "I have been expecting this moment for so long. What happens to me now?"

"We treat all matters of corruption extremely seriously Mr Shaw," Julia told him, "do you want anyone here with you?"

"No. Look, I'm in too deep and they will kill me if they think that I am talking to you. I am sorry but this is bigger than either of you can ever imagine." Stephen butted in at this point before the Governor said too much.

"Okay, stop talking, save it for the police." Barry Shaw sat shaking in his office chair, not saying another word. A knock on the door broke the silence and three police officers entered and officially cautioned him. He was led out of the establishment in handcuffs and taken directly to Paddington Green station, Stephen following. He didn't want to miss one second of this interview.

The recording equipment buzzed into life as Barry Shaw sat sweating with his solicitor. Across the desk sat two experienced police interrogators, veterans of a number of high-profile cases. Shaw had been identified as a soft target for them, with a possible motive of greed but with no sympathies for terror causes. He was afraid of the people manipulating him and terrified of the consequences, and they believed that he would fold like a house of cards.

The interview started with the basic questions, and Stephen took notes from a hidden room as he watched intently through the CCTV. Shaw cleared his throat before singing like a canary. He had amassed gambling debts while working in Milton Keynes, he lived alone and visited the casinos on a regular basis. He had borrowed cash from a number of sources and his line of credit had long run out. He had been approached by a Senior

Prison Service person two years ago and given the prospect of earning a lot of money from a scam that they had concocted. He went in with it as he trusted the person and couldn't see how he would be caught. He had cleared his debt and earned hundreds of thousands of pounds as life changing amounts of money were on offer. But when he tried to stop, he wasn't allowed. He had been brought closer into the group and involved in other activities. He had a lot of information but wanted a plea deal before he would share anything else. Stephen continued to write the transcript of the interview, and realised that this man was the key to the whole operation set up by James. With Shaw's co-operation, Stephen could be re-joining his family sooner than he had thought.

Shaw then continued with information that none of them were expecting. "I also have information on a front bench politician, three senior prison service managers, terror cells operating under the Prison Service's nose, alongside gun smuggling, drugs and corruption in the police force. I can smash the largest organised crime racket that you have ever seen but what are you going to give me in return?"

Stephen sat in total shock, one piece of information had led to an avalanche which would strike right into the heart of Government. The interviewers also sat dumbfounded before the recorders were turned off hastily, the lead interrogator explaining.

"We need to take advice, give us half an hour and we will be back with you. If what you are saying is true, we can do business."

Taken back to his cell, Shaw lay on the uncomfortable bed. He had realised that his scam would one day be uncovered and he had kept details of every interaction that he'd had with anyone connected to it during the past two years. He had gathered a ton of evidence securely hidden in a big brown envelope in a safe deposit box. He always knew that he would need a get out of jail free card and this was it. Meanwhile in the interview room, Stephen talked to the two senior police officers.

"Is there anything we can do to help him share this information?" he asked them. "It's in the interest of national security." The station Inspector, who had become involved when they had realized the importance of this interviewee, nodded.

"Yes, we can definitely get him a good deal, maybe even avoid a prison sentence. However, these things have to have government approval and this won't be until tomorrow afternoon at the earliest." Stephen had experience in how these things worked through gaining immunity for Karen Matthews, the woman who had been involved in the kidnapping of his twins a few months previously so knew it would take time.

"Okay, you have my number, give me a call before you re-interview him please." Gathering his things, he headed back into the busy London streets towards Paddington tube station where he got on the underground to Whitehall. This time room twelve was locked so heading back down to reception, Stephen asked the receptionist if James was in the building. He wasn't and hadn't been seen all day. *Bloody typical, not picking up his calls and suddenly dropping off the radar, just as things were heating up,* Stephen muttered to himself as he left, and walking towards Westminster Bridge, he flagged down an empty taxi. "Muswell Hill please," he asked as this was a ten minute walk from the safe house and as he knew the streets would not be crowded, he would easily spot anyone following him.

Paying the driver, he slowly walked towards the house, stopping and looking in shops, always vigilant, just as James had instructed him. As he placed the key in the front door, he heard a faint cry, and then a louder one, coming from the garage. Cautiously entering the house, he gently swung the interconnecting door to the garage open to see James standing at the far end of the garage, both hands chained above his head so that he was almost on tiptoes. Fastened across his torso was the unmistakable sight of an explosive device. As soon as James saw him, he shouted.

"Stephen, don't come any closer. This thing could go off at any time."

"I'm going for help," Stephen promised as he backed out of the garage and out of the house. Once back in the street, Stephen phoned the reception desk at the Whitehall office, giving his instructions the second it was picked up.

"Listen, it's Stephen Byfield. I have just found James Childs at my safe house. He's strung up in the garage with an I.E.D. strapped to his chest. We need immediate help."

"Stay exactly where you are. We will have someone there straight away," came the calm voice of the woman on reception. He placed his mouth to the garage door, eager to reassure James. "Help is coming, I am staying out here."

In a very short space of time, a non-descript white transit van pulled up fifty metres away, and a man and a woman resembling builders got out with their tool kits. They approached Stephen.

"Where is he?"

"In the garage chained to the ceiling. He thinks it will detonate soon."

"Okay, wait in the van please," they ordered, tossing him the keys. He sat in his own surreal world watching people walk past, oblivious to the drama unfolding in the garage. Lovers holding hands, two men arguing about Brexit, all unaware that this could be their last moments on earth. And suddenly James appeared and ordered, "Get out of the van, we are moving." He didn't give a second glance to the workers getting back into the van as a black car pulled up and the driver ushered them in. Once safely in the back seat, James explained what had happened to him.

"I had a visitor this morning. The English guy appeared in the kitchen as I was eating my Frosties. Don't know how he found us or how he got in, but he did. He wanted information about you and your family. When I didn't tell him, he decided to leave me to think about it for a bit. It was a fake device but I didn't know that at the time. We found a camera in the garage, he had watched the whole show."

"I've had an eventful time too," Stephen told him. "I have a senior prison Governor willing to give names of all corrupt prison managers, police, terror cells and most significantly, a front bench politician."

"Bloody hell! Shaw came up trumps then?" James exclaimed.

"Apparently he has evidence in a safe deposit box," Stephen continued. "It will give us everything if he can cut a deal. The police are negotiating with Government as we speak."

"We need to be there when they open that box Stephen."

"They're going to phone me when the deal is agreed, do you want to come with me?"

"Too right!"

"So, tell me more about the English Guy, what's going on with him? He could have killed you easily but he let you live."

"Not sure. The weapon he was using was interesting. HS2000, standard issue for Iranian agents so he's working for the Iran Government I think."

"That's bizzare! Did he find anything in the house?" Stephen asked. James looked at him.

"That's where we have a problem. He accessed your laptop and Tanya's flight details were on the system. Have you spoken to her yet?"

"No, her phone is off."

"She needs to know." Stephen's heart sank at the prospect of this but James' next words made him feel slightly better.

"Listen she is in a secure compound somewhere in Cape Town from what you've told me and he hasn't a clue where she is. She just needs to stay inside for a bit and not put herself in any unnecessary danger."

"Okay, I will get a message to her. What's the plan for us now?" James thought briefly before replying. "I have two priority jobs. One, move into a new place with upgraded security and two, kill that English bastard."

Ernie sat in room twelve, he had been summoned by James at short notice.

"How's your Spanish Ernie?" He pushed an envelope over the desk. Ernie took it and departed.

The busy beach bar in Llafranc in the South of Spain sat in an idyllic town somehow forgotten by the worst of the mass tourism trade. The golden sandy beach lapped gently by the blue waters of the Mediterranean was flanked by a pretty promenade and a town square which made picture postcard material. He sipped on an icy glass of cold coke while watching his target.

The smartly dressed man sat with a beautiful olive-skinned woman in her early twenties. They ate expensive looking food and drank chilled white wine while whispering to one another. Occasionally, his gentle English accent managed to drift across the three other tables to where Ernie sat and listened. He couldn't pick anything up but guessed that it was just small talk. It was unbelievable to think that less than forty-eight hours previously, this man had been strapping an explosive devise onto the chest of Ernie's new boss.

Activating a small listening device, Ernie silently walked behind the chatting couple placing the microphone out of sight on the branch of a palm tree by the table. By chance, their hotel room keys were on the table and with a quick unseen glance as he passed by, Ernie was able to read *Hotel BlauMar, Room 128* on the over-large key fob. Unseen and looking like a holiday maker, Ernie made his way to the hotel to conduct a recce, a five-star place, easily accessible and busy enough for him to move in and out of unnoticed. Once he had found everything he needed to know, he made his way back to his hire car where he could listen in to their conversation without being seen. It was parked on the beachfront where he had an uninterrupted view of the couple as they enjoyed their cozy lunch.

It soon became apparent that the woman was a high-class call girl employed by the Englishman who she referred to as Lance. If this was his real name then this was a development in what they knew about this man. Ernie soon realized that it was pointless listening to the remainder of the chat, he was going to shag her in his luxury hotel room and she was going to charge him five thousand Euros for the pleasure. All Ernie had to do was wait for them to finish their ice cream and then get to business.

He lay back in the car seat and closed his eyes. It had been a long day. This was to be his second confrontation with the Englishman, he had hoped to kill him in Tunisia but he had escaped and he had strict instructions to keep him alive this time until he revealed all his dirty secrets. A shiver of anticipation crawled down Ernie's spine as he contemplated his enemy. The Englishman was a true professional, he had worked for numerous security agencies including the British and American, he was ruthless but sat within the sights of an equally ferocious competitor. Ernie had hunted him down and found him, possibly with his trousers down. He chuckled at the prospect as years of Special Force training kicked in and he checked his equipment again. The Glock 19 pistol was a good choice giving good firepower and accuracy and was ideal for close up action. He also checked the syringes of strong sedatives, these had to be easily to hand as it was vital to incapacitate this man quickly. The girl, well her fate would depend on how sensible she was.

At last, it seemed the meal had ended and the couple settled the bill before strolling hand in hand away from the town centre heading towards the hotel. Ernie drove to the hotel car park and parked the car before walking back a short way and sitting on a bench with a Spanish newspaper. He knew exactly where they were heading and what they were going to do. If he allowed them half an hour to settle down and get to business, he could go in and prove that two was company and three just ruined a good time.

Giving them time to get up to their room, Ernie entered the hotel, and settling in at the large hotel bar, he continued to second guess their timetable until it felt like it may be a good time to spoil the party. He checked his pockets one last time, looking at the entry card to the room stolen from the cleaning team on his earlier visit, the Glock tucked into its holster out of sight and the syringes in a padded wallet ready for use.

He stood outside the room and scanning the card across the reader as the green light flashed, he opened the door to the suite silently. The bedroom door was ajar and the action was clearly lively. Party music screamed from the speakers, a thumping beat, ideal for disguising any noises that may occur in the next few minutes. Drawing the pistol, he pushed the bedroom door open to the disbelief of the couple inside.

"Stay exactly where you are and nobody gets killed," he ordered as the music continued, almost drowning out his voice.

"Okay big shot. Have we met?" Lance seemed defiant. He lay in bed looking at Ernie, his brain calculating if he could reach his gun before getting plugged by a 9mm round. Not a hope.

"You," Ernie looked at the prostitute, "get on the floor, face down." She screamed one short scream before Ernie dropped her with a single shot. Pointing the gun back in the man's direction he warned him, "Don't be a hero Lance."

"Very good, you have really done your homework. What do you want? Money?"

"Get your shorts and t-shirt on, take your time. If you reach for the gun that I know is in your drawer, I will shoot you." The Englishman complied with this request, not taking his eyes off Ernie.

"I will remember your face," he warned Ernie. Ernie nodded and gave his second instruction.

"Lie face down on the bed." The man complied. Ernie took the first syringe and emptied it into the man's arm. It took effect immediately incapacitating him. Ernie helped him off the bed and dragged him into the lift before leading him through reception. For all observers, he looked like a very drunk man and Ernie shrugged and apologised to the guests as he did so. Legs finally collapsing as they reached the car, Lance's eyes flickered open before closing for a few hours. The car had been positioned in such a way that the boot was partially hidden, Ernie opened it and pushed the almost unconscious body in. With a gag placed on his mouth and feet and hands bound, he would get the second shot of drugs as and when needed. The car pulled out onto the main road and headed for the ferry that would take them to Morocco.

The short trip across the Strait took less than an hour, and

Lance was still out cold with no sign of waking up despite the cramped conditions, as they drove off the ferry and headed for Tangiers. Ernie followed the satnav directions before pulling into a disused industrial site in the middle of nowhere. The sun had set an hour or so ago so the flashlight beckoning the car over was easy to see. Pulling into the old factory building, Ernie was met by three rugged looking men who wore camouflaged clothing and looked in good shape. It was an educated guess that these guys were professionals in their chosen trade, torture. He parked in a small, covered area before they dragged the body out of the boot and into a large high-ceilinged warehouse.

Lance came to from his slumped position on the dirty floor. His hands were restrained by heavy chains which were in turn attached to a pulley system. Old blood stains covered the flooring around where he lay and a large gas canister and an oxyfuel cutting device sat beside him. A primitive electric shock device rested, ready for use on a wooden table nearby.

"What do you want from him boss?" One of the three men asked Ernie. Ernie looked straight at the Englishman. "I need to know what he is looking for in the UK, who is employing him and why he is chasing Stephen Byfield."

"Do you want to stay, or shall we report it back to you?"

"I will stay for the first session, then we will see." Lance glared up at Ernie.

"You callous bastard, I will come back for you, that I promise." The rattle of the chains running through the pulley ripped through the room as he was hoisted into the air by his arms, screaming with the intense pain. Swinging only inches from the floor, the lead torturer looked into his face spitting into his eyes.

"Let's start with an easy question. What is your name?"

"Lance Mitchell."

"Good, Mr Mitchell. Who are you working for?"

"I am self-employed, presently not working."

"Let's try that one again shall we? Who are you working for?"

"I was on holiday, this guy has kidnapped me." The interrogator produced a small spray canister. "Do you know what acid feels like when it burns your bare skin?" Without waiting for an answer, he ripped Lance's shirt open before spraying his stomach with the burning liquid. Flesh bubbled instantly and began to fall onto the floor. Lance screamed as the pain grew.

"Who are you working for?"

"Iranian Government," Lance panted through the pain.

"Good, but we knew that already. You have given yourself a lot of pain for things that I already knew. What are you looking for in the UK?"

"Nothing, I am not looking for anything." The remainder of his clothes were cut off leaving him naked. Another spray of acid onto his testicles was followed by indescribable pain that seemed to burn into his entire body.

"A parcel, a fucking parcel," he yelled. "I don't know what's in it, I just have to get a parcel that was sent to Byfield."

"Umm, I think that you know a bit more than that." The interrogator nodded to one of his accomplices, and electric wires were clamped onto Lance's tongue.

"We can stop this at any time Mr Mitchell." Flipping a switch, a jolt of lightning shot through his head and smoke came from his mouth as he fell unconscious. They prepared the next implements of torture and then lowered him to a kneeling position where one man held him from behind while water was thrown into his face. He woke up as Ernie sat watching, he hadn't heard enough yet and knew the guy was stalling for time. He was not adverse to torture if it had a purpose and he still needed to know what was in the parcel. "Give him more until he talks," he ordered.

"What is in the parcel Lance? Tell me or I start cutting you into pieces, beginning with your toes." He lit the gas cutter and showed him the blue cutting flame. "This will go through flesh and bone in seconds, and it is a painful way to die." Lance cracked.

"Photos and evidence. Evidence on corrupt officials in all areas of the UK. The British Government wants the evidence back. The Iraqis support this. That's all I know."

"Enough for now," ordered Ernie. "Let me confirm this information." He went back to the car and phoned James.

"I have our man, he has told us what is in the package and you were right, it's dynamite."

"Well done!"

"What now?"

"Leave him to die."

While Ernie was in the car, Lance hung burning and in agony. He pleaded for a drink. One of the men urinated into a cup and laughing, he took it over and made him drink it. Lance fell unconscious again and the man slapped his face trying to bring him round to prolong the pain. He hit him once more before a head butt split the Moroccan man's nose and at the same time, Lance threw his legs around him bringing the automatic weapon into his grasp. The first burst took the lead torturer off his feet and panic set in amongst the men as the third guy opened fire. Lance swung his captive into the line of fire killing him instantly, and he then fired another burst killing the last of the men. Climbing back onto his unsteady feet he unwound the chains from his wrists. "Fucking amateurs," he muttered to himself as he gathered his torn clothes and put them on.

Ernie heard the first shots and guessing what was happening, he threw the car into reverse and out into the forecourt before speeding away. A burst of fire took out the rear window and thudded into the passenger seat as he looked in the rearview window to see Lance Mitchell throwing the now empty weapon down. *This fucker is using all nine of his nine lives* he thought, as he picked up the phone and pressed the number for James.

"They fucked up. He is on the run."

CHAPTER EIGHT

Lance Mitchell lay in an Iranian hospital bed, flown back by private plane and offered the privileges normally associated with high-ranking dignitaries. The searing pain had begun to subside with the painkillers as an official sat at his bedside, debriefing their top agent. The acid burns had been quickly treated and were healing although horrific scaring would be left as a memory. His hatred of the man who took him to Morocco also burnt into his heart. Once the business was dealt with, he would love to settle the score with this man, particularly as he knew that another meeting was inevitable.

Mitchell had been a promising school boy, attending Eton after the death of his wealthy parents in a car crash in 2006. Progressing to Oxford University, he was part of the winning boat race team as well as a promising boxer. After attaining top marks in Politics and International Business, he was asked to attend Whitehall for a series of meetings with the security services. Fluent in Arabic, Mandarin and Russian, he was exactly the type of recruit the service coveted. He joined GCHQ, monitoring communications across the Middle East before his real qualities were spotted.

MI6 took him into their agency and trained him to act as a field operator where he was a natural and excelled. A number of other operations followed until he was uncovered in Libya during the uprising. Abandoned by the Government and another undercover operative who had handed him over to the Benghazi Militias in order to spare his own life, he was brutally beaten before an American SEAL team rescued him and returned him to the British Government.

Disillusioned, he resigned from all UK Security groups and began freelance work, a mercenary who would do the dirty work for any government. He still had links with the UK and US but had plied his trade in the Middle East for the past five years.

This job was his most complicated, he was up against MI5 and MI6 but also representing the interests of those same groups. He was expected to protect some of the very people who had left him to rot in the desert. And why were Iran interested in protecting the UK? The same reason Iran were interested in anything. The people in power in the UK were about to make Iran a wealthy country again, deals were ready to be signed and if corruption was discovered, it could be game over. This one job would make him rich for life with the prospect of retirement in Dubai and possible marriage and a settled family life. After his recent torture, this was becoming more appealing and he could picture a time when his life in the shadows would be over.

Stephen's phone rang, he looked at the number and recognised that it was the lead investigator in the Barry Shaw case. "Hello, Stephen Byfield."

"Hello Stephen, Detective Inspector Clements here, we met yesterday. I have some good news, we have been offered a deal in the case of Shaw. If he can produce the evidence, he will be offered a non-custodial sentence and a life in hiding. He has agreed to this and has provided us with the location of the key to the safe deposit box. Do you want to meet us at the address given for the key?" Stephen took the details and phoned James before the pair made their separate ways to a small semi-detached house on the outskirts of Newbury, Berkshire. They waited until everyone was present with every move filmed by staff trained in evidence preservation. Entering the front door, they took the first door on the left into what was obviously a garage conversion. On the right of the large en-suite bedroom was a walk-in wardrobe. On the shelf just inside of the door was a built-in safe. Shaw had given them the number and a police officer tapped it in and opened the door. There sat the safe deposit box key.

Following the police car along the A4, they headed back to West London to visit Safe Deposit Box London and Storage Lockers UK. DI Clements produced a court warrant before they were escorted to the private viewing room. A woman appeared five minutes later carrying the box as though the crown jewels were inside. Potentially the contents could be of far more value. She placed the box on the table. "Do you have the key sir?" Clements produced it and quickly opened it. It was empty and the feeling of anticlimax washed over everyone present.

"You are not the first policeman to look in the box sir," the woman informed him.

"What do you mean?"

"Another gentleman came yesterday afternoon, a Superintendent Jacobs. He didn't have a key but had the paperwork from the court. He asked to be left alone while he looked."

"I don't suppose you have him on CCTV?" DI Clements asked.

"Yes sir, if you'd follow me please." They all stood in the security office looking at the screen in disbelief as a uniformed man opened the box using a set of lockpick tools and took out the contents. He placed it in a briefcase he had with him before closing and relocking the box.

"I have never seen this guy in my life," DI Clements announced as he stood up. "I think I need to get back to the station to find out what is going on." He turned to Stephen, "I'll be in touch with you as soon as I have cleared this up." The sound of the police car siren told its own story as he hurtled back to Paddington Green.

Half an hour later Stephen's phone rang. It was DI Clements but not with the news Stephen was expecting. "Stephen, Shaw has been found dead in his cell, we have a doctor enroute but it's too late to save him. And more bad news, whoever took the package from the security box was not one of us."

Stephen wasted no time in getting down to Paddington Green where he was ushered into the DI's office, finding it a hive of activity. The phone rang incessantly as Clements tried to get a grip on the developing crisis. He quickly filled Stephen in on what had happened since he left him earlier.

"I had asked to speak to Shaw to find out who else could know about the box. When my staff tried to wake him up, they realised that he was dead. The doctor has just confirmed death and we are waiting for the coroner's office to remove the body. It's a crime scene at the moment so no one can go in apart from Scenes of Crime officers. Apparently it looks like a heart attack but they'll hold a post mortem tomorrow.

"I don't believe in coincidences. For him to die at this time and in this manner is suspicious wouldn't you agree?" Stephen suggested. Clements nodded, "My thoughts too to be honest. What have we stumbled into Stephen?"

"I don't know, but whatever it is, it's even bigger than we thought."

CHAPTER NINE

The plane touched down in Cape Town, a busy airport but smaller than Tanya had expected, as she made her way to the passport area, struggling with three very tired children. Harry was dragging his feet, exhausted after a long wait at Gatwick and a boring flight. Hector had cried for the last two hours and he was shattered as well. They had seen Mummy argue with Daddy and then they had left him at the hotel in Brighton.

"Mummy, when is Daddy coming to Africa?" Ellie asked.

"He is busy sweetheart, maybe in a few weeks when he has finished his work."

"That's ages Mummy," she whined as she tried to keep up with Tanya and the pushchair. Tanya found herself having to have eyes in the back of her head as hundreds of people were heading in the same direction and Harry was in danger of being swallowed up by the throng.

"Harry, for God's sake get a move on. You will get lost," she snapped as a smart looking Englishman approached her.

"Can I give you a hand there? I'm travelling alone, my wife is waiting in Arrivals. Maybe I can help push the buggy, that is if you don't mind?" Tanya's senses sparked to red alert. She had faced danger too many times over the past two years and she had learned to trust nobody.

"No, it's fine, I can manage thank you." She felt herself looking for the nearest point of help as the man went to take the buggy. "No, I insist, I really don't mind." She had heard enough, tired, irritated and thousands of miles from home and on top of that, a stranger was trying to take control of her children.

"Listen, fuck off and sort your own problems out. Go or I will call a Security Guard." She glared at him.

"Okay, okay," he held his hands up in surrender, "Sorry for trying to help." He carried on walking and Tanya passed through passport control and into the main arrival area. She saw Sally waving frantically and shouting her name. She also saw the helpful man with his wife and as she passed by, she overheard the woman saying. "Don't worry darling, some people just can't be helped." Feeling a little embarrassed by her outburst which she now realised was totally unfounded, she hurried past and into the arms of her excited friend. Hugging Sally, Tanya had never felt so relieved to see a friendly face so far from home.

They set off into the afternoon traffic, temperatures just touching twenty degrees with a blue sunny sky. As they drove further away from the airport, Tanya gazed out at the passing landscape, noticing the contrasts evident between wealth and poverty in the region. The road seemed to be lined with single storey breeze-block buildings strung with cloth make-shift awnings, an endless snake of colours interspersed with the drabness of grey blocks. Sometimes, in the distance, a magnificent house would spring into view and around the larger houses and estates, which seemed to cover miles of green gardens, were tin shacks in groups of maybe five or six sitting in the shadows of the big house.

"Why are these little shanty villages so close to the land owners?" Tanya wondered out loud.

"He has given them jobs, maybe in the fields tending the vines, or keeping the garden tidy. Wherever there is wealth and work, the locals find it and move close. It's the way of the land here," Sally explained. It seemed absurd to Tanya that the local black population were still begging at the table of the rich white families but she knew it was something she would have to get used to if they were to stay out here in South Africa.

They soon reached the village where Sally lived, a high wall surrounding the secure estate, giving it the medieval appearance of the old castle days where the wealthy hid behind fortified walls. Armed guards checked cars in and out and an electrified fence sat just inside the walls. Tanya looked at it all, somewhat perturbed.

"Is this all necessary Sally? It's a lot of security." Sally laughed, "I don't notice it anymore Tanya, it's just part of life here." She chatted briefly to the security officer, sharing a joke with him before driving through the gates and along the road, pulling into her driveway a few hundred yards later. The house in front of them was a magnificent colonial style building, with a wrap-around veranda and sweeping lawns with sprinklers sending sprays of water in every direction, ensuring the grass remained emerald green. The area surrounding the property was also beautifully manicured and lead down to a large lake. Taking it all in, Tanya estimated it to be a good two mile circuit and ideal for her morning run. She woke the children who had fallen asleep during the journey from the airport and they entered the house where they were met by bright white walls covered with vividly painted African scenes, landscapes with delicately painted skies of all shades, markets thronging with brightly dressed people and over-flowing stalls of local produce, and a few exquisite sketches of native animals gazing out of their frames. Sally ushered them through to two, light, airy bedrooms with ceiling fans positioned over beds with crisp white linen. Tanya looked around her with awe, before asking "How on earth do you keep on top of all this work? The garden alone would keep me busy full time."

"I have a little help during the week and I admit that I do have a gardener," she smiled at Tanya. "I also have a part time job that I do as a volunteer, I remember that you have a nursing background Tanya and wondered if you'd like to come with me tomorrow and help out?"

"I can try, what do you do?"

"I work in the township giving medical help for free. A charity provides the equipment, I provide the expertise. It's up to you of course, but we always take any help we can get."

"What about the children? It doesn't sound the sort of thing I can take them to."

"Most people in the village work and they have young children as well. Life is a little different here but I will show you more after we have eaten, you must be starving."

They had a leisurely lunch on the veranda, and after the children had spent some time charging up and down the garden, avoiding the sprinklers, Tanya put Hector to bed for an afternoon sleep while Sally made a quick call. A short while later, a stunning, young black woman appeared at the front door, around thirty years old with the most disarming smile Tanya had ever seen. She had a little girl with her dressed in the prettiest pink dress you could have ever imagined who gazed with wide eyes at Harry and Ellie. Sally introduced them all.

"This is Jenny, Tanya, she is a trusted nursery worker and looks after a lot of the younger children while their parents work. She can look after Harry, Ellie and Hector for three mornings a week if you would like? They would meet the other children and learn about Africa. Wouldn't that be fun?" She turned and looked at Harry and Ellie, "And this is Bella who can help show you around and be your friend while you are here." Jenny smiled at them all.

"It would be a pleasure to teach your children about our beautiful country. Would you like to come and see the school?" Tanya went with her while Sally watched the children who had already started playing together with some toys she had borrowed for them to use during their stay. It was a short, two-minute walk to the single-story white school house. Five children sat in a small classroom, the walls covered with their artwork depicting the animals of the country, interspersed with posters of far off mountains and waterfalls, beckoning you into the paradise that was South Africa. Zulu shields fastened to the ceiling reminded the children of their heritage, and it was obvious that everyone connected to the school took pride in their country.

"We are small but we get very good results. The children and parents are happy here," Jenny explained.

"I'm not surprised," Tanya agreed, watching the children sing together while clapping along to the tune.

"Can the children give it a try tomorrow to see if they like it?" Tanya was impressed with what she saw and could picture the twins joining in with the local children.

"Of course, we can deal with all ages; we are not pressured by exams and curriculum. This is Cape Town, we have time for everyone, and unlike the UK, we have lots of helpers. Through here, we have another room for the younger children where they can play safely and sleep when necessary." Here she led Tanya through to a nursery type room, perfect for Hector.

"Bring them over at nine tomorrow, they can spend the morning and see how they get on."

Tanya walked back deep in her own thoughts. They had been here for just two hours, and already had a school arranged and a part time job with Sally. It felt as though this was meant to be. All she needed to do was work out where Stephen still fitted into her life.

CHAPTER TEN

"We have the reports from the coroner Stephen, you were right, it wasn't natural causes," DI Clements informed Stephen over the phone. "She spotted a small injection mark on his neck and tests showed a lethal cocktail of drugs had been administered shortly before we found him. There were no defensive marks on his body so it is assumed that whoever killed him must have been trusted to get close to him."

"Obviously someone working within the team then."

"It would seem so."

"CCTV?" Stephen asked hopefully.

"Wiped out. This stinks Stephen, the authority needed to wipe CCTV from the most secure police station in London can only come from the highest sources. Nobody has access to that type of evidence so we're really up against it."

"Welcome to my new world," Stephen replied without humour as he hung up, contemplating what this new information meant to both his safety and his investigation.

The young couple took their normal Sunday morning route along the Grand Union Canal near their Brentford home. The puppy loved chasing the sticks thrown, and at this time of the morning there were rarely any other people around to spoil the silence. The canal wasn't the type of water that you'd fancy falling in, but for somewhere so close to central London it was amazing how peaceful it could be, and if you were patient, how many wild animals you could spot along the bank.

The man hurled a well chewed stick underneath the graffiti-strewn bridge. Normally it would be retrieved in seconds, but not this time. The incessant yap of the little Jack Russell echoed out from the shadows.

"Come on Buster, bring it back," he shouted but still the barking continued. He jogged forwards to stop the noise before the people in the flats adjoining the canal began to complain. As his eyes adjusted to the gloom, he could make out a human shape hanging from the girders of the bridge, feet dangling around fifteen feet above the path. The dog stood underneath it and continued to bark. "Mollie, phone the police," he shouted to his girlfriend, "there's a dead body hanging here. Wait! Fuck me it's a Policeman!"

James's phone rang. It was a little after eight o'clock on Sunday morning.

"Sorry to wake you up James. I think we have found Superintendent Jacobs," Stephen greeted him.

"Where is he?"

"In the mortuary, Brentford."

"I am guessing he didn't have the parcel?"

"No, but the police have a match for his finger prints already. Have you ever come across a man named Gary King?"

"Not an uncommon name, but I can't think of anyone at the moment."

"GCHQ intelligence analyst, presently on secondment with Westminster. Isn't that convenient?"

"So whoever killed him has the papers?"

"Yes, and they knew who he was, where he was and what he was looking for."

"We have a major breach of security from within our team then Stephen. Only a handful of people knew of the existence of the safe deposit box. Whoever it is knew that they had to get there quickly to beat us to the evidence."

"Find that answer James and we find the mole."

After his call to James, Stephen checked his phone. There was no missed call from Tanya. The worrying thing is that this was the first time he had thought of her and the children since they left. She was right, he was so hooked up in the moment that everything else had become irrelevant. After all that she had suffered whilst still remaining strong, she had become inconvenient to him. What was he turning into? His mind twisted back to James, he had no one in his life, his country first and foremost. He sighed, knowing that for the moment at least, he would have to follow suit. He phoned James back.

"James, I've had a thought."

"On what Stephen?"

"Maybe I am supposed to get that parcel. Barry Shaw was ready to send me the evidence, so when the government guys got wind of it, they handed him over to you to prevent him doing so. Then they stole the documents back only to be double crossed. That could mean that they are now on route to me." James laughed, "You should write a book buddy. On the other hand, it is not impossible. How would they contact you?"

"I have an idea, I will get back to you." He gathered his keys and wallet and made his way out of the safe house onto the street before making a call.

"Terry can we meet up, I need a bit of help?"

Three hours later Terry walked into the Charles Dickins pub near Paddington station. He quickly spotted Stephen and walked over, giving him a hug like only old friends do.

"What have you got yourself into this time Stephen? I heard that you had a cushy job somewhere behind a desk."

"Pipe and slippers Terry, how is the prison going?"

"Much better since the last guy left." They both laughed before Terry continued.

"So what are you getting me involved in this time?"

"Not a lot to be honest, I need to go home and check on something but I need you to come with me."

"Why?"

"People are trying to kill me and Tanya has taken the children half way around the world to avoid being caught up in it. Apart from that life is good." Terry didn't even flinch.

"Who is chasing you?"

"Not sure, Security services from a couple of continents I

think."

"Why?"

"Terry, if I could tell you, I would," Stephen apologized. He knew he had no right to ask Terry to get embroiled yet again with his problems. Terry had gone beyond the bounds of friendship too many times already. However, he had no need to worry and Terry didn't waste a moment in agreeing.

"Okay, let's go."

Pulling up at Stephen's home a couple of hours later, Terry noticed the gates were open.

"Were they open before?"

"Yes, they broke a while go and I haven't got around to fixing them yet. The last time I went into the house my dog was hanging gutted in the pantry Terry. Hopefully it has all been cleaned by the Government."

"Fucking hell Stephen, that's a bit drastic!" They entered the hallway where the strong smell of cleaning materials told their story. He checked around for any obvious packages but found nothing.

"Terry, I am looking for a parcel," he explained opening the door to the cupboard under the stairs.

"Have you checked your post box?"

"Good point Terry, no I haven't. Because the gates were broken the postman has been coming straight up to the house. I had forgotten about the box."

Finding the key, he walked across the driveway to where the back of the box was half hidden in the hedge. He opened it and finding it empty, started closing the door when a slip of soaking paper stuck to the side of the box caught his eye. *'Sorry we tried to deliver a parcel but you were out.....'*

Checking the small print, he realised they had thirty minutes to get into the village post office to collect it before they closed.

"Terry, we need to go."

Pulling into the lay-by, Stephen hopped out of the car and went into the shop. The door chimed as he entered and a kindly face smiled at him from behind the shop counter.

"Hi, I have a parcel to pick up, Stephen Byfield."

"Yes, I do have one Mr Byfield, it arrived this morning. Let me get it for you." She came back with a thick brown envelope and handed it to him. It felt strange to hold a parcel that had cost at least one man his life and put a death threat against so many others. He nodded to the lady and thanked her before getting back into the car.

"Terry, this parcel is the most important delivery that I have ever had. I am going to trust in you for it's safe keeping. Let's drive to the prison and put it into your own safe right now. That way, no one else can get to it until I need it. I don't know who to trust apart from you mate."

"Good plan," Terry agreed. They drove through the familiar country roads before the prison loomed into view. It felt like yesterday that Stephen walked out for the last time, so many good and bad memories within the formidable walls.

"Am I coming in with you?" Stephen asked as they parked up.

"Damn right. I want you to see that this thing is safe." They entered the main gate where a couple of staff recognised him but there had obviously been a high staff turn around since he was last there. Walking across the forecourt, they arrived in Terry's office. He was temporary in charge while the Governor was away on holiday for a month. He took an evidence bag from his desk drawer and placed the parcel into it. Taking a seal with a serial number on it he securely fastened the top of the bag closed before locking it into the safe.

"There you go mate, safe and sound. Give me a call when you need it."

"Thanks Terry, it's good to know it's safe and out of the way from all those looking for it. Now, I must get back to London, can you give me a lift?"

"No problem, just do me a favour Stephen. Stay alive and contact Tanya as apart from me, she is the best thing in your life."

The drive back to London was uneventful, Stephen's mind was in overdrive until he fell into a deep sleep, waking as the car pulled up at Paddington Green Police station. This place was starting to feel like home. The Detective Inspector had phoned an hour ago, he wanted to talk but in a secure place and face to face. Stephen thanked Terry and made his way to the reception desk. DI Clements quickly came down to greet him and the two men disappeared into an empty interview room where the DI wasted no time in voicing his concerns.

"Stephen, the incident in which James was attacked, you mentioned it to me but it hasn't officially been reported as a crime."

"Okay that's not unusual though for secret services is it?" Stephen asked.

"No, it's not. What is unusual is that we have looked at the CCTV from the street which has a good line of sight on the safe house."

"What are you suggesting?"

"We have examined twenty-four hours of footage and you are seen coming and going a number of times."

"I live there!"

"You, James and briefly your father are the only three people who enter or leave. In the period of you leaving the house and returning to find the bomb, no one else enters the property, front or back."

"That's impossible, I saw James tied up in the garage with my own eyes."

"Stephen, I have checked the evidence myself. No one enters or leaves. Either the attacker was always in the house and didn't leave, or..."

"Or the attack didn't happen."

"Bingo Stephen, I have not shared this information, but please be careful. I don't think all is as it seems. Do not trust anyone at the moment. There is no chance that an intruder entered the house to carry out that attack." Stephen's mind whirled as he considered what this might mean.

"Okay, let's keep this to ourselves at the moment. I have been having doubts myself," he admitted.

Making his way back to Whitehall, he had more questions

than answers buzzing around in his head as he made his way up to see James.

"Hi Stephen. Any developments?" Stephen looked at James and made a decision.

"Nothing, I went back to the house to look for any evidence of a parcel, absolutely nothing."

"Interesting, it may still turn up."

"I have redirected all mail to a mail box, so if it is coming, it will arrive there."

"Good thinking, that way you won't miss it and you can let me know if you get it." Stephen decided to dig a little.

"How are you after the scare James? It certainly had my pulse racing."

"And mine, I thought my time was up for a second, thank God you arrived back when you did."

"I must have just missed him, how did he leave? We may have passed on the street."

"You probably did, he walked out of the front door, bold as brass. Heard him slam the door and whistle as he walked past the garage door. Callous bastard."

"How long had he been gone?"

"Five minutes at most. Why, do you have an idea on where he might be?"

"No, just trying to put the puzzle together. Anyway, I think that I will head back, I still need to try to talk to Tanya to warn her."

He was dreading this call. Tanya heard the phone vibrating, it had been dead since her arrival as her charger was still in the UK and she had only just managed to borrow one from Sally's friend. She'd had a day or two to calm down and was wondering if she'd done the right thing in taking the children away from Stephen.

"Hi Stephen, how is it going back there?"

"Busy sweetheart. How are you and the children?"

"We are settling in. It is lovely here and I've already volunteered to work with Sally for her charity. It's great, you would love it here." Stephen knew it was now or never, "I am missing you all like crazy, Tanya, but we have a problem." Tanya froze, "What sort of problem?"

"The people following us know you are in Cape Town."

"How?"

"They saw your details on my laptop." A silence followed, Stephen could tell she was thinking deeply but was not prepared for what came next.

"Let's take a break Stephen. I told you that I have had enough of the danger you bring, now you are phoning me to tell me that you have caused me and my children more harm. I don't want to hear from you until everything is settled. Then, and only then, we can talk about whether we still have a future. I just can't do this anymore."

"Tanya, I need you. Don't go!"

"You follow your dream action man, I will follow mine out here. Let's see where it takes us both."

She hung up the call and tossed the phone onto the couch, angrily muttering to herself, *"If anyone comes to find me out here, they are in for one hell of a fight."*

CHAPTER ELEVEN

Tanya climbed into Sally's car. They were heading out to the local township, and full of trepidation, she asked constant questions, the most pressing was one of safety.

"How many people live in the township?"

"Forty-four thousand people share the town, twice as many as it should hold."

"What are the main issues they face?"

"HIV is rife along with drug and alcohol issues. Sexual abuse is common in the families unfortunately and STD's are everywhere. There are the usual mental health problems and the normal complaints we see from rough sleepers as essentially, that's what lots of them are." Sally glanced over to see what reaction her words were having on Tanya who was absorbing everything she was hearing.

"Is it safe?"

"We are not guaranteed safety Tanya, we are mixing in a difficult population, abused for centuries and mistrustful of strangers. We are performing a helpful service though, which goes some way towards being accepted. One thing that we can't do is take any medication into the drop-in centre that can be abused so we mainly provide first aid and advice."

Entering the township, the poverty shocked Tanya. Rubbish strewn alleyways and tin shacks sprung out from the wasteland in every direction. Crowds gathered on corners looking menacing, many drinking from cans or plastic un-labelled bottles, and some looking under the influence of other things stronger than alcohol. It was surreal, a thrown together ugly, makeshift town, with the awe-inspiring backdrop of towering mountains, hiding their summit in fluffy white clouds set in a brilliant blue sky.

A large tarmacked road divided the centre of the vast town, where electric street lights showed that the grid had made it here. The corrugated buildings were ramshackle in appearance, with splashes of colour dancing between the greys and browns of rusting iron. There were the occasional shops selling second hand appliances at low prices, a builder plying his trade for an extortionate price, but without him and his mafia, new homes were not allowed. Some brick buildings had sprung up in the more central areas, and these housed the drop-in centre, a small school battling against a lack of government funding and looking a little sorry for itself, and surprisingly, a crèche backing onto the school building. Tanya, taking it all in, pointed to the crèche.

"I didn't expect to see that here," she commented.

"No, but nearly ninety percent of the men are unemployed, so some of the mums have found work out of necessity. A local woman started out with this for children between one and five and it's a life saver for them."

"What do the men do if they aren't employed?"

"Gangs are a big thing out here, life is cheap, there is very little work and kids as young as ten are forced to work with the gangs to deal drugs and steal from tourists. It's a dog-eat-dog world I'm afraid." Tanya felt such a sadness gripping her stomach and she ached to help these disadvantaged children.

Sally parked up in a small secure carpark area and getting out, she walked to the fence to talk to a boy, perhaps fifteen or sixteen years old who was sitting on the ground just outside the enclosure. She took a handful of change from her pocket and gave it to him before walking back to the car.

"What was that about?" Tanya asked her.

"Keeping the car in one piece for another day. He will sit and guard it all morning for the equivalent of a couple of pounds," Sally replied as she grabbed her bag from the back seat and locked the car.

They entered the front door of the clinic, where already

a queue of men, women and children all looking in desperate need of attention, was developing. They worked non-stop until midday, Tanya following Sally's instructions as she picked up what needed doing, when a large man stopped any more people joining the line.

"Come back tomorrow, make sure you are early or the doctor can't see you," he instructed as he shepherded the latecomers out of the door. Tanya watched him in dismay before going to find Sally who was in the treatment room.

"Sally, this is heartbreaking, all these people with no health care apart from us and we're turning them away." Sally stopped what she was doing and beckoned Tanya over to sit down next to her.

"We can only do our best, I hate leaving while people still need me, but if I stayed, I would be here twenty-four hours every day. At least if two of us are here we can see twice the numbers once you are up to speed."

"Count me in, I can help you for three mornings a week but I still wish we could do more," Tanya sighed.

"Whatever we do, it will never be enough," Sally smiled as she got up, gathering her things together before heading for the door. "The doctor will be in tomorrow, Jack Cookson, a young Australian who has given up a year to help us here. He's an angel and him being here means we can treat a lot more conditions that would otherwise go untreated. So just remember, we are making a difference." They walked back out to the car where the boy still sat watching.

"Miss, who is the other lady?" he called over to them.

"This is Tanya, she is going to help me in the clinic so be nice to her."

"Yes Miss. Hello Miss Tanya. You are fine looking," he smiled as he looked at Tanya.

"Thank you, and thank you for looking after the car. I see you are an important man in the area."

"Anything you need Miss Tanya come speak to Bandile." She laughed but the irony of their very different worlds was not lost on her as they drove back to the luxury village.

The following day they returned to the clinic, Tanya excited to help again. They walked in and saw that the doctor's office was open. Sally popped her head in and spoke to him before he appeared at the doorway with a beaming bright, white smile.

"Hi Tanya, thanks for coming in and helping out. We need all the help we can get," Jack gave her a grin as he shook her hand. Mid-thirties, standing six feet two and built like a professional sportsman, he was an impressive figure. His warm outgoing personality oozed charm and their eyes locked for a second longer than maybe they should before Tanya busied herself with preparing for the queue.

"Hey, maybe we can all grab a coffee after clinic and get to know each other, how does that sound?" Jack suggested, his eyes still following Tanya. Sally looked up, "If you're paying Jack, I'm sure we can fit you in with our busy schedule."

"Fab, let's get cracking then."

They worked through the queue of patients, Tanya confident enough to deal with many things herself, either giving advice, first aid or making an appointment with Jack. It was good to be wanted again. Midday came around in a flash and Sally spoke to the large guard on the door. "No more for today please." He opened the door and beckoned her over.

"There are no more, you three have cleared the queue for the first time ever. So many happy faces." Sally called Tanya over, "See Tanya, that is the difference you have made already."

They left the centre and reclaimed their cars from the unofficial secure car parking attendant. Sally spoke to Jack before they got in.

"We'll follow you, where are you taking us?"

"Thought we would go to Haas Coffee today, push the boat out to welcome Tanya."

"You are spoiling us," she teased, having noticed the attraction between the two of them. Tanya got into the car with Sally and they drove into central Cape Town. Parking up, they found their way to the coffee bar, a smart place on the ground floor of an art deco building. Jack was already seated looking at the menu.

"I know what I am having. Come on ladies, share a cake with me then I won't feel such a pig."

"It's okay for you Jack, us ladies need to work hard to keep slim, you seem to do it naturally," Tanya replied, showing him she had noticed his impressive physique.

"Nonsense, you are both naturally goddess looking. I need the gym five time a week or I will end up like my dad, a real lard arse." He laughed as he said it. What he didn't add was that his dad had represented Australia at Rugby over a hundred times and Jack had made twenty appearances before following his career as a doctor. He didn't feel he could balance the two things and give a hundred percent to either, so the rugby was dropped.

They spent an entertaining hour together before heading their separate ways, "See you two next week, take care," Jack instructed them both before getting in his car and driving off with a final wave out the window. Sally and Tanya headed back to the village. Tanya wanted to know more about the doctor and wasted no time in quizzing her friend.

"He's a nice man Sally, does he have family here?"

"He has a wife but they have been separated for six months, the strain of working away has taken its toll. I think he hopes it will work out when he gets back to Australia. No children though. He's the best doctor we have had here." She glanced across at Tanya. "It's a pleasure to go into work, I must say."

"You can say that again Sally," Tanya agreed, with a big grin.

"Tanya Byfield, you are a married woman!" They both broke out in a fit of the giggles and a little bit of Australia stuck in Tanya's imagination. Tomorrow would be the final day of the week at the centre, and there would just be Tanya and Sally to deal with the crowds. They discussed what needed doing and Sally warned Tanya that she had a visit she needed to make so would drop Tanya off first before going on to the house call. Tanya had gained confidence during the day and was quite happy to work on her own for the time it would take.

Once they were home, Tanya picked the children up from the nursery. The buzz of the school filled her with joy, especially as the children seemed to love the place. They had made some friends and had even learnt some new words which they proudly showed off over dinner.

"Mummy, we love it here, can Daddy come over and then it will be perfect?" Ellie asked as she picked peas up individually with her fork before popping them in her mouth. Tanya, although glad the children were happy, felt a bit guilty at taking them away from their father.

"He has some work to finish first and then maybe he can join us. Shall we phone him?"

The phone rang a few times before Stephen answered. He was sitting alone in the safe house and his heart leapt when he saw Tanya's number displayed.

"Tanya, I am missing you all so much, how are things?" he greeted her.

"Going well, the kids are very excited to talk to you."

"Me too, how about you? Are you excited?"

"Stephen, I do love you, we just need to work things out. We can't be stuck in second place behind your work and in constant danger." The children came onto the phone and chatted for a few minutes before running out of things to tell him and Tanya came back onto the phone.

"They seem very happy, it seems like paradise there, if they are to be believed," he laughed.

A call waiting flashed up on his screen, it was James. Fuck, it must be important or he wouldn't call.

"Tanya, I have an important call waiting, can I phone you back?"

"More important than us Stephen? Glad you have sorted your priorities out."

"I will only be a second, don't go anywhere," he begged before he hung up and took the call.

"James, how can I help you?"

"Oh bugger, sorry Stephen, wrong number." He ended the call.

Stephen tried to phone Tanya back but she didn't pick up.

The early morning sun woke Tanya up. She looked at her phone and saw that she had missed seven calls from Stephen, she didn't care, she was beyond angry with him. He was a class one arsehole and could wait until she was ready for another chance to talk, all she knew was that it wouldn't be any time soon.

Sally dropped Tanya off in the centre parking area and drove away. The young car park attendant was not there which she thought seemed strange as she had understood that he would always be around. However, as she unlocked the clinic door, he rushed into the compound.

"Miss, Miss Tanya, come quick, I think my brother is dead." He was sobbing and his eyes were wild with panic as sweat poured from his forehead.

"Please help me," he begged, "he can't die." Tanya relocked the clinic door, her bag still in her hand, and turned to the boy.

"Take me there, quick as you can." They raced along the tarmac road before dipping into the narrow alleyways between the huts, taking so many twists and turns that Tanya had no idea where she was. They arrived at a non-descript tin building with a blanket over the doorway and dashing in, Tanya noticed a number of young men who were staring down at a lifeless body. Drug paraphernalia littered the floor and it was obvious the other guys were high.

"Move!" she ordered. She pushed them out of the way and crouching down by the body, quickly cleared his airway before checking breathing and pulse. There were no signs and looking up for help she realised that these people were either clueless or off their heads so she was on her own. She gave CPR and worked tirelessly until, after what seemed an age, he spluttered and vomited over Tanya's arm. She quickly re-cleared his airway and placed him in the recovery position, checking his pulse constantly. Slowly he regained consciousness before sitting up, dazed and confused. He was still high and had no idea what had happened. He looked at Tanya and his eyes flashed with anger.

"Get the fuck out of my house, who the fuck are you?"

"Your brother asked me ...." He cut her off and slapped her across the face.

"Leave while you still can, leave before we rape your white arse," he spat at her while trying to get to his feet. She got up and ran out into the alleyways hearing laughing and cheering behind her. Lost and totally disorientated, she stumbled from one alley to another before noticing music coming from a shack. Pushing the blanket that covered the doorway to one side, she saw that she was in an illegal bar. One of the customers looked up at her with glazed eyes which widened as he took in the attractive white woman in the doorway.

"What you doing here white girl? Why are you in our town? You know what happens to pretty white girls in our town?" He took a step towards her while at the same time, a massive guy came out from behind the makeshift bar.

"Shut up you fool, this lady helped my mother yesterday, she is the nurse I told you about. Can I help you lady?" Tanya almost sobbed with relief.

"I am lost, I need to find the drop-in centre. Can you help me?" The big guy came over and ducked through the curtain. "Follow me Nurse, it is only a minute away. I will take you there personally."

CHAPTER TWELVE

Stephen was back in room twelve. He was beginning to dislike this office as the trust he once had in James was stretched with so many unanswered questions about the assault.

"James, when I first came here there were a number of other people in the office. Where have they disappeared to?"

"A couple have finished their investigations and I am going through their evidence. Some were not needed so I sent them back to their normal day jobs."

"Is that normal?"

"It's the first time we have conducted such a large scale operation. At the moment the team consists of us two although I do sub contract some parts of the work out, for instance when we saved your arse in the ship."

"You hire people willing to kill," Stephen suggested.

"If that's how you want to put it, although looking through your history, I don't think that you were too bothered when Martin Heard was shot by a hired killer. It saved the lives of you and your family. Unfortunately, the world of guns for hire doesn't come with a manual or a series of risk assessments, it's a murky world and one that you are better staying clear of. Do your own investigation, get the parcel of evidence that people are killing each other over, hand it to me and go home to live out your life. It really is that simple. Do you have the package Stephen?" His tone had changed and the question was asked in a way that the answer was already known.

"Why are you asking me that again? You asked the other day and I said no."

"Someone has got it, the Royal Mail have told me that it was signed for and collected close to your home address. Now, do you have it?" Stephen now knew that James doubted him as he was obviously checking up on him, contacting the post office directly.

"No, I do not have it. When it arrives you will be the first to know."

"Make sure that's the case. As I have said, too many have died for its secrets." It was a chilling statement. Did James believe him? Could he bluff it out, and more importantly, if he handed it over what would be the result? If anyone thought that Stephen had looked inside the package and had seen the dirty secrets, would he be expendable? Of course he would. He too would be found dead in unexplained circumstances. He needed advice urgently but was all alone with no one to trust. He realized James was saying something and focused.

"Stephen, we are having a few drinks over here with the Iranian minister on Friday evening next week, eight o'clock. Can you make it?"

"Yes, I am available, any dress code?"

"Normal attire."

"No problem. I'm going to take a few days off if that's okay? Thought that I would fly up to see Dad and get a game of golf in. I will be back for Friday evening though."

Stephen sat in the departure lounge at Heathrow as a call came over the tannoy. *'Last call for passengers flying to Aberdeen.'* He didn't move, his flight was scheduled for three fifty, a nine hour flight to Tunis on Air France. He had questions he needed answering and he knew the man he needed to talk to, Trevor Hinton, the Embassy official.

Managing to sleep on the flight was a blessing, and as the plane touched down and he looked out across the floodlit tarmac, it dawned on him that he was now sitting on the same continent as Tanya and the children. He wondered what they would be doing in a few hours once the sun came back up and became more determined to get this whole thing resolved so that he could get them back.

Gathering his sports bag from the overhead locker, he made his way through the airport before finally reaching the cab rank outside, the warm, humid night air wrapping around him like a blanket as he left the air conditioning of the arrivals hall. The last trip to this city seemed like only yesterday instead of three months ago and he hoped that the staff in the Embassy had not changed. It was a possibility, and he had no fall back plan if Trevor had moved onto another job. He just knew he needed answers if he was to get to the bottom of this and more importantly, come out of it alive.

Stephen remembered the lesson that he'd learned the first time he'd come through this airport and chose an official taxi, rather than one of the many unregistered cars which hung around the exit. The short drive to the Ibis Hotel took half the time and cost half the price as last time and checking in, he found his room and unpacked the few belongings he had taken with him. He hoped this would be a short trip and had booked the return flight for two days' time.

Plugging his phone into the charger, he phoned the Embassy number hoping that he could get a lead on Trevor Hinton. The phone rang for a long minute, and just as he was about to hang up, it was answered.

"Good evening British Embassy, Tunisia, how can I help you?" He had expected an answer machine message and it threw him for a second.

"Good evening, I have just arrived in the city and I was hoping to speak to Trevor Hinton."

"Who is calling?"

"Can you tell him it is Mr Byfield, we met a few weeks ago."

"I will leave him a message sir, he is on duty in the morning."

The following morning, Stephen sat in the square outside the Embassy building, drinking a coffee when he noticed Trevor walking past him. He stopped him before he reached the Embassy doors.

"Good morning Mr Hinton, remember me?"

"Oh gosh yes, Mr Byfield. What on earth are you doing back

here again?"

"I'm just tying up a couple of loose ends for a report that I'm submitting in regard to my last painful visit. I have another meeting later in the day so I wondered if I could I pop in this morning to make sure that I have got the correct information. I need to submit everything to my boss by the weekend." Trevor glanced at his watch.

"I'm a little early so I could join you for a quick coffee now if that's any use?"

"Sensitive information Trevor, do you mind if we went inside?"

"Of course, follow me." The inside of the building seemed different to the last visit, with the day time hours bringing a real buzz in the air in contrast to the old colonial bastion, and passing through security, they retreated to a small office on the second floor. Again, there were no real indications as to what job Trevor performed in this organisation as the desk was cleared of any evidence.

"You look a bit healthier this time around Mr Byfield," Trevor commented as he sat down in the chair behind the desk. "What on earth happened the last time you were here?"

"That's what I am hoping to find out," Stephen explained as he too sat down.

"I have already helped you more than you realise, I just picked up the pieces on that night," said Trevor.

"What does that mean?"

"As I said, I think that I have done my bit. So, how else can the Embassy assist you?" Stephen started to feel a bit frustrated with the Embassy official's unwillingness to help him and thought he might try spelling out his situation.

"I was tricked into going into the port area, kidnapped and nearly killed. But you already knew that. You had arranged for me to be rescued, for a doctor to be on hand on my arrival here, and you knew who I was. I thought that I was here for a quick meeting, you knew differently. How?"

"I don't think that I can share that information, I'm sorry."

Stephen looked him straight in the eye.

"My life depends upon it, my family have been threatened and have left me and my world is falling apart. I need to get answers to get my life back together again." Trevor met his gaze.

"It really is not a good idea to ask me to help Stephen, we could both be in a lot of danger. I think that you should go now and return to the UK. Maybe you can find your answers there."

"Please, don't you have a family? We need help, please help us." Stephen passed him his phone number.

"I am only here for two days, if you decide that there is anything you can tell me that will help, please contact me." Trevor stood and opened the office door.

"Thank you for coming by to catch up Stephen, take care now." He escorted him back down and through the reception area. And suddenly he was back into the bustle of a busy city. The one lead he had was gone. No plan B.

His phone rang, it was James.

"Where are you Stephen? I thought that you were in Scotland."

"Just catching up with a school friend in Rome, Scotland tomorrow, everything okay back there?"

"Yes, just had the post mortem results on Barry Shaw. He was murdered, single injection mark to his neck and a large dose of a particularly nasty substance was given. Toxicology tests should show us what later. Are you managing to stay out of the rain over there? Just saw a news stream from the city, it looks terrible."

"Yes, staying in the cafe drinking lots of good coffee watching tourists get soaked. See you on Friday."

"Take care." James rung off leaving Stephen thinking that he was the second person to tell him to take care in the last few minutes. And fuck it, did he know he was lying about Rome? He clicked onto the BBC weather forecast for Rome. Shit! Twenty eight degrees and sunny, he knew alright. The phone rang again, it was an unknown number.

"Stephen Byfield speaking."

"Hello Stephen, it's Trevor. I have booked a table for lunch. Meet me in the square outside the Embassy at twelve thirty."

They sat in a French restaurant sipping on a Bordeaux white wine, the place was empty except for the waitress who busied herself behind the bar flirting with the manager.

"Why the change of heart Trevor?"

"A few reasons, I lost my marriage and family to this damn job. Believe it or not I worked undercover for a few years in Libya posing as an oil refinery manager, I was of course spying on Gaddafi and his regime. I loved the cloak and dagger stuff until I realised that I had left my life in the UK behind me. I lost everything. Gaddafi went, the administration crumbled and I was withdrawn to this place, bored out of my mind. When I was briefed that you were in the country and about to be taken by the local mafia, it reminded me of my earlier days."

"How did you know that I was in danger?"

"We had a call from Whitehall would you believe, we didn't arrange your escape, they did everything."

"Who did you speak to?"

"Didn't catch a name, some young guy who seemed to know your movements." Stephen took another sip of his wine while he contemplated what he had been told.

"This is starting to add up, who was the guy with you while you were questioning me?"

"He flew in from London the day before, he's a senior manager from GCHQ. I don't know anything else."

"He wanted information about a parcel," Stephen recalled and reminded Trevor.

"When we spoke before you were delivered to us, all he talked about was that parcel. If you had told him where the parcel was, my orders were to keep you in the Embassy until he had phoned the UK and the package was in their hands, I knew that you couldn't tell them where the parcel was. It was obvious to me."

"So he also believed me?"

"Yes, it was clear that you didn't know anything about it. He was furious when he left." Stephen still had questions that needed answering and he continued quizzing Trevor.

"How much more do you know about me? The guy said he knew everything."

"We knew you were on secondment to Whitehall from HMP. We also knew that you had spoken to a tribal leader about past arms deals and that he had names for you. He was found dead later the same day by the way. We also knew about an investigation you were undertaking into high level corruption."

"Bloody hell, the guy from Whitehall told you all of this?" Stephen was incredulous that so much of his supposed confidential role had been divulged.

"No, he didn't tell us that."

"Who did?"

"The Foreign Secretary. As I said, this could get both of us into very deep water Stephen." Stephen grimaced as he replied,

"I've got a feeling we're already there." Two plates of food arrived at the table then, and they talked more generally as they ate. Finishing the meal, Trevor got up to go back to work and the two men shook hands.

"Not a word to anyone about this Stephen, it will end what is left of my career."

"I understand and you have my word," Stephen promised.

"Thank you and good luck." Trevor turned and left without a backward glance. Stephen returned to his hotel room, his brain processing all the information he had received. All was starting to become clear as he realized that there were two separate camps at work. James and his team needing the parcel, presumably to sweep the evidence under the carpet and protect the government officials made up one team, and then he, and whoever was helping him, needed to keep control of the parcel and expose the corruption. The problem was, he didn't yet know who was helping him.

Trevor stood at the junction in front of the Embassy, waiting for the traffic lights to change, when a heavy hand fell onto his shoulder and another took his arm as he was guided into the back of a Range Rover waiting at the lights. Roughly pushed into the central seat, he was punched heavily on the jaw.

"Now sit still and say nothing," he was ordered. The accent was Eastern European and brooked no argument. He was in no doubt that if he resisted, the consequences would be grave. The car drove through the streets before disappearing through an archway and into an open courtyard. Two men stood waiting, and as the car drew to a halt, they pulled the door open and dragged the panicking Embassy man out and down into a cellar. He was strapped to a chair with a solitary exposed bulb hanging above his head. A small stocky man stood in front of him, his thick Newcastle accent surprising Trevor for a second before a gloved fist broke his nose open. A second blow hit him hard on the left ear, a harsh ringing blocking out all other noise for a moment. He lifted his head and a third blow broke his jaw, stars flashing in his head as the taste of blood trickled down his throat making him gag. A darkness descended over him before a bucket of cold water in his face pulled him back to reality.

Lance Mitchell came into the room pulling on a pair of thick, black, leather gloves.

"What do we have here?" He nodded to the stocky man who instantly took two steps back.

"I hear that you have been giving secrets away Mr Hinton." He looked down at the bound man and saw that his jaw was beginning to swell, showing the signs of the beating.

"What have you said Trevor, what little tales have you told?" He took a bottle from a table set at the side of the room.

"Now, I need to know what has been said and if you don't tell me, I have learnt to my cost how much acid hurts when it burns and you will share my pain. Do you want that?" Trevor shook his head.

"No, no I don't want that to happen to me. I don't know anything," he mumbled through swiftly swelling lips. "I just arrange meetings and functions, I have nothing to give you," he repeated, trying to come across as the grey Embassy official with the boring job.

"But we saw you having your little lunch meeting. It looked

to me as if you had plenty to give Stephen Byfield."

"We are old friends, we were just catching up."

"Bullshit, you tried to have me killed in the boat, so don't insult me." He poured some of the liquid onto Trevor's thighs, and his trousers melted away as smoke rose up from them. A high-pitched scream was lost in the sound protected room as the flesh underneath blistered up, red and swollen.

"Please, no more," Trevor begged, tears of pain running down his cheeks.

"What did you tell him?"

"Nothing, we just chatted about what happened to him last time. I didn't know anything."

"Okay, as you wish." Mitchell walked to the back of the room, where a hissing sound and a red glow emitted. He turned holding a poker glowing white with heat.

"Let's see how this goes," he said, holding it centimetres from Trevor's exposed eye. "What did you tell him?" Trevor closed his eyes, hoping that in some way it would help. The heat was intense before burning through his eye lid and into the eye. He passed out again before another bucket of water brought him around.

"I told him nothing, you fucking bastard," he managed to gasp. Mitchell disappeared to the back of the room to reheat the metal.

"Okay, if you know nothing I may as well kill you," he said, returning with the white hot poker. Trevor broke.

"I told him about the Foreign Secretary, about GCHQ, about you, about the parcel. I told him what I knew."

"Good, Good." He nodded to the other man. "Untie him and bend him over." The thug untied him and pulled his torn trousers down before pushing him over a table.

"You have tried to fuck me up the arse twice office boy. Let me now reciprocate." Ramming the bar into Trevor's anus, the white hot metal screeched as it penetrated his bowel. Trevor screamed for a few seconds before death took the pain away. Mitchell looked at the other man.

"Geordie, get yourself back to the UK. I have a job for you to do. When was the last time you were in prison?"

The runway in Aberdeen felt a million miles away from where he had left twelve hours before. Chris was waiting for him in the small arrivals area. They quickly made their way to the car.

"Good trip over?"

"Busy Dad, I only have a day with you as I need to be in London tomorrow evening. How's the break going?"

"Nice, How's the family?"

"Don't know Dad, she won't speak to me at the moment. I can't blame her, fucking misery I have caused everyone."

"Sort it out, she is a brilliant wife and mum. You need to look at your priorities." Stephen nodded.

"If I get through this job Dad, I am out of the service. It has broken me."

CHAPTER THIRTEEN

Tanya entered the drop-in centre, the doctor's door was open and Jack was busy working at his desk. He glanced up and saw her walking past.

"Hey, how are you doing Tanya? The locals are telling me great stories about your exploits." She laughed. "Bit of a stupid thing to do, nearly got myself into trouble."

"My carpark boy says you are a hero. Anyway, Sally has to leave early today, she has asked if I can give you a lift back to hers. I thought a quick coffee after work before I drop you off?"

"Sure Jack, sounds good."

The clinic buzzed all morning with stories of Tanya saving a man's life and she was quite embarrassed with the exaggerated tales. The achievement was made greater by the fact that this man's money fed two families. If he had died, it would have caused a real crisis. Tanya knew he was a drug dealer and local gangster but didn't mention the fact when questioned by the patients. The morning slipped by before Sally poked her head into Tanya's room.

"Just going out, see you at home," she waved as she left the door.

With the last patient treated, Tanya cleaned up her room in preparation for tomorrow with a real feeling of achievement. It was such a rewarding job, and with her elevated status, she felt like a true member of the team. Jack drove her to the same coffee bar in the city centre. "What do you fancy Tanya?" He had a boyish glint in his eye as he asked.

"I need a strong coffee please, we've had a hectic few hours."

"Strong coming up." He made his way to the counter and gave the order. As he put the coffee in front of her, she noticed that her name was written on the top of the coffee with a swirl of cream.

"How sweet," she said before discarding it with a swish of the spoon.

"What, me or the guy's writing?" Not replying she took a sip from the cup and opened the small biscuit resting on the saucer. Jack took a sip from his own cup, looking at her over the rim.

"Tanya, I am at a loose end tonight, do you fancy a drink or two?" Laughing she replied.

"What, I'm only good enough to fill your spare time?" As soon as the words left her lips, she knew it sounded like a come on.

"No of course not, just a drink as mates. I don't know many people around here, to be honest only you and Sally, but I guess that if you come out, you will need someone to look after the kids." Tanya smiled, thinking she deserved some time to herself.

"I'll let you know, I will send you a text."

"If it's a yes I'll pick you up at seven thirty." They drove back to the village chatting about the townships and problems faced by the clinic and the local's life styles. He pulled up outside the house and instead of driving off, he got out of the car and walked up to the door.

"Thought that I would say hi to Sally," he explained to Tanya as Sally opened the door.

"Jack, thank you for dropping Tanya off, can I get you a drink?"

"No thanks Sally, I am planning on having a couple tonight in town and I am trying to persuade Tanya to come with me."

"You used to take me out Jack, am I too old for you now?" Sally replied with a pout and a laugh.

"Never Sally, you will always be my bestie." He gave Sally a big bear hug causing her to squeal. Tanya laughed at the two of them messing around.

"Sally, can you keep an eye on the children tonight? I might just go out and see something of the town."

"Sure Tanya, In that case Jack, you may as well stay here and have dinner before you go out. It will save you another trip." She turned and led them both inside. The children came running in, stopping quickly when they saw Jack in the kitchen.

"Hey guys, how are you doing?" he asked them, giving them a big smile. Tanya kissed the twins hello and picked up Hector. "This is Jack, he is a doctor."

"Cool, do you do operations?" Harry asked.

"Not today, but a more important question, can you catch a ball?" Jack replied. They disappeared into the garden throwing a rugby ball to each other, Hector toddling between them all, getting in the way. Tanya saw Jack pick him up and pretend to throw him like a ball causing great peals of laughter from all three kids as the twins begged for their turn. Sally saw a look of sadness pass over Tanya's face and she knew she was thinking that it should be their father playing with them. She put her arm around her, giving her a quick squeeze.

"You'll sort things out with Stephen, in the meantime, have some fun, it's just a drink." Tanya hugged her back.

"I know but I can see just how much the kids are missing him and then I wonder if I am doing the right thing." They stood watching for a few moments more before Tanya pulled herself together.

"It'll be nice to see the city at night and as you say, it's just a drink."

Sally called everyone into the kitchen, where a huge bowl of tomato pasta sat on the table, waiting for them all to dig in.

"Sally, how did you know this is my favourite meal?" Jack asked as he sat down, the twins clambering up to sit on either side of him.

"You say that every time Jack," Sally replied, dishing out large bowls for everyone. Jack poured wine for the adults and they ate and chatted until it was time to leave. Tanya came back into the kitchen, having put Hector to bed. She wore smart jeans and a shirt which showed her figure off.

"You scrub up well Tanya" Jack joked.

"Make sure that you get her home in good time," Sally looked at him sternly.

"Yes Mum!" They drove off waving to Sally and the twins until they were out of sight.

Stephen sat in the Scottish cottage, he had tried Tanya's phone again but it was off. He hadn't spoken to her for over a week as she had constantly ignored his calls and he guessed that she was still pretty angry with him. Checking through his contacts on his phone, he found Sally's number, he hadn't seen her for years and hoped it was still current. It was and Sally answered,

"Hello Stephen, it's a long time since we spoke.

"Too long, I have been trying to contact Tanya but she still isn't picking up. I wondered if you might persuade her to talk to me?" In the background, he could hear the twins chatting and laughing as Sally replied.

"She's just popped out Stephen, I will tell her that you rang and ask her to give you a call."

"Thank you Sally, I appreciate it. I can hear the children, can I have a quick chat with them?"

"Sure. Kids, Daddy's on the phone." He could hear them arguing about who was going to talk first before Ellie took the phone.

"Hi Daddy, I'm missing you."

"Missing you too darling, what have you been doing today?"

"School and then learning to catch and kick a rugby ball with Jack. He's a doctor."

"Fantastic sweetheart, where is Mummy now?"

"She has gone out for a drink with Jack, he has got a nice car Daddy, it's like yours."

"Can you let me speak to Sally again darling?" He heard the phone being passed back before demanding, "Who is this Jack, Sally?"

"Oh, he's the doctor from the clinic, he is just showing her the city. It's all very innocent, he has taken me out dozens of times. He's a lovely lad."

"Lad?"

"Well not a lad exactly, about your age I would guess." She

gave an embarrassed laugh, hoping she hadn't made things more difficult between Stephen and Tanya.

"Okay Sally, tell her I called, I will try to phone again when she is not so pre occupied."

"It's not like tha....." the phone went dead.

"Can I talk to Daddy now Sally?" Harry's little face looked up at her.

"He had to go sweetheart, he will phone back later."

They sat in the harbourside bar, the lights from surrounding buildings reflecting on the calm water as an impressive array of yachts bobbed gently against their moorings. The quiet buzz of conversation mixed with the flowing music of Africa spilling from unseen speakers, made an intoxicating atmosphere. The long, cold cocktails helped the flow of conversation between them as they sat on high bar stools, the bartender standing unobtrusively at the far end of the long counter. Occasionally making small talk with the couple, he felt very at ease with them, they were fun, intelligent and good tippers and he would make sure that their glasses were never left empty for long.

"So Jack, why were you at a loose end tonight?" Tanya asked, wanting to understand why he would be in this beautiful city alone.

"It's a long story; it's my fifth wedding anniversary of a presently failing marriage, I am here and Kate is in Sydney, that says it all really. I was planning on flying back for the week as a surprise but when I told her that I was coming home she said that she had made other plans and was going to see friends in Perth. I wasn't wanted, hence I am sat here with my new friend. That's my story, although I feel that yours may be a little more complicated."

"Jack, if I were to tell you about the last two years of my life, you wouldn't want to be anywhere near me. When the dust settles, I may write a book and it will be a bloody best seller with all the drama I've had."

"And your husband? You have never mentioned him."

"He's a good man, just very preoccupied with work. Things have got a little sticky at home and we needed a break for a number of reasons."

"Sticky in regards to what?" Tanya felt a little protective about her situation, she had drunk three good cocktails but her senses were still in place. She didn't want to give him the wrong idea.

"Not marriage wise. His work was causing some security issues as normal."

"What does he do?"

"I'm not sure anymore. I think he may be involved in government issues that are beyond him, but it's all so secretive that I really don't know a lot."

"A spy?"

Tanya laughed, "No nothing so romantic, more a fall guy I think." She sipped the last of the cocktail and stirred the bottom of the glass with the straw.

"Another cocktail guys?" The attentive barman had noticed her empty glass.

"Yes, last one please, same again Tanya?" She looked at her watch, the evening had flown by and it was approaching midnight.p"Why not, it's been a lovely evening and so nice to have an adult night out for once." They chinked glasses and laughed. The noise in the street outside the bar was growing. At first the people inside thought that a fight had broken out but the approaching police sirens indicated that it might be more.

Jack turned to the barman. "What's going on out there?"

"I will go look, one second." The bar had emptied out except for a dozen or so people whose conversation had turned to one of anxiety over the increasing sounds of trouble outside. The barman returned, a look of consternation on his face. The fact that he locked the door as he came in and turned the lights down was an indication of a problem.

"It's a township issue," he explained. "The police have arrested a number of gang leaders and one has died in the police cells. There are hundreds of people rioting down the road and there is a cordon but the police guy that I spoke with doesn't know if it will hold. If it doesn't, it will be chaos. I have never seen this before. We are on lockdown and they have told us not to move at all. It could be a few hours before we can get out."

"So what do we do?" Tanya asked, worrying about Sally being left alone with the children.

"Stay here with me I guess. We have hotel rooms upstairs but I don't think that is a good idea, we may have to move quickly if we are told too." Tanya phoned Sally who was still awake and watching the news.

"The locals are rioting in the street, we are locked in the bar and the police have advised us to stay put. I'm not sure how long it will be before we can get out."

"I thought it was a bit tense down there earlier, I saw on the news that there was a problem, I just didn't realise it was in your area. Talking of problems, Stephen phoned."

"What did he say?"

"It's what the children said that is more of an issue. They told him that you were out with Jack. He wasn't happy. He said he would phone you when you were not so pre occupied."

"Oh bollocks! Okay, I will deal with that if we survive this riot. See you later Sally, keep watching the news and I will phone if there are any developments." As she rang off, another surge of police and army vehicles sped down the main street to shore up the area before the bark of police dogs was eventually lost in the wail of the mob. A banging on the bar door sent the barman over to investigate before turning and addressing those sheltering inside.

"Okay everyone, follow me. The police are moving us out, get your stuff and get on the trucks outside." He turned off the remaining light and following everyone out, locked the door saying a silent prayer for the business as he looked over the tail gate of the truck towards a burning barricade not far down the road.

It was three in the morning before the taxi arrived back at Sally's. Jack had stayed in a city centre hotel as the protesters had been pushed away and returned home, but Tanya was eager to get back to the children. She silently climbed into bed thinking about Jack, still slightly intoxicated from the alcohol and excitement of the evening as she thought about what she wanted from life.

Jack clearly liked her, he had made that clear from the first minute and although Tanya had been very careful not to give out any signals, she was secretly flattered that someone else had found her attractive and it had been an ego boost for her. Where was this heading though? She didn't need extra complications in her life and anyway, Jack hadn't made any advance on her. She drifted off into a heavy slumber thinking it wasn't every day that your evening was disturbed by a rioting mob. It could only happen to a Byfield. She jolted back awake. *I am a bloody Byfield, I love Stephen and I need to sort this out before he gets the wrong message.* With that firm resolution in her mind, she let herself return to sleep.

CHAPTER FOURTEEN

Stephen had a sleepless night, worried sick that Tanya was out on the town with another man. He had tried to call her but the phone had cut to answer message. He planned to fly down to Heathrow in time for dinner with the Iranians, where he would not be drinking as he intended to drive back up to Scotland for the remainder of the weekend. There were no available flights and the car was easier than messing about with a late-night rail service. With luck he would be back at Dad's before lunchtime and could then focus on an uninterrupted call with Tanya.

Arriving at Aberdeen Airport, he noticed that there were no delays although he had hoped that by some miracle, all flights would be cancelled. He had to face James who would question him as to why he was not in Rome, where he had really been and where the parcel was. How long could he keep this bullshit going? He was concerned that his marriage was falling to pieces as he sat in yet another departure area surrounded with people he didn't care about, contemplating that his life was unravelling around him. He dragged his heavy heart onto a packed plane, noticing from the chatter around him that they were mainly oil workers and a plethora of I.T. experts discussing stuff from another world that Stephen had no hope of understanding, plus a few soldiers heading back south for the weekend. He rested his head against the window and managed to get some much needed sleep, waking to check his phone in the hope that Tanya had contacted him.

The plane touched down in afternoon drizzle and he planned on getting the train into the city before collecting his car and driving to the secure parking used by Whitehall staff. He would then make a quick getaway and drive the nine hours back up to Aberdeen. Half hoping to see a friendly driver holding out a card stating his name, he was quickly disappointed and made his way to the station.

The short train journey and cab ride from Paddington to the new safe house didn't take long but it gave him enough time to think of a plausible story to keep James at bay. Quickly checking the rooms in the house to ensure that he had no unwanted surprises waiting, he showered and changed before packing a sports bag for the weekend. Checking himself out in the hall mirror, a feeling ran through his mind that this whole thing was coming to a climax and it felt as though it would explode in Stephen's face at any minute.

He locked up the house and gunning the engine, headed out into the afternoon traffic. With no holdups, he reached the office with an hour to spare so headed straight up to face James. His boss was still working and looked up when he saw Stephen enter the room.

"Hi Stephen, how was the trip?"

"Scotland was great, in fact I'm driving back up there tonight after the dinner, back on Monday morning."

"And Rome?" he looked pointedly at Stephen.

"Don't know about Rome, I didn't go there. Sorry I lied to you. I was actually in Amsterdam seeing an old girlfriend, and you freaked me out a bit when you phoned."

"You crafty old git, Tanya has only been away a short while and you are out chasing an ex. I am shocked."

"Yes, let's keep this between us, I have been seeing her for a few months but nothing serious." James nodded.

"So long as it doesn't impact on our work. Any news of the parcel?"

"I was going to ask you, have you checked the box?"

"Yep, nothing, and I don't expect it to appear as someone has it already." Stephen kept his face expressionless.

"Who?" he asked.

"I will find out shortly, the Post Office have the guy on CCTV.

When I see it I will know for sure." He looked at Stephen hoping for a response, a tic that gave him away or a downward glance but he maintained eye contact and was unreadable. He logged off his computor and stood up.

"Let's get downstairs and greet our guests, just the normal courtesies. This is the end of a long week for them, the Foreign Office have tied up a multi-billion pound deal so let's show them a good time." James laughed to himself as they took the lift down to the conference room.

"In the time it took you to screw your ex and play a couple of games of golf, the Government have made us three hundred billion pounds, it's a crazy world." Stephen was just thankful James had believed his story, even if he did now have the reputation of a cheating bastard.

The evening passed in a blur for Stephen, constantly checking his phone in the hope of a response from Tanya, yet afraid to phone her in case they argued again. James worked the room all evening, shaking hands and making small talk, and following suit, Stephen did his best to socialize. An Iranian official eventually cornered him making inane chatter about the sale of equipment to help the war in The Yemen. Three hundred billion pounds to pummel a penniless population, with many more defence orders to follow. As Stephen listened with half an ear, he mused over the fact that the Foreign Secretary had certainly earned his money this week. Such a shame that Stephen knew a front bench politician was corrupt and the Foreign Secretary had been taking an active interest in Stephen and his parcel. Again, he remembered advice given to him as a young prison Governor. *There is no such thing as coincidence, everything happens for a reason.*

The evening was due to end at ten thirty, and as always seemed to be the case in diplomatic functions, both sides were eager to get out, the Whitehall staff to go home, the visiting delegation to hit the casinos and bars. As the clock hit the finishing time, there were only a handful of people still chatting as staff gathered up empty glasses and plates while the last few stragglers disappeared into the London night. Eventually the catering staff slipped away leaving just Stephen and James, neither of whom had taken a drink all evening as business came first. James headed towards the door.

"Right, I'm going up to the office to send my report through to the Foreign Secretary and then I'm going home. How about you?"

"I'll be setting off for Scotland shortly, hope to be there before lunch time. I couldn't get a flight so I'm going to have to drive all night."

"Wow, that's a tough drive, good luck with that one," James said as he patted Stephen on the back. He then casually asked, "Do you want to come and identify the person picking up the parcel Stephen? You may know him."

"When are you going to do that?"

"Now, it was being sent through to my system while we were entertaining. Shall we check?" His head spun, if he refused, James would know for sure that it was him, if he went with him and saw himself on the CCTV, the game was up. Both ways, he was screwed. Why hadn't he thought of this and sent Terry in? He decided it was better to know for sure if he had been found out, he could then think of a way out.

"Sure, I can spare a few minutes, like you say I may know the face. If Barry Shaw hid it in a safe deposit box he may have told a friend who has tracked it down."

The lift seemed to take an age to get to the floor, the walk to the office twice as long. Stephen's heart thumped as James unlocked the oak door and flicked the florescent lighting on. They both went behind the desk as James logged onto the system.

"Here we go, the footage is here, direct from the Post Office." Double clicking on the link they waited for it to download, the circle spinning in the centre of the screen in time with Stephen's stomach.

Finally, the footage appeared, but it was poor quality as it appeared that a spider had spun its web across the lens. James complained out loud.

"Why do we give these fucking idiots security when they don't maintain it properly?" The image of the back of a man talking to the staff member filled the screen, any other details had been hidden by the silk of the web. The man could have been anyone, the lighting was poor, the lens was blocked and the angle of the camera was wrong as it only showed the rear of the customer. Stephen started to pray, if he hadn't looked up at the camera he was safe. Holding his breath, he continued to watch and saw with relief that head down, he had walked out of the shop without an upwards glance. He was unrecognisable.

"Can we just run that back James? I couldn't pick up any clear details," he requested. They looked through it again but it was such a bad recording that they couldn't even tell if the man was white or black. They would need more proof. "Maybe a statement from the postmaster may help," suggested Stephen.

"The postmistress must have had identification or the parcel would not have been handed over to its intended owner unless they knew them. It was in your village Stephen."

"Someone else was expecting me to have the delivery and they must have claimed it. I have never used the Post Office. Tanya took care of all that side of life. Why can't you ask the woman?" James closed the file and looked up at Stephen.

"Because she has gone missing, she didn't unlock the shop this morning and no one has seen her for a couple of days."

Lance Mitchell took a familiar pose, standing in front of a terrified victim as they pleaded for their life. The woman was in tears. The plastic straps were digging into her wrists and the hard metal chair cut into the backs of her legs as he asked her the first question.

"Who picked up a parcel from you last week? It was a large padded, brown envelope possibly addressed to Mr Stephen Byfield. Do you remember it?"

"I have a lot of parcels left with me, I can't remember," she sobbed. He laughed. "I knew that response was coming so let me help you remember." The cut throat razor flashing its deadly blade in the light of the room was a terrifying sight.

"Do you know how much make up you will need to hide what I am going to do to your face?" She sobbed, head down and back arched trying to move her head as far away from him as possible.

"One last time, did Byfield pick up the parcel?" What Lance Mitchell hadn't realised is that this innocent looking lady had been a senior police officer during her younger days and she had a strong will and even stronger resilience. She knew that he was the enemy and Stephen Byfield represented the good. There was no way that she was going to give him up.

"I don't know who picked up what parcels without looking," she told him, looking straight at him.

"Yes you do lady, yes you do!" Slicing the blade through her right cheek, blood flowed down onto her light blue cotton jacket.

"Was Byfield alone?" She didn't answer, sitting defiantly in front of her potential killer.

"Was he fucking alone you bitch, talk to me?" He cut her again, she screamed once before catching her breath as the blood flowed from her wounds, onto the floor.

"If I need to cut you into little pieces I will, now tell me what happened." She lifted her head, eyes blazing with anger at him.

"You really feel that hurting me so badly is going to help you. Only God can help you and I sincerely hope that you have the chance to meet your maker quicker than you anticipate. I doubt that he will be welcoming you though." Enraged he sliced through her white throat leaving a dark oozing gash before blood squirted out and over his shirt. He cursed and cut her again, disappearing into a blood lust frenzy, only stopping as he became tired. Fatigue spread through his body as he looked down on the mess that had been an honest wife, worker and mother only minutes before. He looked into the mirror and saw the face of a monster looking back at him and for the first time, he questioned himself. He had killed many times before, enemy agents, enemy soldiers, but this was the first time he had taken the life of an innocent civilian. He had taken an innocent life because one person had demanded it. He would kill again on this mission, as many times as he needed to in order to achieve it and then no more. His day had come.

CHAPTER FIFTEEN

Stephen headed north, he'd had a lucky escape as someone seemed to be on his side. However, if James found the Post Office worker, she would identify him easily. He had used the shop dozens of times and always cursed himself that she knew his name but he didn't know hers. The adrenalin of the last few hours was seeping out of his body and stopping at the services, he filled up the tank and took a walk into the shop for a sandwich and a couple of cold drinks. Ploughing on towards the border, he struggled to stay awake and drove with the window open and the radio blaring. He stopped once more, walking around the car a few times, breathing in the cold night air before he drove on into the approaching dawn and crossed the Scottish border. It was a real boost to his morale to be in his destined country and off the motorway.

The blue lights flashed behind his car and with nobody else on the road, he pulled over into a layby. He knew that he was struggling and maybe looked like a drunk driver for anyone following him, an easy mistake for a tired policeman to make at this time in the morning. He sat in the driver's seat watching the policeman come up to the side of the car.

"Do you know why we have stopped you sir?"

"My bad driving, I guess. Sorry, I'm tired, I'll take a break for an hour."

"Have you been drinking sir?" The other policeman was on his radio but Stephen was unable to hear what was said although the officer seemed to be concentrating.

"No, I haven't had a drink," he replied to the question.

"Turn off the engine sir. Give me the keys and then keep your hands on the wheel." He obliged as another police car pulled up in a blaze of lights and dust. Two armed police officers appeared out of the car pointing their weapons at him.

"What the fuck is going on?" he asked in disbelief.

"Do you have any weapons on you?"

"No, of course not."

"Get out of the car and keep your hands on your head," he was ordered as the door was thrown open.

"Lie down, face down, do it now." It felt the most bizarre thing to ever happen but he complied as the policemen proceeded to search his car, opening the boot and bonnet and checking every inch of the interior.

"Sir, you told us that you didn't have a weapon, why do you have a pistol in your boot?"

"I don't know what you are talking about," Stephen twisted his head round, trying to look up at what was going on.

"I am talking about this." The officer dangled a gun in a clear plastic bag in front of his face.

Stephen knew he had been set up and lay listening to his rights being read to him as the dust from the road crept into his throat.

"Someone has made a mistake; I work for the security services," he tried explaining as he was lifted on to his feet and bundled into the back of the police car.

"That's not the information we have on you so I suggest that you save it for the duty solicitor," was the reply.

Paraded in front of a high desk, the duty police sergeant spoke with Stephen before he was questioned in the interview room where the duty solicitor in attendance seemed more concerned with making him state no comment than actually getting to the truth of the matter. Left alone in the room as the interviewers took a break, Stephen asked,

"Will you get me bail?" The duty solicitor looked at him in surprise.

"I doubt it Mr Byfield. With your extensive criminal record and failure to abide by bail conditions last time, I think that you will be remanded without a doubt." Stephen looked at him in horror.

"What criminal record? You have made a mistake, I have

never broken the law in my life."

"I have your previous convictions here Mr Byfield and they are extensive."

"No chance, Google me."

"I have everything I need here Mr Byfield, you will be going into custody. The weapon found in your car was used in a murder in Glasgow last week. I'm afraid that you are in a lot of trouble this time." Stephen was not giving up.

"Just humour me, Google me. Stephen Byfield, Prison Governor."

The duty solicitor gave a resigned sigh and clicked onto his laptop.

"Nothing under Stephen Byfield, Prison Governor but plenty under Stephen Byfield, arrested Peckham, Stephen Byfield, arrested in Holland, plus many more. They even have your arrest pictures. Please don't waste any more of my time."

"No, let me show you," Stephen insisted, holding his hand out for the computer. The solicitor pushed the laptop over to him, "Click away Stephen." He looked at the screen in amazement. His whole online life had been deleted and replaced with fake news. He knew this collusion was from the top and it was as if the real him had never existed.

Standing back in front of the custody desk, he was charged with possession of a firearm and murder, and as events became blurred and confused, he was bundled into a secure van and driven off into the traffic. The cramped cell in the van brought his situation into sharp reality. He had been used by James and he was now surplus to Whitehall's requirements. The government security services could do whatever they wanted to him and there was nothing at all that Stephen could do about it. No one knew where he was, he had been taken off the grid, the parcel would be discovered eventually and Stephen would be killed in prison without anyone knowing or caring.

He had heard the same story from two other prisoners during his time in the Prison Service and had discounted the first man as an imposter. The second occasion he had taken the time to dig into the story and the man had been telling the truth and was eventually released. Nobody was going to dig for him though and a complete nightmare was unfolding in front of his eyes.

Standing in the dock, Stephen heard a prefabricated criminal history revealed, he had been offending for twenty years and was involved in gang warfare in London and Manchester. He had served a number of sentences both in the United Kingdom and abroad and when the question arose as to if he should be granted bail, police believed he would flee the country as he had done in 2006.

Remanded into custody, he was placed back into the van and driven out into the city traffic. He looked through the van window at the families shopping on the busy streets and his thoughts returned to Tanya. How could he contact her?

To his surprise, instead of delivering him into custody, he was taken back to the original police station. It seemed strange to him that they would not want to get rid of him straight away and even the escorting staff didn't know what was happening other than they had been given specific orders to follow. Arriving at the station, he was bustled directly into a cell with no furniture other than a concrete bed.

"Cup of tea and a sandwich?" he was offered.

"Yes please, why am I here?"

"Legal visit that would have taken too long to arrange with the prison," the officer explained before shutting the door. This made even less sense, he had seen his so-called legal team in the court and everything had been discussed. The door reopened revealing James standing there with the tea and sandwich. Stephen looked at him in disgust.

"You have screwed me over James."

"You should have just given me what I was looking for Stephen, I knew that you had it, all you had to do was pass it over and walk away."

"And allow them to win?"

"As I said to you, the good guys don't always win. It's all for the good of the country and you seem to have forgotten that."

"So, what happens to me now?"

"Give me the parcel and you will get bail and have all charges dropped. Keep playing the hero and you go to jail." James then added another threat, "Don't forget, I know where your family are hiding."

"No, you don't, you just have the name of the city and it's a big place. Tanya will lie low, you won't find her."

"No, I won't, but my English friend on the other hand, is very good at hide and seek. Shall I make him count to ten?" Stephen slumped in resignation.

"James, why me?"

"Because we thought that you were washed up after the treatment you've received over the last couple of years. We thought that every ounce of resilience had been stripped from your body and you were not supposed to uncover the evidence, that was my job. Find it, make it go away. Someone decided to make you a central character for whatever reason. Did you look in the parcel?" Stephen thought quickly.

"Yes, I've seen it all and if anything happens to me, it will be sent to the BBC."

"No, it won't as no one knows where you are. That's why I have had you arrested in Scotland, it's a completely different prison service to England and you have no friends here to help you out. Whoever you have trusted with it will either die hiding it or leave it where it is because you have run for cover. Either way, it is useless to you." Stephen tried one last ditch attempt.

"If you hurt my family you will never get it."

"I will take my chances. You have a week to consider your options, I'll be in contact with you then."

James turned and walked out of the cell leaving Stephen to consider both options. He got up and banged on the cell door.

"Officer, can I have a phone call please? I need to tell my wife where I am."

"No, you are not allowed any calls, orders from the boss. Sorry." He sat back down, head spinning with the choices facing him. Give up the evidence and see the corruption covered up but get home to see the family, or keep silent and die in prison. Sod them, he would rather die a lion than live as a sheep and he lay on the concrete bed to wait for what came next.

Finally, he was told that he was going to be moved to a prison where he would be allowed a call and he would get everything that he was supposed to get. He was led outside and climbed back into the secure van. He was surprised to see that it was already dark again.

"What time is it?"

"Ten o'clock."

"Why so late?"

"No idea, we are just moving you at the time that we were told to do it. We don't want to be driving on a Saturday night either and the prison certainly doesn't like receiving new receptions this late." Of course Stephen was well aware of this fact but didn't think it would do him any good to point this out. They drove back into the city and soon reached the vast, formidable Victorian prison. He was very used to seeing a prison that was locked up for the night and wasn't surprised that it took a while for the gate staff to open the huge wooden gates, the clunk of the locks ringing out in the silent gate area. A radio crackled in the distance as the night manager came down to meet the escort.

"Okay, get him off here and I will take him through reception. Any property?"

"Nothing at all, straight off the street." The van door opened and the cell door was unlocked, Stephen being the only person on board.

"Okay, follow me," he was ordered. "It'll be a quick reception process tonight as the staff went home hours ago. I will give you your stuff, you will see a nurse and then straight to your cell. You can get a shower in the morning."

Standing in front of the reception desk was a strange experience, he knew every question that would be asked, knew every answer to get himself a single cell instead of sharing, or even to manipulate a place on the hospital wing. Instead, he just listened to the script. Tired, worried and very frightened, he just wanted to sleep. The nurse came into the reception building and ushered him into a separate room where she quickly ran through the standard form.

"Any mental health problems?"

"No."

"History of self-harm or recent thoughts of hurting yourself?"

"No."

"Substance abuse, drugs or alcohol?"

"No."

"Okay, you will see a doctor on Monday morning, they're not in the prison on Sunday." Sent back out into the main room, the Prison Officer continued.

"Any reason why you can't share a cell, bearing in mind I do not have any single cells available?"

Stephen decided to make him work for his money.

"If you put me in a cell with anyone, I can't guarantee that I won't harm them. I have a history of acting out violent episodes when I am locked in a cell with someone who I don't know."

"What do you mean by that?" the Officer asked, looking concerned.

"Just what I said. I can't control my temper once locked in a cell, but it's your call."

"Okay, wait there, I will see what we have available." Stephen sat in a waiting area, a small holding room covered in graffiti and stinking of tobacco and stale clothing. The Perspex windows separating him from the main corridor were scratched with gang insignia and threats towards the prison staff. He knew they wouldn't risk putting him in a shared cell and sure enough the officer soon returned.

"Right, you're in luck, I have found a single room. Here is a small pack of essentials, toothpaste, shower gel and so forth, you have been in prison before so I don't need to remind you not to borrow anything and do not lend anything out or you will be fleeced." He led Stephen onto the Induction Unit, a smallish wing, four landings high but only thirty cells on each landing.

They climbed the harsh metal stairs up to the third landing, and along to cell 28.

The door was unlocked, and he was ushered in. The floor was filthy, the window was broken allowing the cold air to sweep in, and the glare of the external security lights flooded all areas of the room. Any furniture in there was broken and it was a miserable scene. The officer, seeing his face, shrugged his shoulders.

"It is all I can offer you tonight, make your bed up and get some sleep, they will let you clean it up tomorrow."

Throwing his things onto the bed as the door thumped shut, Stephen looked around. It was a dive of the highest order, the bed was broken, there was no TV and the main light in the cell was not working. Blood seemed to be splattered on the back wall and names and dates were written on every available surface. He tried to use the toilet but when he finished, it wouldn't flush. Frustrated, he rang his cell bell. After five minutes a face appeared outside of the door.

"What's the emergency?"

"I have no toilet, no bed, no pillow and no light. This place is a shit hole and I want another cell."

"It's midnight and we haven't got another cell. This one is normally off line but you insisted on having a single cell and this is all we have. Get your head down and we can try sort you out tomorrow. Stay off the bell." The observation flap was closed and the officer walked away. He had no choice other than to try to sleep, the broken bed frame making this nearly impossible.

"Oy, twenty eight, what's your name?" Stephen ignored the call.

"Twenty Eight, where are you from?" He ignored it again.

"Okay, you fucking prick, it's on tomorrow." There was a howl of laughter from some of the other cells. Others started to shout at him. Stephen had heard this happen a million times, he just didn't realise how intimidating it could be. He still ignored the calls. Another voice from a cell bellowed out.

"I am sleeping you fucking smack heads, shut the fuck up." The noise stopped instantly.

The drone of a hundred radios playing throughout the night filled the loneliness. Stephen strained his ears to pick out news reports and time checks. He counted every half hour off during that first long, cold night. At last a weak sun tried to raise its head over the old brick wall surrounding the prison, and the noise of night staff counting the prisoners and sorting out the paperwork before handing over to the day staff joined the cacophony from the radios. Every alarm bell was checked at six o'clock with control confirming it had registered. Stephen listened to all the activity, wanting to learn the routine in order to make life easier for himself. Sitting carefully on the broken bed, he thought about James. If he handed over the parcel, this would all be over, however, too many people had died and he doubted very much that he would be allowed to live. He had to get a message to Terry.

CHAPTER SIXTEEN

This was Terry's third week in charge of the prison as the regular Governor still had one more week left on his long-haul holiday. The regular drive in that day was enhanced by a magnificent sunrise which made him feel good to be alive. He enjoyed getting into work and making a difference and although retirement was approaching fast, he wasn't sure that he was ready to give up his job. His wife Jo, however, had other ideas. She was looking forward to seeing the last of the Prison Service and the stress that it brought. She had seen far too much trouble during the past two years as they had shared every twist and turn with the Byfield family and it had nearly broken them on more than one occasion. Luckily, they were made of tougher stuff, which is just as well, as trouble was coming up the pathway.

The two men had waited unseen in the road outside the house, they had seen Terry leave for work and guessed that Jo would be inside alone. Their son Tom had left for a school trip skiing in France two days earlier and the men had followed Terry as he dropped him off at the school gates.

The doorbell rang and Jo could see the silhouettes of two people standing on her doorstep. She wasn't expecting guests and looking at her watch, she noticed it was only eight o'clock. Her heart started to thump, as her immediate thought was that there must be a problem with either Terry or Tom and, forgetting all the lessons learnt from past traumas, she opened the door without first fitting the safety chain. Her first awareness that she was in trouble came as they pushed past her, and although shocked, she tried to push them back through the door. The first man in, who was short and stocky, grabbed her by the arm and dragged her into the kitchen, forcing her onto a chair. The other man quickly handcuffed her, and placing a finger to his lips, he gave her the international hush sign, warning her not to scream. The first man spoke to her in a broad Geordie accent.

"We are about to have a look around your house as we want a parcel that your husband is looking after. If we find it, we will leave you alone."

"I don't know what you are talking about," Jo replied, furious that she had let herself be held hostage again. After her run in with Martin Heard, the serial killer a couple of years ago, she had taken self defence lessons but they were proving pretty useless in her current situation. She was slapped fiercely across the face, blood dripping from her split lip. The Geordie pulled up a chair as his accomplice began the search.

"I am staying here with you, so if there is anything you want to tell me, go ahead."

"Look, I honestly don't know what you are talking about, we haven't got anything of yours. I would have seen it if anything had been delivered here." The searcher came back downstairs and shook his head, before starting to rummage through the cupboards in the kitchen. Jo watched the mess he was making as he turned drawers upside down and hurtled packets and tins out of cupboards, and spoke again.

"I am telling you the truth, I am not hiding a parcel." The Geordie stared at her for a few moments.

"Okay, I believe you," he said as he took his phone from his pocket and dialled. The phone rang briefly before being answered. He kept his eyes on Jo as he spoke.

"It's not here, she is telling us the truth. What do you want me to do with her?" Her heart thumped out of her chest and she could barely catch her breath as sobbing, she pleaded.

"I have a husband and child, just leave me alone. I don't know what you are looking for, but it is certainly not here." He ended the call and placed his phone on the table spinning it as he stared at her.

"Are you expecting any visitors this morning?"

"No, I was going shopping."

"Will you be missed?"

"I was going alone, no, I am not meeting anyone. What do you want with me?"

"We are staying right here. If your husband is a smart man, we will be gone in an hour." He turned the kettle on and found the tea bags. "I'll make us a brew while we wait."

Terry was sitting at his desk, he had held the morning meeting and was in the process of planning for a meeting that afternoon with the Healthcare providers when his phone rang. It was the manager of the main gate area.

"Governor, we have a visitor demanding entry, he is Mr Uden, Deputy Director, National Security Group. Shall I escort him in?"

"Yes please, straight up to my office." Terry quickly alerted his Head of Operations of the visit, within five minutes the whole team would be aware and whatever he was coming in to look at would be working like clockwork. The tap on the office door signalled the arrival of Mr Uden.

"Good morning sir, this is a pleasant surprise, how can we help you?"

"I am carrying out some unannounced visits, just to get a feel of the estate. How are things running here Mr Davies?"

"Seems to be going okay in the absence of the Governor. We have had no dramas to date I'm happy to report."

"I would like to go through your contingency plans for staff going on strike, if you wouldn't mind." Thinking this was a strange request, Terry was happy to oblige.

"Sure, they are kept in the main safe, I will get them for you. Are we expecting a union problem?"

"Perhaps," Mr Uden answered in a non-committal manner. Terry took the safe key from the secure key box by his desk and walked across to the other wall. It always felt like a piece of theatre opening such a heavy safe and turning the key, he then twisted the handle pulling the door wide open. Moving two files out of the way, he reached in to retrieve the contingency planning file. The safe was large, perhaps three feet across and four feet high and it contained a lot of confidential information that was to be kept out of the eyesight of prying people.

Suddenly Terry became aware that Mr Uden was standing behind him staring directly into the safe, his eyes scanning the contents. He moved to block the view.

"I am sorry sir, I don't think that you should be looking in here." Udin moved Terry to one side.

"I say what I look at and what I don't," he insisted, as reaching in, he grabbed a large brown envelope and held it close to his chest. He turned back to Terry.

"I am taking this with me Governor. I am not sure that it is official Prison Service documentation, are you?"

"No sir, it is not prison service work and I'm sorry."

"I think that I have found what I came for so please escort me back to the gate. We are done."

The Geordie's phone vibrated on the table and he answered before quickly hanging up and placing the phone back in his pocket. "Okay, we are going. It seems that your husband came up trumps." They released Jo from the handcuffs and left. She ran to the door and placed the security chain on it before phoning Terry's office.

"Terry, two men have just broken into the house, they were looking for a parcel. Please come home, I don't know what to do." She broke down sobbing again.

"I am coming back now Jo, have the men left?" She looked out of the lounge window. "Yes, they have just pulled off."

"Get out of the house now, drive to the petrol station on Turnpike Road and I will meet you there. Have they hurt you?"

"Not really, just a bloody nose and a split lip."

"Bastards, they will be back Jo, so move quickly."

"Why will they come back? I thought that they had got what they wanted from you."

"They have got this month's supply of my running magazines and my entry form for the London Marathon. I knew that this would happen." Terry packed his sports bag and headed for the gate, he was pleased that he had followed his gut instincts and taken the parcel to another location but was furious they had attacked Jo. Whatever was in there must be dynamite.

He pulled out of the car park passing Mr Udin who was still sitting there in his new Mercedes. The running magazines were sprawled on the tarmac beside the car and Udin was shouting into his phone not noticing that Terry had just driven past him. Quickly phoning the Duty Governor, Terry passed on the message that Mr Udin was not to be allowed entry back into the prison and fifteen minutes later, he entered the forecourt of the Esso garage. Jumping from his car he hugged Jo tightly.

"I am so sorry darling, lock up the car and get in with me, we are sticking together. I need to give Stephen a ring to find out what the hell is going on." Stephen's phone didn't ring and it was obvious that it was turned off. Terry noticed that he had a voicemail message waiting and when he heard it was from Tanya, he played the message through the car speakers so Jo could hear too.

"Hi Terry, it's Tanya. This is probably a silly call but I'm worried about Stephen. We've been having a bit of a tough time and now he seems to have disappeared. I am not sure if he is just ignoring me, so could you phone him please and ask him to ring me? I know he will listen to you." Terry phoned her back, but it immediately went to answer machine so he left a return message.

"Tanya, hi, it's Terry. I've tried phoning him but his phone is off. Something is wrong as we have just been threatened by people looking for Stephen's parcel. I will try find him and when I have news, I will phone you. When you are free call me back."

Tanya finished her morning shift at the drop-in centre, it had been a manic morning and the talk of every patient had been the riot in the city centre. The police had released the gang leaders and two metro policemen from the gang unit had been suspended from duty and were going to face criminal charges for the murder of the young man. The Chief of Police had quickly called township meetings which he personally attended and his pro activity had averted a real crisis.

Unfortunately, it seemed that not all of the police officers shared his passion for working with the local families and one sat on the bonnet of Sally's car as they walked out of the centre to return home. Sally spotted him first, tugging on Tanya's sleeve. "This doesn't look good," she muttered quietly.

"Morning ladies, wasting your time dealing with the Kaffirs, hear you kept one alive?" They ignored him and placed their bags in the car. He looked at Tanya.

"You think those Kaffirs are going to help you, think again. One day you will know I am right." He strode off and got back into his patrol van, high fiving his colleague.

"What a charming man," hissed Tanya.

"We need to be careful, bad things can happen out here Tanya," Sally warned her. Tanya felt her phone vibrate and taking it out of her pocket, listened to the voice mail.

"Everything alright? Your face has dropped," Sally asked.

"I think there is a problem with Stephen, I need to make a call."

Terry's phone rang and seeing it was Tanya, he answered it straight away.

"Hi Tanya, I am not sure what is going on, Stephen wouldn't tell me the last time we met, but I think he's in trouble."

"We were followed in Brighton Terry, Security Services wanted to put us into a safe house but I wouldn't do it and came out here to South Africa instead."

"He did say that he was under surveillance when we went to pick up this parcel. It's got to be pretty important as it seems everyone wants to get their hands on it."

"I don't know anything about it Terry, he seems lost in another world and I'm not even sure that he wants us around anymore," Tanya replied and Terry heard the withheld tears in her voice.

"He wants you and the children more than anything in the world Tanya," he reassured her, "he's just hopelessly out of his depth. I will try and find out what's happening, do you have any names that I can go on?"

"I only met one person and Stephen seemed to trust him, I think his name is James. He works in Whitehall somewhere."

"Okay, good. Someone from the Prison Service will know where he was sent on secondment, so that will be a starting point."

"Thanks Terry. Please let me know when you find anything." She ended the call thinking hard about what may have happened. There were too many questions to be answered, but hopefully if Terry found a starting point, the rest might unroll.

They pulled up outside the house, Tanya had been so preoccupied that she didn't even realise that they were in the compound. She turned to her friend.

"Shall we go and pick the children up from school and have a nice lunch? I need to feel a touch of normality again as it seems that everything is spinning out of control." Sally reached across and took Tanya's hand.

"It will work out darling, Stephen will not leave you, he will not ignore you, and there will be an explanation for everything. He was a bit angry about Jack but that is just normal, he doesn't understand the pressures we face out here. Let's get him out here and show him." Tanya smiled sadly, "I need to find him first Sally."

CHAPTER SEVENTEEN

James sat in a hotel room in Bordeaux, facing the Grand Theatre Opera House, a stunning white building overlooking a pretty square in the centre of a delightful city. He had arrived that morning on an Easyjet flight from Gatwick, one hour and twenty minutes and here he was in a cultural dreamland.

He had arranged a meeting with someone who he had not seen for a long time, their situations being such, that any previous face to face contact had been impossible. The only surviving member of his family since their parents had died in a horrific car crash, he was looking forward to seeing his brother. Often separated by continents, hardly ever in the same country, they had both received a private education as children, but had ended up going in different directions in later life. Now, both were experts in their given field. There was a knock on the door, four o'clock exactly.

"Come in." The door swung open, slightly bouncing back from the wall, and there stood his brother, Lance Mitchell. Dressed immaculately in a new Armani suit, he strode in, taking a glass of champagne from the table before shaking James by the hand.

"James, you are looking well. Thanks for choosing somewhere out of the UK to meet, it makes life a bit easier." James smiled at his brother.

"Easier for both of us I think at the moment when it's difficult to know who to trust."

"Talking of trust," Lance said, inadvertently put his right hand over the scaring on his stomach, "I need to ask you a question that has been eating away at me for a while."

"You're going to ask me why I had you kidnapped and tortured," James interrupted.

"Yes, I've been wondering why you would want that to happen when I was working for you?"

"The acid was not supposed to happen, it got out of hand and I was unable to stop it, You were supposed to kill Ernie Stocken as he's become a real fly in the ointment and knows too much. He's just missed out on killing you twice Lance and he must be taken care of. Apologies anyway for the added pain....good thing you're such a hard man!" The two of them chinked glasses to show that there were no hard feelings and they sat down in front of the window to observe the comings and goings of the city and continue their conversation.

"Why have you started using the surname Mitchell, what's wrong with the family name?" James asked.

"Couldn't have two men named Childs trying to rule the world, it makes life confusing. Anyway, I sometimes feel we're like the Mitchell brothers in EastEnders so thought I would use their moniker."

"You can be the small, fat bald one."

"Fuck you James."

"How is the money in Iran holding up?"

"Nicely hidden away thanks to you and your Special Forces bank robbers. Only you could have thought of robbing the two biggest banks in the city during a fire fight, pure genius." James nodded his agreement.

"Made us a lot of money Lance, we just need to get it all back over to the UK so we can spend it."

"Well, when the Foreign Secretary gets his backside in gear and arranges for the Iranian Government to turn a blind eye to me driving ten million dollars of cash through the border, we can get on with spending it. Until then, you'll have to make do with the cash transfer I'm able to send you each year."

"And there's the problem, he's a greedy bastard mate, he's demanding four million to smooth the deal, and he knows nothing can happen until we agree to it."

"Will he negotiate on the cut?"

"Nope, he is retiring from politics after the next election and this is his nest egg."

Lance shrugged, "We have no choice then do we."

"That's what I have been thinking, without him we can't get all the cash and a bit here and there is nice, but not life changing."

Lance looked deep in thought.

"We need to talk about where this mission is heading. I expect to hunt and kill people, it is part of the job and I get paid well to do it. I just feel that we are in mission creep and too many people are being killed on both sides. The tribal chief was about to give up a lot of information and he had to be dealt with, as did Barry Shaw. The Embassy Official had already crossed the line, he had let me down in Libya a number of years ago and he might have forgotten his mistake but I didn't. He nearly cost me my life when he ran away in the desert and he paid dearly for that error.

The last one though was pointless. I took the life of a brave old lady who looked me in the eye as I cut her to ribbons. I can't shake that one from my dreams. I overstepped the mark and killed out of pure evil. I looked at myself in the mirror and saw a monster. This is my last job James." He took another sip from the champagne flute, looking at his brother to see his reaction. James was surprised at his brother's sudden development of a conscience and concerned that he might backout, jeopardizing everything he had put in place to safekeep the establishment. He spoke quickly, wanting to ensure Lance's continued commitment.

"We are in too far and we need to see it through. We need to protect the Foreign Secretary no matter what the cost is to others including ourselves. Anyone else involved in the evidence Byfield has gained is collateral damage. I don't care about them but the Government must be protected."

"Yes, I get the patriotic story about good old England but I don't give a shit about any government. I am freelancing for bloody Iran at the moment and babysitting a shed full of illegal cash that we can't spend. How shit is that? When does the roundabout stop spinning because I honestly want to get off."

"Country first Lance," James insisted, "you are well paid to do what you do, so am I. Finish the job and I will never call on you again. You can go into retirement or retrain to be a plumber, whatever you fucking want to do, you'll be able to afford it." He stood up and taking Lance's face in his hands, he kissed his younger brother's forehead.

"Let's just get this job out of the way first." He walked over to the table and brought over the bottle of champagne, topping up both their glasses. "Did you really stick a red hot poker up that guy's arse?"

"How the hell did you know that I did that?"

"I saw the post mortem report and crime scene photos. That was pretty random, even for you."

"I wanted to send a message to the UK and make Byfield think."

"It's 2019, you could have sent him an email. Anyway, we have Byfield safely tucked away in a Scottish hellhole of a prison, have you managed to get your guy put away yet? I want Byfield to have a friend."

"I have, but not sure it's a friend he'll have, I've sent him in to kill Byfield, not cosy up to him."

"Hold him off until I say, I have given him a few days to think about things so hopefully he'll get me that evidence. Someone is hiding it somewhere."

They embraced again and raised a glass. "To the last time," Lance toasted.

Day Two in Prison

Stephen was sitting on his bed as the door opened and a young fresh faced woman poked her head in.

"Get yourself down to the office, the Induction group are meeting in five minutes."

Cleaning his teeth, he put a list of requests he had for staff into his pocket. He had to get out of that cell today, or if not, ensure the list of things were mended or replaced. Walking out of his cell, he noticed a group of five or so prisoners standing at the end of the landing, who, as the Officer walked towards them, parted allowing her to walk through and down the stairs. When Stephen reached them, they didn't offer him the same courtesy and instead, they stood blocking his path.

"When I call your cell number you fucking answer me, do you understand?" This came from a hard looking Scotsman, around thirty years old and covered in tattoos. He wore gray track suit bottoms and a blue sleeveless vest and was an obvious gym user with enormous arms and a barrel chest, no fat around his stomach and looking every inch a boxer.

"Yes, no problems, I am sorry," Stephen told him, keeping his head down.

"Sorry isn't going to do today English man, you fucking mugged me off in front of my pals. I want your reception pack, go get it."

"No problem." He walked back and picked up the few items given to him the previous night. He handed them over to the Scot who looked at the meagre hoard in disgust.

"What the fuck do you expect me to do with this shit?" He threw the bag into Stephen's face causing the others to laugh.

"Go and get me something I need big man, get me biscuits and shower gel. I want it by tomorrow, you understand?" Picking up the bag from the floor Stephen nodded.

"Good, make sure you do." He produced a small homemade blade and held it towards Stephen's cheek.

"No one gives a fuck about you, remember that." They still refused to move and Stephen wondered what was expected of him next. Suddenly a voice came from behind him, an English voice.

"Is there a fucking problem with my friend here? I hope not because if anything happens to him, I will take it personally." Stephen turned around and saw a stocky man standing directly behind him who looked at least as hard as the Scottish guy.

"So, what are you fucking Scottish pricks saying?" He continued, "Are you going to move or do I move you, and if you bring that little tin opener out again I will split you open."

"Okay man, no problems." They walked back to their cells, the menace gone for the moment but definitely not forgotten. "

"Stick together, they will be back," he said and held out his hand. "I'm Geordie, I came in yesterday."

"Hi, I am Stephen, came in last night and first time inside for me."

"Last time for me," Geordie laughed, "I've had enough of this shit." They walked down the stairs towards the meeting place for the Induction group.

"You need to stick up for yourself Stephen, otherwise you will have a bad time," he advised him. "Stick with me and I'll show you the ropes."

They followed an older Officer into a large classroom where around ten other prisoners sat in a semicircle. Some looked bored because they had done this too many times before, but some were also here for the first time and tried to read every bit of literature being handed out. A couple of skinny men with hollow eyes sat together.

"Smackheads," whispered Geordie, "watch them, they're bad news." The officer briefly left the room to pick up some more leaflets, leaving the prisoners looking around, sussing each other out. One of the smackheads stood and made straight for Stephen.

"Fresh fucking meat," he slurred, his foul breath hitting Stephen in the face. "Bet you've never seen the inside of one of these places before, you English cunt." The rest of the group now focused on the conversation, some laughing. Stephen sprang to his feet and punched him in the face sending him flying into a stack of empty chairs which fell, causing an almighty crash. The Officer ran back in looking around.

"What the fuck is going on?" The smack head was picking himself up from the debris.

"Nothing boss, just lost my footing, nothing going on here." He sat back down rubbing his sore jaw. Geordie tapped Stephen on the arm.

"That's what I'm talking about," he laughed out loud. "I think it's you who should be keeping an eye on me."

The Induction session ended just before lunch time, the Officer asking if anyone had any questions. Stephen had a few but decided to deal with them one to one and he approached the Officer as the others left. "I am in a terrible cell, everything is broken and it's filthy. Is there any chance of moving?"

"Oh, bloody hell, they've put you in there have they? The last guy killed himself and it's been empty ever since. Everyone else refuses to move into it."

"That makes sense. I will share, last night I made up a crap excuse to have a single cell but it backfired. I'm no problem really."

"Oh is that right? Do you think I didn't see what you did to Mr Mulligan this morning? I've hated him on every sentence," he laughed. "He had that coming, tries it on every time he comes in."

"Sorry about that," Stephen laughed, "I was told to stick up for myself, so I did."

"Let me see what I can do, I will have to have another cell sharing risk assessment done but that only takes a few minutes. I will move you after lunch if there are no problems."

Stephen walked back to his cell to find the gang waiting for him on the landing again.

"Heard you put that smackhead on his arse big man, good for you," the lead guy said as they parted and let him pass. Geordie who was five cells further down from Stephen was standing looking over the railings down onto the bottom landing and called him over.

"I think we will be alright, I have had another word with those boys and it's all sorted. We now need to get off the induction wing and get on with securing a job and keeping busy."

"I am moving this afternoon but I'm not sure where they are putting me. My cell is a shit hole, have you seen it?"

"Not really, I was told it was the dead man's cell and I turned it down yesterday before they even opened the door. It stank."

Stephen grimaced in agreement.

"True, anyway, if they move me off the wing, I will catch up with you later."

He didn't bother picking up the lunchtime meal as there were other things he needed to sort out. Firstly, he wanted to speak to a Governor, he needed to get them to clarify who he really was and this should be simple after a couple of phone calls to the English Prison Service. Secondly, he needed to speak to Tanya.

Looking down onto the bottom landing, he saw a man in a suit walk onto the wing, a number of prisoners flocking towards him asking questions. He was obviously one of the Governors, so he made his way down and waited while the Governor fended off another request for a phone call. This wasn't boding well for his next request.

"Governor, can I chat to you for a second please"

"What can I do for you son?"

"It's private, can we talk in the office?"

"If it's quick." He unlocked an office and logged onto the terminal.

"What do you want to talk about?" he looked up at Stephen.

"I shouldn't be here, I am a Governor in the English Prison service and I have been stitched up by the Security Services."

The Governor smiled, "Oh I see, let's have a look. Can you give me your number and name please?" He tapped in the details and read the information.

"You are a Prison Governor you say?"

"Yes."

"And fitted up by the Security Services?"

"I know how this is sounding, but yes."

"Have you seen the mental health team?"

"No, why?"

"I am going to make a referral for them to have a chat with you."

"I don't need to see them."

"Byfield, you have a record as long as my arm, you have been offending since you could toddle your way into Tesco's so stop wasting my time."

"Please, I need to phone my wife, she is overseas."

"You are not allowed to phone anyone or have visits with anyone. It is written on your Security reports, you will have to finish your trial before you can speak with anyone other than your legal team. I also see you have impersonated a police officer and a soldier in the past and have had extensive mental health treatment for these types of fantasies. Anything else?" He started closing down the computer as Stephen gave one last plea.

"Can you phone Governor Terry Davies? He was my Deputy Governor and he will confirm everything I'm telling you." He wasn't listening, "We are done son, go get your dinner and bang up. In future, don't approach me for anything, make an application. You are a fucking Walter Mitty!" He locked the office door and walked away from the wing. Geordie was looking down at him laughing.

"I bet he fucked you off, I could have told you that he would give you fuck all and plenty of it." The gravity of the situation was dawning on Stephen as he faced a fathomless pit of hopelessness and despair. He'd thought that he would be able to resolve this quickly and it should have been simple, a matter of a few calls. But no one believed him and he sounded like a fraud, like a thousand others who had tried to con him during his time working in prisons. James had completely rewritten Stephen's life, a whole, believable back story, so convincing that no one would question it. He was prevented from communicating with anyone and was on a clock to give James the evidence. He had less than one week before things would come to a head.

He returned to his cell and slammed the door shut, tugging on his hair as he let out his frustrations, and kicking the back of his door repeatedly. The din echoed around the wing and prisoners returning to their cells with their dinner opened his observation flap and laughed.

"Go on man, smash the fuck out of that cell." He looked around, there was nothing that hadn't been smashed already, there must have been dozens of people feeling the same anger and frustrations that he felt and a locked cell with nothing in it only encouraged these feelings of despair.

He kicked the door again several times "Fuck, fuck, fucking bastard," he cursed James. The door opened and three staff stood there, looking in.

"Bang that fucking door one more time and I will bang your head," he was warned. The door closed again and the wing entered an eerie silence, the rest of the prisoners willing him to kick the door. After all, it would have been a few minutes of entertainment to break up the monotony. A voice broke through his tormented thoughts.

"Stephen, its Geordie. Forget it man, they will hurt you for fuck all!" He was right, the staff would be waiting for one more bang and then would drag him into segregation and that's not what he wanted. The induction officer then appeared at his door flap.

"Don't be an idiot, if the staff start hating you, I won't be able to do anything to help you move cell so calm yourself down."

"Yeah, sorry. Tell them I'm sorry, I'm just frustrated." He left and after a quick conversation in the office, he convinced the three staff to take a lunch break instead of bouncing Mr Byfield around the prison landing. At two o'clock the cell door opened again, prisoners were going to work and the wing was a buzz of activity. The induction officer stood there.

"Get your gear and follow me, we are going to Hall B. That will be B Wing to you Englishman. I have found you a cell with another guy of a similar age so it should be better." They walked down the landing, Stephen stopping at Geordie's cell to shout through the door that he was moving, then they were gone.

Hall B was a lot bigger and everyone seemed to be going to work in different parts of the prison. Although he was given a few quizzical looks, it was a different atmosphere and appeared a lot calmer. "It seems a lot better on here, more activity," he commented to the officer.

"Yeah, but don't be lulled into a false sense of security, when it goes wrong on here, it really goes wrong, this is Barlinnie after all."

To Stephen's relief, the cell was on the first landing, near the staff office and in an area normally associated with wing cleaners. The cell was already open but the occupant was out, obviously working somewhere close. He put his one plastic bag into the cupboard drawer beside the bed noticing that everything smelt clean, the windows were not broken and had a curtain across them, the bed was in one piece and a small television sat on the shelf in the corner of the cell. He checked the toilet, clean and working. Nearly everything on his list had been resolved.

His cell mate appeared, possibly slightly older than Stephen, dressed in his own clothing and wearing smart black glasses. He was around five feet seven and his shaved head showed off a large pair of ears, hence the nickname as he introduced himself.

"Hi I'm Wingnut, can't think why that one has stuck," he smiled and held out a hand.

The officer walked over to the wing office where he was obviously briefing them about the new face on the wing. The manager clicked onto his terminal and read the information; he nodded to the Induction officer as he left. The information had been handed over, no calls, no visits, a fantasist with no lie to be believed.

CHAPTER EIGHTEEN

Terry sat with Jo in the family holiday rental in the Cotswolds. Normally, it was rented out but this year bookings were slow which was just as well as they needed somewhere to hide out. The family home had been violated by whoever had barged in, someone who Terry knew was connected to Mr Uden. A whole conspiracy was unwrapping itself just as Stephen had hinted, people at the highest levels were involved and obviously suspected Terry to be the key to finding the evidence they were all looking for.

After thinking about Stephen's problems with the brown envelope, he had considered it too obvious that he would be trusted to look after it. Anyone doing their homework would quickly realise that they trusted each other with their lives, and where would the most secure place be to hide a document of such importance? The prison safe of course, so he moved it in secret the following day, not even telling Stephen. He smuggled it away to one of the last places anyone would thing of looking and his hunch had paid off but he now had the issue of a Senior Prison Manager searching for it.

He tried Stephen's phone again finding it still switched off which was a real concern. He had tried every hospital in the area to see if he had been admitted, but then faced another problem, who to trust. If he reported the disappearance to the police then everyone would know Terry was looking for him. He would have to give his contact details to the police which in turn would lead others to his door again. He needed to continue to work, because with the number one Governor still away, he was the glue holding the place together. He just had to be cautious as next time, he wouldn't get away with a pile of magazines.

He showered and dressed for work and they went through the

plans should Jo have any more visits to the house. Tom still had a few days skiing before coming home so there was no pressure on him but Terry was loathed to leave Jo alone in the house.

"Leave the chain on at all times, all windows and doors locked. Any concerns phone the police and I will call you every couple of hours," he instructed her.

"Okay, but can you make me a promise before you leave. When you reach retirement age can we have a normal life? I can't take it anymore. Let's move away and have a normal happy life please." He looked at her, her lip still purple with bruising. "Yes sweetheart, six months and I am out, I promise."

He drove into work, the car park was almost full when he arrived and the pile of magazines still sat where they had been dropped. He picked them up and put them back into his car, pretty pleased that it hadn't rained overnight. Walking through to his office, he had a brainwave regarding Julia Matthews. He knew that she and Stephen still had a working relationship and she was someone to be trusted. He sent her an email requesting help and she answered within the hour with one simple request, *'Phone me ASAP.'*

Terry rang, it was a complex story but she seemed knowledgeable about Stephen's placement in Whitehall. He explained about the package and how Stephen needed it kept secret, so much so that he hadn't even discussed what was in it with him and she supported what he was saying with her own account of her meeting with Stephen and the suspension and death of Barry Shaw. It was like a spy story unfolding around them and at the end of their respective accounts of events, Julia said,

"Terry, something untoward is clearly happening, leave Mr Uden to me and I will ensure that you do not receive any visits until we can clear up this mess. I can find out who Stephen's manager is at Whitehall and take it from there. Trust no one at the moment," she warned as she rang off.

Meanwhile, James was sitting in Whitehall in a sombre frame of mind. He couldn't move forward until he had spoken to Stephen again and he wasn't confident of ever finding the hidden evidence.

Uden had prematurely startled the prey by going into the prison without the authority required and he had compromised James and Lance by using Geordie in the questioning of Jo. If he were recognised by her at a later stage, it could point back to Lance and then to James himself.

In the meantime, the Home Secretary had demanded a separate investigation into the security breach at Northway. This had complicated existing operations as this parallel investigation could come close to uncovering the true motive for James's subterfuge.

The Governor Mark Skinner had been removed with immediate effect and it was clear from information gleaned from Matt Phillips and Barry Shaw that the Prison Service and Government had been corrupted at the highest levels. GCHQ were working overtime to resolve the case but the only known evidence was hidden by Byfield. Lance, his brother, was in Iran waiting for instructions, Geordie was sitting in Barlinnie Prison waiting to kill Byfield and he couldn't take the chance in having anyone else involved. There had already been a high death toll for what appeared to be a simple case of stealing an envelope.

Byfield's family were hiding somewhere in Cape Town and Terry Davies was virtually fire proof due to the bungled search of his house and office, any further intrusion into his life would shine the light in the direction of London.

Ernie Stocken knew too much about the operation but specifically about James and he had gone to ground since Morocco for good reason. Lance Mitchell was a dangerous man and Ernie had blown his chance to kill him and he knew that he would now be hunted. It was imperative that when given the opportunity, Ernie be eliminated.

James still had questions. Who had killed the GCHQ agent on the canal? He hadn't authorised this killing and why had Byfield been selected to receive the information, instead of him? Who had not trusted him? He suspected that someone within the Security Services was aware of the plot and was acting alone to disgrace the Government - he had to uncover the mole as a matter of urgency.

Cape Town

Tanya drove into the city centre with the three children, they planned to visit the Canal Walk shopping centre to buy some clothes for them all and have a bite to eat before heading back to Sally's. Parking at Canal Walk was easy with plenty of family spaces and strapping Hector into the buggy, the other two led the way towards the lifts taking them up to the shops.

The bustle of the busy mall seemed reassuring to Tanya, she liked the feel of being back in civilisation again, making simple choices about fashion rather than where to hide or who she could speak with. A small area had been sectioned off and a number of children's rides and entertainment had been set up. A large contraption which sprung children strapped in harnesses metres into the air, somersaulting and laughing was too much of a temptation for Ellie and Harry.

"Mummy, can we have a go please?" Ellie begged.

"Go on then, join the queue and I will catch you up," Tanya told them as they sprinted off and joined the back of a line of five other children of a similar age. Quickly they began talking to the boy and girl in front of them, pointing at the people already spinning up and down. The boy told a joke and Ellie and Harry laughed along with him. It was nearly their turn so Tanya walked over to pay the attendant, a young black girl, attractive and around twenty years old. Harry carried on laughing.

"What's making you laugh so much mister?" Tanya asked as she bent down to talk to him.

"The boy in front said that his dad wouldn't pay a Kaffir to bounce around like a monkey." He laughed again and Tanya, furious and embarrassed at what she had heard pulled the children out of the line. "You naughty boy, you must never say that again, it is cruel and rude," she told Harry but before she could reprimand him further, a voice came from behind her.

"You sticking up for your little black friends again? Mark my words, it will come back to get you. Kaffirs always try to get the last word." It was the Policeman who had spoken to her outside the drop-in centre. He took his children out of the line and looking at the lady taking the money, he said unblinkingly, "I will save my money to feed a white family," and they all walked away laughing. Tanya was horrified and looked at the girl apologetically.

"I am so sorry Miss, my son didn't mean to be so rude." Taking the children, she hurried away and headed straight back home. The day had been ruined.

She told Sally the story on the drive in to work the next morning and she was disgusted but not surprised. She explained that some of the cops out there still had a bad attitude, and the guy who was so rude to them was probably a regular and he hated the black kids. They pulled up in the secure compound, noticing that the unofficial car park attendant was not there.

"Where is our guy this morning? He doesn't normally miss a chance to earn a few Rand," Sally commented as another older youth came into the compound.

"Nurse, you looking for my brother?" Tanya recognised him as the boy who she had saved in the shack.

"We were wondering where he was, are you doing his job today?"

"No man, I'm too busy but if you want him, he is in the police station, they took him in this morning."

"Why?" Tanya asked.

"They said that he was running an illegal car park scam, getting money from the people working here."

"What? That's ridiculous! Where is he?" Tanya demanded.

"In the cells and that's where he is staying until they put him in jail. They won't believe anything he says." Tanya turned to her friend in alarm. "We need to get down there and sort this out, we need to explain that we asked him to watch our cars." They went in and explained the situation to Jack who had a better idea. They would carry on with the treatments while he went to the station, that way the majority of people would still be seen. He drove off on the short drive and was soon parking up outside the police station. He made his way to the front desk where he spoke to the duty officer.

"I have come to see a young lad that you took in this morning, I think his name is Bandile." The officer glanced at his computer screen.

"He's in court now, if you are quick you may see his case." The small court building ajoined the station so Jack rushed around and found the youth court room where they were about to hear the case. He took a seat just as Bandile was escorted into the dock, Jack noticing him wincing as he sat down. The judge had yet to come in so he walked over and caught his eye.

"You okay buddy? Looks like you have a bit of pain."

"Fell over and hurt my side," Bandile mumbled, not looking up.

"Quick, show me," Jack insisted. He lifted his shirt and showed a number of bruises, evidence that he had been beaten and his ribs broken.

"Pull your shirt down," barked a court official. "Sir, please take your seat," he told Jack. He sat down just as the judge came in. The racist Police Officer, Andy Hicks, took the stand and explained to the court how this person had extorted money from the people at the centre. It was a flimsy case but the judge listened intently.

"It has been going on for a few months but we managed to catch him this morning," Hicks explained. "He put up a fight and assaulted two officers while we were apprehending him." The judge nodded before responding.

"I have listened to all the charges, do you have anything to add?" she looked at the boy.

"No Miss."

"I find you guilty. You will pay a five hundred Rand fine or go to prison for three weeks." The police officer smirked, this was a year's money for the boy's family so he knew he would go to prison and receive further beatings.

"Can you pay?" she demanded.

"No Miss."

Jack stood up, "I will pay." The court fell into silence, the smirk leaving Hicks' face. "And I will be employing him at the Centre where he will be car park security."

"Okay, please speak to the court clerk to arrange payment." The judge stood and left and the court door slammed as a furious Hicks left behind her. Bandile was beaming from ear to ear.

"Thank you doctor, you are a good man." Jack laughed and got his cheque book out. He returned to the Centre and told the others what had happened, Bandile appeared and shook their hands but he looked in a lot of pain.

"Come on in here Bandile, we need to look after our staff," Sally told him as she took a look at his injuries.

The morning rush was over and Jack walked into the treatment room.

"Coffee? My treat," he suggested to the two women.

"Lovely, but we will treat you today, what you did was beyond kind," Tanya smiled.

"Nah, they're just bullies in uniforms." They walked out to their cars, diligently supervised by the new head of car park security. Sally turned to Jack.

"So, what's the deal with payments, can the charity afford this?"

"They are paying him in food vouchers for his family and I'll give him a few rand a day. It keeps everyone happy, well nearly everyone," he added as he glanced through the gates. Across the road from the compound, a police van sat with two men staring at them, the passenger easily recognised.

The van door opened and he stubbed out a cigarette in the dust before he strode across the potholed tarmac road and stood in front of Jack.

"You happy with what you did there, Doctor, overriding the

law with your fat cheque book?"

"I am happy that I got this child away from you, you racist bastard," Jack replied, looking him in the eye. Sally and Tanya both flinched.

"Is that right Doctor? Didn't have you down as a kaffir lover when you first came to the area, looks like I was wrong." Andy Hicks leant in and smelt Jack's shirt. "You even smell like a fucking Kaffir," he said as he shoved Jack back a few steps. Jack pushed him back, his strength taking the policeman by surprise as he staggered back. He rushed forward and punched Jack in the face as the pair of them fell grappling to the floor. The sound of the van door closing made Sally look up as the other Police Officer ran across the carpark wielding a baton which he crashed into Jack's ribs as he tried to get back onto his feet. He fell coughing as the officer struck him again three more times across his chest and back. He finished it off by kicking him in the groin and they both stood above him as he writhed in agony, struggling to get his breath.

"Assaulting a Policeman is a serious charge. You keep your mouth shut or we will finish it here." Hicks spat down onto Jack's shirt.

"You fucking bullies!" screamed Sally. "Always the same." Ignoring her they got back into the van and drove away. Bandile knelt down and stroked Jack's head.

"We need an ambulance Miss," he looked up at Sally.

"No Bandile, I will be fine, too many questions at a hospital," Jack gasped as he knelt before getting to his feet. "Had worse playing Rugby against the Pomms. Let's get that coffee." He climbed into his car before adding, "Don't forget, you're paying," and he was gone.

By the time they reached the usual café, Jack's bravado was vanishing as he tried to climb out of his car but failed. He reckoned he had a few cracked ribs and some damage to his chest while extensive bruising was already developing across his face.

"Sorry Sally, I'm in a bit of a bad way, I need to get back to my place," he said through clenched teeth, lying back in the driver's seat.

"What and suffer alone? Nonsense, you'll come back with us and I'll look after those injuries for the next few weeks, no arguments. Tanya will drive your car, you are coming with me." Jack knew when he was beaten and with some relief, let Sally take charge.

CHAPTER NINETEEN

Day three In Prison

Stephen lay on his bed reading a book which he had just found on top of his locker. It had been well read but still seemed to be in one piece. A shadow crossed the door before an overweight prisoner with receding hair stepped into the cell and pushed the door closed. He was probably early fifties and Stephen didn't think it looked as though he would pose a problem. Putting down the book, he sat on the edge of the bed, ready to jump up if he needed too.

"Hi, how can I help you?" he asked.

"I'm hoping that I can help you Byfield, I hear that you have no way of using the phone?"

"Word spreads quickly around here, what else do you know?"

"You killed a guy in a drugs disagreement and you can also get your hands on weapons."

"Could get my hands on weapons, but it's not true, I'm being set up," Stephen told him.

"So you can phone your wife then?"

"No, no, that bit is true, I am banned from any contact with the outside world."

"Can I make a suggestion?"

"Sure."

"If you look after a number of phones for me, let's say three, I will give you a free call every week."

"Not interested, you've got the wrong man," Stephen lay back on his bed, picking up his book again.

"Okay, no harm done, let me know if you change your mind." He disappeared back onto the landing, leaving Stephen thinking. It was a tempting proposition but one that carried a lot of dangers. If the phones were found by staff, he would be in a lot of hot water especially before his court case, if they were stolen by another entrepreneur he would be expected to replace the loss or face the punishment from the gang. It was a lose-lose situation for a short call every week.

Wingnut came back into the cell, he had seen the large guy leave.

"What did he want Stephen?"

"He wanted me to babysit three phones for him."

"What did you say?"

"No. I can't afford to be caught, though I do need to make a call. My wife will be desperate to find out where I am."

"Good shout, if you had taken them you would have been caught in no time. I'll see if I can borrow a phone for you, but it will cost a few quid."

"How much?"

"Ten pounds for five minutes."

"How do I pay?"

"In the goodies you buy from your weekly money. Get a job and you will pay it off in three weeks."

"Can you sort it out for me?"

"Sure," he lifted his pillow and pulled out a small phone. "Five minutes that's all, but not till tonight when we are all locked away." He placed it back under the pillow.

"Who was that bald guy?"

"Dave Packham, he can get you anything you need at a price. He's harmless though, he won't cause you a problem."

"I will need to phone before it gets too late, around ten-ish?"

"We need to be careful, the screws have phone detectors, if they get a signal they will storm in and take it, then you are in the shit."

"Okay, you keep an ear open tonight and I will make a quick call. It's overseas though."

"Fifteen quid for overseas," Wingnut confirmed. He nodded, what more could he do?

The rest of the day dragged, Wingnut was out working, cleaning the landings and earning eight pounds a week. Stephen needed some money, he had the advantage that his cell door was left open all day as his cell mate needed to be in and out during all hours, so he walked to the office where two female officers sat processing paperwork and writing reports on the computer. They stopped and looked up when he knocked on the door,

"Yes Byfield, what do you want?"

"I need a job please, any going on the wing?"

"No hope, we have a waiting list." The Officer saw the dismay on Stephen's face. "I'll tell you what, I can get you into education next week and on the gym list for tonight if you want?" The thought of being out of his cell all day learning, and having a place in the gym this evening before lock up was too good an opportunity to miss.

"Yes please Miss, sounds great," he smiled at her.

"Okay, go back to your cell and wait for the gym staff to unlock you at six." Walking back to his cell, it felt that his luck had turned, a gym session, a phone call and a job next week. Things were looking up.

He didn't eat the evening meal which was some form of processed chicken nugget, and took a few slices of bread thinking he would make a sandwich with the chicken when he came back from the gym. Wingnut was reading the paper commentating on everything. He looked up and noticed a brighter looking cell companion.

"You are looking very happy this evening Stephen. Are you planning a night out?"

"Maybe Wingnut, thought that I would use the gym tonight, chat to my beautiful wife and start a new job next week."

"Sounds good to me Mr Byfield. I will have the wine chilled for when you return."

"I think a nice crisp New Zealand white tonight which will compliment the chicken perfectly."

"Oh shit never mind, I only have Chilean, let's give it a miss and drink crap tea instead." They both laughed. "I bloody wish," sighed Wingnut. "I'm seeing my wife in a couple of days, she is bringing the baby in, first time I will have seen my little boy."

"Brilliant, a good future for both of us," Stephen smiled as he lay back on the bed thinking of Tanya and the children. He must have dozed off as the next thing he heard was the main gate to the wing crashing open and a voice bellowing out.

"Gym, get yourself ready. If you're not on the list, don't ask." Suddenly his door was opened, "Byfield, get your kit." He had conducted a brief gym induction the day before and he'd had his shorts and t-shirt issued. He grabbed his things and went across to the office where a number of prisoners were waiting.

"Football and weights tonight lads, take your pick," they were informed. They filed through the gate, the staff crossing names from a list. "Byfield, football or weights?"

"Weights please." They were escorted down a brightly lit passage until they reached another barred gate, the sign above it reading *'Gymnasium'*. Three prisoners were already on the gym floor sorting out equipment, and Stephen assumed that they were trusted gym orderlies, one of the best jobs in the prison.

"Get changed, five minutes and in the weights room," he received yet another order. He quickly got changed, the rest had already put their gear on before they left the wing so they were on the equipment first, a good tip for next time he thought. He stood amongst rows of machines not sure where to start as three men near to him were planning a chest training session.
"Hey big man, join us, it gives us the right amount of rest with four of us," he was invited. He smiled and thanked them before laying on the bench to warm up with an empty weights bar. The men were slightly stronger than him but he didn't embarrass himself and forty minutes into the session, the same gym officer bellowed again.

"If you want a shower get one now, last fifteen minutes. Stephen needed one, he hadn't had the chance yesterday so grabbing his shower gel and towel, he walked around to the large old shower area. It was a bit daunting as he noticed it was empty but he took his chance, showering quickly and washing his hair, letting the hot water run down his back. It felt so good to be clean again.

"Were you asked to look after some phones today English man?" the voice seemed to come from nowhere. Stephen wiped the water from his eyes and looked around to see a man in his early twenties standing at the edge of the shower, still clothed.

"Yes," he replied, "but I couldn't do it, I have too much to lose."

"You're going to prison for life, you have fuck all to lose. When you get told to look after things the answer is always yes, understand?" Before Stephen could say anything, he was knocked down by a hard punch to the side of his head.

"Take that as a warning." The man walked away, others came in to shower and looked as he picked himself up from the floor. No one said anything because no one cared. He walked back into the changing area seeing the man again, this time sweeping the gym floor so he knew he was an orderly. If he was going to use the gym, he would have to deal with this man every day so he needed to sort this out now. He walked over to him.

"I am not fucking scared by you or your friends and I'm not hiding fuck all for you. If you want to make an issue of it, let's go back into the shower." The man stared at him for a few seconds then putting his broom down, said, "Fair enough, let's go." They both went into the shower area, out of sight of the staff but this time Stephen was ready. Six other prisoners saw Byfield knock the man down with a heavy blow before the guy sprang up and hit Stephen with two good shots in the face knocking him backwards into the far wall. He waited for the man to come forward again and when he lunged in, Stephen grabbed him and smashed his head into the white tiles of the wall. Blood trickled along the grouting and into the drainage channel as the man lay face down, momentarily stunned. Climbing back to his knees, he shook his head to try to gain his senses but it wasn't happening and the fight was over. He picked himself up.

"Okay man. Enough." He held out a hand, "Billy Penman, you are okay for an old guy," he laughed, and went back to sweeping the floor, dabbing his bleeding head with a tissue as he did so.

The move back to the wing was a bit different and people were clearly giving Stephen a lot more respect. He had earned his stripes tonight.

Getting back to his cell, Wingnut had already heard of the fight, news spread so quickly in prison. The rest of the wing were locked away and the familiar sounds of staff preparing to go home filled the landings, until, like a change in the tide, there was finally silence as the clutter of the day washed away and a lull set in.

"Can I make the call now?" Stephen asked his cell mate.

"Let me guard the door, if anyone comes, hide the phone." He dialled Tanya's number, but the phone didn't ring and he sat looking at a blank screen.

"Mate, I am busting for a shit, hang up and do it in a minute," Wing Nut told him. He rushed past and sat on the toilet just as the phone began to ring.

"Fucking hang up," he yelled at Stephen.

"It's ringing I can't," he replied as Tanya answered the call.

"Stephen!"

"Tanya, it's me, I'm in trouble." The door sprang open and staff leapt on top of Stephen grabbing for the phone until after a brief struggle, he gave up and complied.

"Tanya, I am in prison," he yelled but it was too late, the call had been disconnected. He was bundled out of his cell and taken down to the Segregation area.

"One fucking day son, and you are causing problems, let's see how you get on down the block," he was told as the door to his new cell clanked shut leaving him on his own.

CHAPTER TWENTY

Tanya looked at her phone in disbelief.

"Is everything okay?" Sally had seen the look of bewilderment on Tanya's face.

"It was Stephen, he tried to speak to me but someone took the phone from him. They were fighting Sally, I knew that something was wrong."

"Bloody hell, what did he say?"

"He said that he was in trouble and I could hear him fighting someone. There were raised voices but I couldn't hear what they were shouting and then they cut the phone off. What's going on Sally?" She scrolled through her contacts and found Terry's number, pushing the button in one movement. It was answered immediately.

"Terry, it's Tanya. Stephen just phoned, he was only on the phone for two seconds before it was grabbed from him but he said he was in trouble."

"What else did he say Tanya? I need to know everything."

"Nothing, just that he was in trouble, then a lot of voices shouting at him to give them the phone but I couldn't hear any more than that."

"Well at least we know he's alive, that's good. He has somehow got access to a phone which means that he has some limited freedom, that's good also. Do you have the number that he was using?"

"I hadn't thought of that Terry, wait." She checked the call log. "It's a UK number, so he's still in the country."

"Okay, leave it with me Tanya, text me the number and let me phone it. I'll get back to you as soon as I find out anything." He hung up. *James you fucking lying bastard, what are you hiding.*

Stephen is still in the UK, he muttered to himself. When he had contacted Stephen's boss, he had been reassured that Stephen was fine but was abroad and could not be contacted. He phoned the number Tanya had texted but it went directly to number unobtainable. The phone was off.

Tanya, Sally and Jack watched the late news on TV, the children fast asleep upstairs. Jack was happy that he was staying with Sally, his ribs were aching and he had a thumping headache. He knew that the injuries would heal but the flow of good cooking and motherly love eased the process along. A local news report came on and they watched in shock, the headlines familiar to all three of them.

'Volunteer Doctor Jack Cookson beaten by local police for helping township families, more in a minute.' This was accompanied by a brief CCTV clip of the attack.

"What the hell, who reported this?" spluttered Jack. He looked at the other two.

"Neither of us, we have been with you all the time," exclaimed Sally. They carried on watching, as an in-depth report and a thirty second clip of the attack was shown in its full brutality. It culminated in Bandile speaking to the camera. The reporter ended the clip with a short interview with the Head of Car Park Security, who had sent the clip to show the problems that people helping township families faced.

"These people work here for nothing, they care about the people from around here. The police don't care about any of us," Bandile proudly said. The reporter finished by stating that the Chief of Police was holding a full investigation and the two Officers involved had been suspended without pay. Jack threw his arms into the air and immediately regretted it as he winced in pain.

"Good old Bandile, let's see how the cop likes that."

The next morning, a Senior Police Investigator was already waiting for them at the centre and he had a younger aide with him carrying a digital recorder. They sat in Jack's office where they discussed the events and reviewed the CCTV. It was indisputable proof that Jack had been assaulted badly by both men. They had breached the trust bestowed upon them by the Chief of Police and they would pay the price. The investigator concluded the interview by stating that if the evidence was as strong as he anticipated, the matter would be a criminal prosecution for both of the attackers. The two men had been ordered to stay clear of the Township and Jack, Tanya and Sally and they were not allowed to come within two kilometres of the drop-in centre while they waited for the case to come to court.

Stephen sat in his cell in the Segregation Unit. He had complied with the staff after a brief struggle and they had allowed him to walk there without the need for restraint. He had seen segregation a hundred times as a Governor but little had prepared him for the feeling of desperation it gave him, walking into that bleak, cold empty cell with only a solid, hard, plastic molded bed fixed to the floor.
The door opened and a pile of clothing was thrown in front of him.

"Strip and put these clothes on when we tell you to," he was ordered. He pulled off his t-shirt.

"Put your arms in the air and turn around, good. Now face the front." He picked up the shirt from the floor.

"Put that back down, I will tell you when to get dressed. Take off your shoes and socks and pass them to me." They were inspected by the waiting staff and thrown out of the door along with his original shirt.

"Bottoms and boxers." He took these off, standing naked in front of the staff.

"Turn around, show the bottom of your right foot, now the left, good. Now squat, all the way down." Stephen felt very vulnerable with three people staring at his naked body.

"Get dressed." He quickly put the issued boxershorts on, instantly feeling a little better, and took his time putting the other items on.

"Can I have my trainers back please?" he asked.

"Ay no problems, they are ours anyway," the officer replied as he kicked them back into the cell. A nurse appeared and spoke very gently to him, he had no injuries and no thoughts of self-harm so she told him that he would be out of the seg the following day. Stephen liked her and made a mental note that if he ever got out of this mess and returned home, he would make a point of contacting her manager. The Officer returned to the cell door.

"Can I call you Stephen?"

"Of course, that would be nice."

"Okay Stephen, you're staying here tonight and it's tough enough to be in Segregation so we won't make it any harder than it needs to be." A howl of laughter went up from the other four residents who were listening to every word.

"Don't believe them Englishman, they will stitch you up every time they can. We haven't been out of our cells for two days."

"Don't listen to those clowns. Tomorrow you will be on adjudication in front of the Governor and they will decide what happens to you. Chances are you will be back on the wing by lunchtime."

"Thanks, I will just get some sleep if I can." He was thankful the staff down here seemed to play it by the book. They gave him a hot drink and closed his door. He climbed into bed and closed his eyes only to be woken up ten minutes later by the other four prisoners shouting at each other. It was incessant for the next four hours until they ran out of steam and he could at last sleep.

His door was opened again at eight thirty by a new group of staff.

"Morning Mr Byfield, breakfast and a hot drink?"

"Yes please, I am knackered, didn't get to sleep until four. Where do they get the energy?"

"Sleep all day and take drugs I guess," an Officer replied. "God knows how they keep supplied, one of them must have an arse full." The other staff laughed. "We're putting you in front of the

Governor first. Are you pleading guilty?"

"Don't have much choice, it was in my hand and I was trying to talk."

"No problem, we're going to stick you on the exercise yard and then you can get a shower." The exercise area was a small tarmacked patch, the size of a badminton court. Thick wire ran overhead to prevent anyone climbing onto the roof. A high wall topped with razor wire covered all four sides.

He walked around the area a number of times before staff called him back into the segregation building where he was shown to the small shower area and given a towel and sachets of shower gel/shampoo.

"No rush Stephen, the others are asleep so have a good long shower. We'll give you a shout when we need you back in your cell." He stood and let the hot water wash over him, enjoying the feeling of not being threatened or vulnerable. After a blissful ten minutes, the staff rattled the barred shower gate.

"Okay Stephen, time to finish up in there." He dried himself and walked back to his cell. He turned to the Officer. "Thanks for that, it means a lot." The door closed and Stephen noticed the adjudication paperwork on his bed. He didn't read it because he knew it inside out. He waited on his bed for another two hours until his door opened again.

"You ready?" He walked into the adjudication room and sat facing the Governor. It was the same man he had spoken to a couple of days ago. The formalities were gone through and Stephen was asked how he pleaded.

"Guilty."

"I accept your guilty plea and I am adjourning this for the police. Due to the serious nature of your offences, I am asking them to examine the phone records. Where did the phone come from?"

"I found it on the floor of the gym last night, I panicked and put it in my pocket. Sorry." He could tell that the Governor hadn't believed one word.

"Take him back to the wing please."

Stephen arrived back at his cell where Wingnut was lying on his bed reading. He was still angry.

"I told you to wait and now I am in the shit, the phone wasn't mine. You will need to pay the guy back."

"Who is it?"

"The bald guy, Dave Packham, I told you he was okay and he is, just not all the time."

It was lunch time and Stephen was waiting in line to pick up his meal when Packham joined the queue behind him.

"We need a chat." He turned round and acknowledged the man.

"Yeah, I'll come straight around to your cell when I've eaten."

Stephen stood at Packham's cell door. "Sorry, I messed up. What do I owe?"

"Seven hundred and fifty by next week."

"I haven't got it," Stephen looked at him in dismay.

"In that case, we have a problem…. unless you work the debt off."

"How?"

"Look after a parcel for a couple of days, until a kitchen worker picks it up from you."

"What is it?"

"It doesn't matter, are you going to do it? If so, I'll wipe five hundred from the debt." He thought hard. It must be heroin and he made a decision

"Sure, I'll do it, just don't tell Wingnut."

"Come to the showers tonight and one of my boys will sort it out. Seven twenty, don't be late." He wasn't late, two men stood by the shower door, steam filling the room ensuring that business could not be overseen. A ping pong ball sized package of brown powder was given to him and Stephen placed it in his pocket.

"Not your pocket dumb ass. Put it between your arse cheeks, as tight as you can get it. Staff check pockets, they don't check arses." He took the package from his pocket and wedged it in place.

"In two days, a prisoner working in the kitchen will come to see you, give it to him, job done." He returned to his cell, Wingnut still reading. He looked up from his book.

"Have you seen him?"

"Yes, it's sorted, I'm going to pay him back."

"Is he happy?"

"Yes, trust me Wingnut."

CHAPTER TWENTY-ONE

Wednesday, Day six Prison

After a two-day nervous wait, a prisoner wearing kitchen whites walked into Stephen's cell while Wingnut was out cleaning.
"Byfield?"
"Yes." He took the package and handed it over, happy that it was out of the cell and no longer his responsibility. The first five hundred had been paid back. The prisoner took it back to the main kitchen where it was bagged up and hidden in hot trolleys awaiting delivery all around the prison, a perfect distribution network.

Later that day, Stephen was queueing up for his lunch when Packham appeared in the line again. "One more time Byfield. This time the package will come straight to you as I have a bent screw. Do this and the debt is clear."

"Last time," Stephen sighed.

"She will see you on Friday, same routine with the kitchen guy, got it?" Stephen nodded.

He sat on his bed two days later. It was only seven thirty in the morning but Wingnut had been asked to clean up a cell from a smash up the night before. He had complained but had been offered a five pound bonus, so off he'd trotted with his bucket and mop. The cell door pushed open and a young, tall, skinny female officer with bad skin looked in. She had a notebook in her hand and was looking nervous.

"Mr Byfield?" He nodded feeling sick to the pit of his stomach, this was how easy it was to get drugs into the prison. She stuck her hand into her bra and pulled out an identical package to last time, throwing it on the bed. "You have a legal visit at two thirty Mr Byfield." She turned and walked out. Quickly he wedged the package into his arse cheeks, just in time as Wingnut came back into the cell.

"What did she want?"

"She told me I have a legal visit today, I wasn't expecting it." Suddenly the alarm bell rang out and scared the life out of them both. Stephen clenched his arse cheeks tightly together in case they were after him. Radios crackled and three nurses rushed onto the wing.

"Everyone away!" came the order, and as there were only a few people unlocked, they quickly went back to their cells. Wingnut was chatting through the pipes connecting the heating along the cells, a simple way to pass messages. Stephen lay reading the paper. "What's the news mate?"

"Smack head on the landing was found dead at unlock, still had the needle in his arm." He felt sick, he was part of this and could have made the very drug that killed him available. The coroners came and took the body away before the wing could be unlocked. Eventually his door was opened and he walked straight onto the landing and bumped into Dave Packham.

"Keep your mouth shut, your latest package will be picked up in an hour. We need it away from here ASAP." He looked at Stephen's face. "Don't get on a guilt trip, he was a junkie."

"No more Dave, this is the last time," he told him.

"No sweat, I have your replacement already. Fucking cheaper than you too!"

"We are all square on the debt?" Stephen asked him.

"No worries." The package was dispatched in the same way as before and Stephen breathed a sigh of relief. Never again.

Things on the wing returned to normal and for lunch Stephen lay on his bed eating a sandwich with no filling as he chatted to Wingnut who seemed a bit distracted.

"You're not with it today mate, you need a sleep. I have a legal visit after lunch, but we can chat about it later." He got no reply, his cell buddy had already fallen asleep. Two thirty came and he was unlocked for his legal visit. It was the same corrupt officer, and she behaved as if they had never set eyes on each other. They entered the legal visit area and Stephen was not surprised to see James sitting smiling, a briefcase by his feet. He stood and held out his hand, Stephen declined the offer. James wasted no time in getting down to business.

"So, what's it to be Stephen, yes or no?" Stephen sat down, staring at him.

"No James, I will not be handing anything to you so you can do whatever you want." There were a few seconds of frosty silence.

"You would rather stay here?" he asked in disbelief. "I could take all this away in seconds and you could be on a flight to Cape Town on a full pension and with your family. Think of it, a full pension in your thirties, it is all arranged for you. You know what I want, tell me where it is and you can come with me today." Stephen shook his head.

"I would be dead in two minutes the moment I gave it to you. No, I will keep it and when I'm able to talk to somebody not corrupt, it will be used to send you and others into prison. Let's see how you like it." Without another word, James signalled to the office that they were finished and Stephen was taken back to his cell. James sat, thinking about their conversation as his second client was escorted in.

"Hi James."

"Hello Geordie, how are you?"

"Good thanks. Is it time?"

"Yes it is."

"Do I get out of here when it is done?"

"Before his worthless body is cold my friend." He signalled to the office again and Geordie was gone.

Stephen wanted to use the gym that evening so he changed in the cell and left Wingnut to sleep. He waited at the gate as normal, but this time when he tried to get through, he found that his name was not on the list and no amount of persuasion could change the officer's mind. His session was over before it started and returning to his cell, he pushed the door open.

"Wingnut, what are you doing?" He was sitting on his bed and the undeniable stench told Stephen he was smoking heroin.

"Sorry buddy, I was clean for five years but Packham gave me some this morning. I have to look after his gear for him now and this is how he pays me." Stephen's head spun, his only mate in the prison had fallen off the wagon and he knew it was Packham's revenge for losing the phone. He had turned Wingnut back into a drug addict.

"I am only doing one package mate," Wingnut told him, "It's coming in on Saturday morning, through one of Packham's bent officers." He saw the disappointed look on Stephen's face. "Don't get all holier than thou on me, anyway, he told me you did it twice."

"To pay off our dept you idiot. This has to stop or I move out."

"Okay, last time on Saturday, deal?" It went against everything Stephen believed in as to him, bent staff were the lowest of the low. As his gym session was off, he went down to the ground floor to play pool. This was the first time he had bothered to mix on the wing in the evening but after his recent fight in the gym, he now had a reputation that he wasn't a man to try and bully. He noticed a Governor come onto the wing, and seeing him enter the office, Stephen knocked on the door.

"Can I talk to you about the gym list this evening boss?"

"No you can't, I am too busy, take it up with the gym staff," the Governor replied, not even bothering to look up from signing a variety of documents.

"How about a bent member of staff bringing drugs in this week?" Sure enough, this made him lift his head.

"I will be back in ten minutes, we need to do this without raising suspicion, so go back out and wait," he explained before he left the office and walked away without looking back.

He returned ten minutes later, Stephen saw but made no move to approach him, he would leave that up to the Governor.

Sure enough, one of the Officers soon came over to him.

"Byfield, the Governor wants to discuss your complaint about the gym list."

"Tell him I'm playing pool." One of the others interjected, "Speak with him man, that gym list is shit, sort it out." Stephen put down his cue and walked over into the office where the Governor was sitting alone.

"So, what do you have to tell me?" he asked once Stephen had closed the door.

"You have a lot of heroin coming into the prison, two shipments a week."

"How do they get in?"

"Your female legal visit officer, tall skinny one with spots, she is bringing a package in on Saturday."

"How is it passed around the jail?"

"Through the hot food trolleys coming from the kitchen, each one is packed up with the wing's supply."

"And why are you telling me?"

"I don't like bent staff, simple. I don't want anything but you could sort the gym list out though."

"I will look at the list. Do not tell anyone else about this issue, I will take it from here. Understand?"

"No problem." He walked back to the pool table, and the prisoners looked at him in anticipation.

"He is going to look at the gym list system," Stephen told them, picking up his cue.

Saturday, Day Nine, Prison

Stephen was unlocked early the next morning, it was Saturday and one of the gym orderlies had just been bailed. The gym officer was shaking Stephen's leg to wake him up.

"Oy Byfield, if you want a job in the gym you better get out of your bed and follow me, we have stuff to do, first class is in an hour." He was out of bed in a second, pulling his clothes on and brushing his teeth at the same time. He looked at Wingnut, lying yawning in his bed. "Remember your promise."

They walked around to the gym gate, the officer chatting all the way. He was amazed that Byfield had been chosen in such a short time but the other orderlies had wanted him, they thought he was a good guy. He reached the main gym and was given a list of jobs that needed to be done, the bonus was that he could have as many sessions working out as he liked and he could even train when the gym was empty. Hard work but rewarding. However, the message of warning was clear from the officer.

"We trust you guys, but do not get too familiar and don't take the piss. Okay?" He nodded, it was brilliant news, a backhander from the Governor for stopping the flow of drugs. Working hard all morning, he returned to the wing and bounded into his cell before lunch.

"How's it going mate?" he looked down on a pissed off Wingnut who was lying on his bed.

"Fucking shit, that's how. The Officer bringing in the gear has been nicked and apparently taken away in a police van. Stopped in her car in the car park. Packham has been moved to another jail as she grassed him up." Stephen tried to act shocked and it worked. "Course she grassed him up, she's looking at ten years for this." Wingnut tossed the book he had been reading down onto the floor.

"I'm in trouble now, the drugs have been intercepted but the money has already been paid out. I'll have to ask my wife to bring a package in tomorrow otherwise I am totally in the shit. I have smoked my share of this one already so I'm in debt again."

"How much do you owe?"

"Hundreds, fuck knows, whatever they tell me."

"So this package coming in tomorrow pays that off?"

"Yeah, we're straight after that and Packham's men will let me live."

"Well make it the last time and good luck mate." He went out and grabbed his sandwich, this time it had a good filling which made him smile as he contemplated how the gym orderlies were well looked after. Wingnut was asleep when he returned, having probably just smoked the last of the heroin as the cell stank of it again. He went back into the gym after lunch, and was soon on the last job of the day and contemplating having a short training session before going back to his cell. He took the heavy steel bucket and mop and set about cleaning the changing room and shower area. A dozen guys were still showering as he picked up discarded clothing and threw it into the laundry bin.

Glancing up, he saw Geordie had come in and was looking around the room, he hadn't seen Stephen yet so he shouted over to him. "Geordie, how is it going?" They were ten paces apart, Stephen still smiling, when he saw the blade come from his sleeve directly into the palm of his hand as Geordie moved quickly towards him. The blade plunged towards his chest, which was only protected by a blue gym vest but at the last minute, Stephen managed to spin slightly to one side deflecting the knife on its journey. Missing his heart by an inch, it sliced deeply into his left bicep and through an artery causing a fountain of blood to hit the wall next to him. Grabbing the steel bucket, he swung it at Geordie's wrist, knocking the knife out of his hand. The vicious homemade blade slid into the showers and Geordie followed on his hands and knees looking for it. He couldn't find it and fled back into the main gym hall to avoid being caught at the scene.

Dizziness overwhelmed Stephen and feeling faint, he vomited into the bin before staggering to the staff office. The alarm bell rang and nurses rushed to the scene to stem the bleeding. Prisoners who were showering had witnessed the assault, they had kicked the knife under discarded clothing to help Stephen and pointed Geordie out to the staff and orderlies. Before the officers could take him to Segregation, he received several good punches to the face from other prisoners, breaking his nose and jaw. "That one is for Byfield you cowardly cunt!" they shouted as he was dragged away.

Drifting in and out of consciousness and barely aware of what had happened, Stephen recognised the blue lights of the waiting ambulance illuminating the sports hall and a stretcher was wheeled in before a set of handcuffs were applied to his good arm. Minutes later he was on his way to A&E, unresponsive with bags of fluid pumping life back into his body. In the emergency department, the doctor examined the cut before he spoke to the escorting staff and told them he would need an urgent operation to repair the damage. At ten twenty that evening, Stephen Byfield was once again under the knife, this time to save his life.

He awoke sometime just before midnight, the handcuffs having been replaced by a long chain. Two officers sat at his bedside and noticed him open his eyes.

"You were lucky there Byfield, that bastard wanted to kill you. What the fuck have you done to him to deserve that?"

"No idea, where is he?"

"Charged with attempted murder and moved out to another prison, you won't be seeing him again." He was too tired to answer and just lifted his eyebrows.

"I'm going to sleep boss, it's been a bad day," he murmured as, closing his eyes, he once again slipped into unconsciousness. The lights in the single room were lowered and one officer sat reading by the door, the other attached to the other end of the chain. It was going to be a long night.

CHAPTER TWENTY-TWO

Sunday, Day Ten, Prison

As the sun rose, his arm throbbed painfully, and while he waited for the requested pain relief, he tried to work out what was coming next. Obviously James had arranged the attempted murder, but it had failed and the man had been moved away. There could be no other immediate danger to him but the other targets to hit would be Terry and Tanya and he would need to get a message to them somehow. The pain relief kicked in, and he dozed back off for another couple of hours.

The staff changed over at eight o'clock that morning, Stephen was asleep when the new guys came in and he didn't even feel the chain being reattached to the next team. He woke up as a nurse checked his blood pressure, the new staff looking very disinterested.

"Good news Mr Byfield," she told him as she took his temperature, "we are able to transfer you back to the prison this morning. You will go into your prison hospital where the nurses will do the same as we are doing here." The staff looked annoyed with this news and when the nurse left, one turned to Stephen. "Fuck's sake Byfield, I have given up my day off for overtime to watch you suffer. If you go back this morning, it will cost me fifty quid in wages and I will have to cut the grass. Tell them you feel too ill to go back now."

"I don't think it's up to me, I'm sorry," he apologised.

Later that morning a prison van arrived in the car park of the hospital and to the bemusement of the waiting patients and families, a handcuffed prisoner in a wheelchair was paraded through the main hospital corridors. They drove through the city centre which was peaceful with few cars on the road. Stephen had forgotten that it was Sunday, in prison every day was pretty much the same, and his mind drifted back to the weekends out with the family and how he had taken even simple things like going to the park for granted. He was amazed at how quickly his conception of life had shrunk to what occurred behind the four walls of the prison, and it came as a shock to see the outside world in its continuum.

They were soon driving back through the gloomy gates of the prison, the Sunday morning tranquility quickly evaporating. A small line of visitors were waiting to come in for family visits, and as Stephen glanced at them through the small van window, he remembered Wingnut's wife and child, and wondered how she would be feeling smuggling the drugs into the prison. Was she an addict herself? What would she think when she saw her husband had started using again as the signs were very obvious? And what would happen to the baby if she was caught? What a complicated life these people led, and he supposed that he was now considered one of them.

The van drove through the prison courtyard and through a series of double gates. Stephen lost count of how many times the driver had stopped before they reached the hospital wing. He climbed out of the sliding van door and entered the building which was an old Victorian two floor wing, small by prison standards, perhaps only twenty-five cells. With no wheelchair available here, he walked slowly past the administration office and was asked to follow a nurse towards his new cell.

Passing a large cell with a barred gate, just off the main corridor, Stephen recognised this as the constant watch cell. Only people at risk of killing themselves could be placed in there under twenty-four hour a day observation. He knew that if a prisoner ended up in these cells, he had reached the end of his tether. Not a good place to be and he gave an involuntary shudder at the thought of being held in there. No staff were outside at the moment so he guessed it was empty. He carried on walking, having to take momentary pauses to regain his energy until they reached cell four, a larger cell than normal, and it was all for him. On the scale of prison cells that he had seen in this place, this one was good and better than most. He entered and sat on the bed while the nurse looked at his dressing.

"Okay Mr Byfield, you are going to be with us until the doctor says that you can go back to the main prison which will probably be a few days, so take it easy and take the time to recover. It was a nasty cut." She left the cell and he lay down and turned the TV on while dozing. It had been less than twenty-four hours since the attack and he was in a lot of pain and still some shock. His arm throbbed and he was pleased to see the nurse return with some pain relief. "And you will need a few of these before it stops hurting," she gave him two tablets. "I need to see you swallow them please," she insisted. Opening his mouth he stuck out his tongue. "Thank you nurse," he said before laying back down and waiting for them to kick in. Drifting in and out of sleep, the day slipped past until he was woken up by the same nurse.

"Do you want a bit of fresh air Mr Byfield?" Standing unsteadily, he followed her to the door and back down the corridor. Passing the constant watch cell again, a voice spoke to him and looking up, he saw it was the disgruntled officer from that morning.

"No grass cutting for me Byfield!" He saw the overweight officer smiling broadly as though he had won a prize in the raffle. Suddenly another voice hailed him. "Stephen!" and looking through the barred front of the cell, Stephen saw that it was Wingnut.

"Can I talk to him officer?" Stephen asked, looking in horror at his old cell mate.

"If you want son, but be quick." Wingnut was sitting on the bed, wearing only a blue rip proof gown with bandages covering his arms and a red ligature mark around his neck.

"What's happened?" Stephen asked.

"She was caught coming in at lunch time, she's in custody and the baby has been taken away." He looked at Stephen, his face ravaged with the thought of what he had done. "She's looking at two years mate, I can't cope with that. If I hadn't asked her, none of this would have happened." He started crying again.

"On your way Byfield, that is long enough," the officer intervened, not wanting to have his suicidal prisoner upset further.

He sat outside in the hospital exercise area, along with ten other prisoners sitting on benches or walking around in the sunshine, a mixture of mental health problems and people recovering from operations. He reflected on Wingnut's world, within the space of a week he had gone from a respected sensible friend on the wing to a heroin addicted moron who had dropped his own wife in prison and his child into care for the sake of a couple of hundreds of pounds for drugs. Three lives wrecked in a few short days. Then he thought of his own life, he had done nothing any different but instead of heroin, his drug of choice was adrenaline and ego. He was no different to Wingnut, just another moron addicted to a different God.

He had to get out of this mess and start life again, easier said than done while James was pulling the strings. Even as he sat in the Scottish sunshine pondering the situation, James must be sitting in London planning a way to get his evidence or kill him. In truth this had gone too far and James would have no option but to do both.

He returned to his hospital cell just as a new nurse came in with a jug of water. He was an older man, craggy looking who at first did not look up at Stephen, too busy looking at the TV showing the London marathon. He finally did acknowledge him, and when he did, he did a double take.

"Bloody hell, you're a dead ringer for one of my old Governors from England," he said as he walked out and checked the cell card on the wall next to the door.

"Same flippin name too, it can't be you!" Stephen was dumbfounded, it was happening like a dream, finding someone who knew his real identity.

"Yes, it is me, I am a prison Governor, it is me," Stephen repeated with excitement. What prison was I working in when we met? I have forgotten your name but remember your face." The officer put the water jug down, taking another look at him.

"No, I think I have got it wrong, no one forgets prison names and you definitely would not forget where we first met," he laughed, "but it's like seeing a ghost, you're so alike." He walked out chuckling and telling the cleaner that he had just seen a double of his old boss.

The fog of the medication had dulled Stephen's thinking, but as he lay there, willing himself to remember, the name Jeff Allen came to him and with it, the memories of their meeting. They had met during a short spell working in Brixton on F Wing. Stephen had just been given his first promotion and was spending six months in Brixton prison. The first time he had walked onto the notorious F wing, or 'Fraggle rock' as staff called it due to its role as a mental health unit, a prisoner had tried to pull him into a cell and Jeff had dragged him back out by the skin of his teeth. How could he have forgotten that?

Jeff was doubting himself as he sat in the office so he checked on the records for Byfield and saw a long history of offending and fraud. He kicked himself for being so stupid. "Nearly forty years in these places and I still nearly get taken in by a conman," he told his fellow nurse. She laughed. "You'll get the hang of it one day Jeff, anyway you need to take your conman's blood pressure, just don't go giving him your bank account details."

He went back into the cell and pulling the monitor over to the bed, fastened the cuff around Stephen's uninjured arm. "You had me there, I thought I was going mad," he laughed as he started the machine. Stephen tried to sit up.

"No Jeff, I do remember you and I remember what you did for me on F Wing in Brixton. I need help, please!"

"Fuck me lightly it is you, I fucking knew it!" he exclaimed. Stephen motioned for him to keep quiet.

"Jeff, I need you to phone Terry Davies at HMP Marwood, tell him that I am here and that I need the parcel. He will understand."

"I am not sure that I am allowed to do that Mr Byfield. I could get into a lot of trouble and I'm coming up to retirement."

"Jeff, you will not get into any trouble at all, trust me on that. Please phone Terry tomorrow morning," he begged.

"I will think about it, I'm off duty in a minute and not in tomorrow. Don't pressure me, your charges are so serious including murder and possession of firearms, I could end up in prison myself." He packed up the machine totally forgetting to take the blood pressure. Stephen wasn't sure that Jeff would phone, he knew that he believed him, but the prospect of phoning Terry might be a step too far. He had a comfortable life so why rock the boat. A female nurse came into the room to speak to him.

"Mr Byfield, a prisoner calling himself Wingnut is going outside on exercise, he has asked if you want to go out with him?" Sitting in the early evening sun was pleasant, the chat with Wingnut was not. He was at rock bottom and sat there berating himself.

"Why did I get involved in this bollocks? Why did I allow heroin to creep back into my life, it was shit last time and even worse this time round. It has cost me everything. I don't know what is happening to my wife, but she'll go to jail, I'm sure, she has a bit of history with drugs. My little baby though, put into care and never knowing his parents, how could I do that to my little boy?"

"So what happened?" Stephen asked.

"I was waiting to be called for my visit when the screws rushed in and spun my cell looking for another phone. The Governor came in and told me that a drug dog had indicated on Sue, by the time the police arrived to search her, she had handed over the pack of gear. She was nicked and little Billy was taken away by social services. It looks like she'll be bailed until the court case, but she's going to jail for sure. Fuck knows where Billy is."

"Bloody hell mate, anything I can do?"

"No, you're in a worse state than me, you're cut to fuck and not allowed to phone anyone. I'm surprised you haven't done what I tried to do." Stephen looked at the red raw line around

Wingnut's neck. "Your neck looks bad."

"And I cut myself with a blade on both arms, don't know what I was thinking, probably nothing, I was wasted on that shit. Then strung myself up. It was only because a screw walked in that I'm here, silly bitch cut me down, I was fucked, blacked out. The doctor told me I was seconds away. They had to restart my fucking heart three times. Why am I still alive?" Stephen put his good arm around his shoulders.

"Wasn't your time mate, maybe you are supposed to get clean, get out of jail and fight for your child?"

"You think?"

"How long have you got left?"

"Six months."

"Let's try together, let's try win your son back. We can start tomorrow."

"Would you do that for me?"

"If you clean yourself up again, yes."

"Top man Stephen, I owe you for this."

CHAPTER TWENTY-THREE

Tanya woke up, it was a little after seven thirty on Monday morning and she had the day to herself as the children were in play school and it was her turn to have a day off during the week. The centre had become so busy during the past two weeks that the three mornings a week had turned into four or sometimes five. The township had bought into the health care revolution and felt that these people were firmly on their side. They were right and Jack, Sally and Tanya all loved the work. It was just a pity that Jack was due to fly back home shortly to try and patch up his marriage.

It had been a little over a week since the frantic call from Stephen, and they were no nearer to finding out what had happened to him but she was sure he was still alive, she just felt it. And this morning there seemed to be extra hope in her body, although she couldn't explain why she had such positivity surging through her. The worry over what had happened to him made her realise how much she loved him and wanted him back in her life.

At the same time, Terry was sitting at his desk at work when the switchboard contacted him, saying they had a call waiting from a man named Jeff Allen. He worked in the Scottish prison service and was asking to speak directly to Terry.

"I don't know a guy called Jeff Allen and it's a busy day today. Can you take a number and I will try and call him back later?" Terry sighed thinking it was probably someone wanting a move south and wondering if they had any jobs going.

"We have tried that Governor, he is insistent. He is talking about you retrieving a parcel for Stephen Byfield. Is that our old Governor?" Terry sat forward in his seat, gripping the phone tightly.

"Put him through," he ordered, "I will take the call." There was a small pause and a click before Terry heard a voice.

"Hello is that Mr Terry Davies?"

"Yes it is, Mr Allen. How can I help you?" His heart was thumping as if something monumental was about to occur.

"This might sound crazy Mr Davies but I have just been speaking to Stephen Byfield."

"Where?"

"In Barlinnie prison, Glasgow. He is on remand for murder and possession of firearms but he has told me he has been set up and that you should get him the parcel. I haven't got a clue what he is talking about but I recognised him from our time together working in Brixton."

"Mr Allen, you are a hero. Listen to me, do not tell anyone about Stephen, please keep it secret as his life might be in danger. If anyone asks you about it, you say nothing, treat him like any other prisoner and do not tell him that I know where he is under any circumstances. Is that clear?"

"Yes, but don't worry, I have just booked a week's holiday and we are heading down to Greece. Mr Byfield will know nothing about this. Can you also keep it quiet that I phoned you? I can't afford to be in trouble this close to my retirement and you know the consequences of making a call for a prisoner."

"No problem Jeff, you have a good break and thanks again for calling me." He hung up and immediately phoned Julia Matthews where he wasted no time in telling her the news

"He is in prison in Scotland. I'm going to get the package if you can find a way to get him back to London."

"Okay Terry, I have an idea on how we can resolve the Scottish problem. Leave that to me and I will call you when things are sorted. I suggest we don't tell Tanya yet as she may unintentionally give the game away."

"No problems, I will have my end sorted out by lunch time."

Terry slipped out of the prison and drove to his home address, he hadn't been back since the attack on Jo and he was hesitant as he parked outside. The noise of a lawn mower took him by surprise, and suggested that someone was in his back garden. He walked around the side of the house almost scaring his neighbour to death.

"Bloody hell Terry! Sorry, we thought that you were on holiday so I decided to keep on top of the lawn for you."

"Thanks Simon, that's very kind of you," Terry smiled at him, looking around as he did so. "Have we had any callers since we went away?"

"Bugger all Terry, I have been in all day, and our dog goes mad when people come up your path. Absolutely nothing." To Simon's amazement, Terry then walked across the lawn and climbed up the large tree by the fence and into the treehouse he had built a few years ago for his son. He remembered how Tom used to play up there with his grandchildren during the summer holidays.

"You okay up there Terry?" he called.

"Just looking for one of Tom's old memories, he hid all sorts up here," Terry replied. Inside the wooden house, he slid out a plank of wood on the floor, revealing a metal box with a combination code padlock on it. He dialled in the number 007 and it opened. Inside was a large brown sealed envelope.

"Found it," shouted Terry and climbed back down. "Thanks for the help Simon, we'll be back soon buddy, maybe another week or so. I'll tell you about it later." His neighbour, looking somewhat bemused, restarted the lawnmower.

"Take care Terry, don't rush back, we can have a chat when you're home. I'll put the bins out on Thursday for you." Terry shook his hand and got into the car heading back to the prison. Once again in his office, he took the envelope and placed into the main safe. This time he was sure that it would be secure.

Stephen was lying dozing in bed in the hospital wing, he had taken another dose of pain killers, the wound was healing and he was certainly on the mend. Wingnut had been allowed out of the constant watch cell as he had promised that he would not kill himself, and was back on the wing under observation. The nurse came into his cell to speak to him.

"Sorry Stephen, I have some bad news to give you. The Met Police from London have asked for you to be produced back to Paddington Green station to help in their enquiries into an unsolved murder last year. You will be going soon but I'm afraid I can't tell you when due to the security aspects."

Stephen thanked her while his brain whirled over what this might mean. This must be the last roll of the dice from James, he thought. The escort would be attacked en route, and it would be made to look like a gangland hit, he'd be dead and everyone would be in the clear. If he refused to go, they would force him into the van, if he just accepted it, he would be a sitting duck so either way, he was in trouble. He asked to see the Governor before they came to take him, and although he didn't consider a meeting with the Governor would be possible, against all odds he turned up in the hospital the next morning. Stephen was taken into the office to talk to him.

"How can I help you Mr Byfield?"

"The Police Production down to London, I'm worried that the escort will be attacked en route. They have already tried to kill me once and they will try again. Can we not fly down direct to Heathrow and come back the same day? I'm pretty sure the whole thing is a trap." The Governor stared at him, shaking his head.

"Byfield, stop the bullshit. You are a nobody, you were attacked in the gym because you were involved in losing the guy's mobile phone, that's all. No conspiracy theory, no secret agents chasing you, you will be just fine."

"Okay, well I'm just telling you before it happens." Stephen knew this guy was never going to believe him but it had been worth a try.

"Thanks James Bond, I will bear it in mind."

He went back to his cell furious that he would be made to spend a full day sitting in the back of the van, just waiting for trouble. How fucking stupid! He lay back on his bed, his arm and head now throbbing. He rang his bell for more pain killers, but when the door opened, instead of the nurse, there were three staff with handcuffs and an overnight bag. They gave him a few minutes to pack his things into a clear plastic bag and use the toilet as they were in for a long journey and he didn't think they'd let him out for a pee.

They climbed into the secure prison van and headed out of the prison. The cell in the back was not made for comfort, and the thought of sitting there for the next seven or so hours with the pain in his arm and his recently thumping head would make any attempt at sleep almost impossible. He was thankful that the nurse had given him some pain relief before he left and he waited for them to kick in.

After only half an hour, to his surprise and alarm, the van stopped. He hadn't been looking out of the window, as seeing the normality of real life last time had depressed him and brought back too many memories of his freedom and family. The door opened and the two staff were standing there, smiling at him with an obvious airport terminal building behind them.

"Surprise, surprise Byfield, you are getting on the big bird to fly down. The Governor was pissing himself when you asked him if you could fly, he thought you were a mind reader."

Bypassing the standard security, he was soon seated at the rear of a small airplane, with only a dozen other people on board. The sense of relief was massive as he thanked his guards.

"Don't thank us Byfield, we were ready for a long drive and two or three days out of the jail. The police arranged this flight about an hour ago, so you've had a result and will be back in our little jail by lunchtime tomorrow." He decided that he'd had enough of these morons, so slept the remainder of the flight, only waking up as they approached Heathrow.

A secure police van was waiting on the runway tarmac and he was driven directly to Paddington Green where he had been just a few weeks ago, only in very different circumstances. As the van pulled up in an underground parking area, he was still mystified as to why he would be flown down to London for charges that didn't exist. Barry Shaw had died in this station and maybe that was to be his fate too.

The doors opened, and instead of members of the Met Police waiting for him, Stephen saw Terry and Julia and he wasn't sure whose smile was wider. An immense sense of relief rushed over him and to his embarrassment, he began to cry. In Terry's hand was the brown envelope. It was all over and at last he could explain. However, the prison staff were having none of it. He was their prisoner and Julia and Terry had no jurisdiction to intervene. Julia was quick to put them right and court papers were given to them from the Scottish Court saying that Stephen Byfield was to be released on bail into the custody of Julia Matthews. They read the information and phoned back to the prison to verify this unusual situation. After what seemed like an eternity, they took his handcuffs off and he was a free man. They shook his hand. "No hard feelings Mr Byfield, all the best," they told him as they got into the van and headed back to Heathrow.

Stephen turned to Julia, "Can I phone Tanya please?"

"Of course, Stephen, we just need to take a look in the envelope with the Chief Constable first, before anyone else takes an opportunity to get hold of it." They disappeared up to her office where the senior officer insisted that Stephen phone his wife before they opened the envelope.

Tanya had just arrived home from buying the week's groceries with Sally, and Jack was studying a medical journal in preparation for his return to Australia. He was hoping to work in a leading H.I.V. centre in Sydney and wanted to impress during a skype interview later that week. He was healing nicely and getting itchy feet to get back to his rented home by the coast.

Her mobile rang, and seeing that it was a UK number that she didn't recognize, she answered with a tentative, "Hello?" There was silence for a few seconds and she was about to hang up thinking that it was another call centre when an emotional voice burst out of her phone.

"Tanya, it's me, I have missed you so much!"

"Stephen, where are you, are you safe?" She spoke quickly remembering the last call she had received.

"Yes, I'm safe. I am back in London with Terry. I am so sorry I took you all for granted, please forgive me." They were both crying now. Sally and Jack looked at her in concern, not being able to work out if it was good news or bad.

"We'll fly back home tomorrow Stephen, let me look at flights," Tanya managed to say through her tears.

"Just hang on a sec Tanya, I'm on police bail at the moment but it should all be cleared up in a couple of days and I'll fly out to see you all. I need to get out of the UK for now and just want to be with my family. As far as I'm concerned, this job is finished."

"Bail, why are you on police bail. What is going on?" Sally and Jack were even more concerned now at the sound of Tanya's shriek.

"It's such a long story Tanya and it involves that guy James, from the Brighton hotel. He's an evil son of a bitch and had me totally hoodwinked."

"Stephen, are we safe out here?" Tanya asked with concern, "he's the one person who knew where we were going."

"We are just sorting that out, so carry on doing what you are doing, I'm pretty sure nobody will be able to find you out there. Are the kids all okay?"

"They're in bed, do you want me to wake them up?" Stephen looked at the three people sitting quietly in the next office, waiting for him.

"I would love to chat with them but can I do it tomorrow? I'm in the police station at the moment, and they are waiting for me to help them put all this to bed. I will be at Julia's tomorrow though so can talk then."

"Course sweetheart, I am so relieved that you are safe. I love you so much Stephen."

"Love you too darling." They hung up and he walked through into the adjoining office to discover the cause of his last two weeks of living hell.

CHAPTER TWENTY-FOUR

Stephen sat in the plush office, Julia to his left, Terry to his right, and behind the desk sat Janice Lyons, the Met Police Chief Constable, the highest ranking police officer in London, with a barrister by her side, ready to study the evidence. A senior police officer sat at another desk at the back of the room, he was there to document the meeting and ensure that the process was transparent in all aspects. He also had the responsibility for recording every detail covered, both orally and digitally. Nothing was being left to chance.

"Stephen, am I right in thinking that nobody has seen the evidence that is in the envelope since Barry Shaw left it at the safe deposit building?" Janice started, speaking in a measured way.

"I haven't looked in it, how about you Terry?" Stephen asked his friend.

"No, I just took it and hid it," Terry confirmed.

"And we believe that at least three people have died trying to protect this package," Janice stated for the record.

"I hope that it's worth it," Stephen commented nervously as he was now starting to doubt what they might find inside.

"Well, let's have a look but before we open it, let me remind you that the contents of this envelope will be held in utmost secrecy regardless of the outcome of any upcoming police investigations, court cases or prosecutions." They all agreed and a contract was passed to each person in the room by the barrister.

"Please read and sign the form before we can proceed," he instructed them. Silence fell over the room as they all read and signed, the noise of scribbled signatures heard before they were collected back by the barrister.

"Okay, let's see what we've got," Janice said as she pulled the envelope towards her and carefully opened it. Sliding the contents out and placing them on the green, leather desk top, the policeman in charge of the collation of the evidence stood ready to film and take photographs of each document in turn. Janice talked through each photo in front of her.

"Photograph one is of Mr Uden a senior prison service manager socialising with a known criminal believed to be Kevin Brood, deceased.

Photograph two is of Mr Uden taking a parcel from a yet unidentified man but believed to be Gulmurod Khalimov, commander and recruiter of a terror group operating from Syria.

Photograph three is the current Foreign Secretary meeting with a known terror target, Mr Abu Bakr al-Baghdadi, ISIS leader.

Photograph four is the Foreign Secretary with a man believed to be Waleed al-Alwani member of Military Shura, Iraq." She then flicked through a number of other photos and tapes before continuing.

"There are a number of other photographs which I believe to be of senior prison service managers meeting with men we believe to be a high risk to the security of the United Kingdom.

We also have three audio recordings documented as a meeting between the Foreign Secretary and members of terrorist organisations in Iran, aimed at securing trade deals for the United Kingdom.

We also have a hand written note which is addressed to Stephen Byfield." She stopped and looked up at Stephen who nodded his consent. She continued. "It reads,

Dear Stephen, this information was sent to me from my good friend at GCHQ. He died shortly after posting this so paid the ultimate sacrifice.
I thought that this may be of use to you in resolving the problems that you have faced during your duties.
I wish you God's speed and good luck.
Kind Regards Trevor."

She picked up the envelope and turned it over so she could view the postmark.

"The parcel is postmarked Tunis, Tunisia. Is this man known to you Stephen?"

"Yes, he works in the British Embassy in Tunisia." He still had no idea of the fate Trevor had suffered after meeting him. Janice gathered all the documents and photos together and looked up at those sitting opposite her.

"Okay everyone, we need to verify the evidence presented to us and we will conduct what I feel will be the most in depth and complex investigation we have held for a number of years. People identified in the evidence will not be approached until the team are ready to make arrests. It is imperative that our targets have no opportunity to subvert the course of natural justice. Is that clear?" They nodded. She turned her cool gaze on Stephen.

"I understand that you are having an ongoing issue with James Childs, a Security Services MI6 agent working from Whitehall?" Stephen grimaced.

"He was the reason that I was locked up and my whole life history rewritten. He is a dangerous man who ordered me dead and has done the same for others."

"He will not present a risk to you anymore. MI5 are dealing with the problem as we speak. We hope to draw this line of enquiry to a close very soon.

"That's good news," Stephen said with relief.

"Maybe not such good news, we have information that he has arranged for your wife to be targeted and killed, so we need her exact location." Stephen's recent feeling of relief was short lived.

"Cape Town but I don't have a clue of the address." He borrowed Terry's phone and tried to call Tanya again, but there was no ring tone, just a recorded voice saying that the network was down.

"I can't get through," Stephen told her, a familiar feeling of panic beginning to rise within his chest.

"Don't worry, we can try again later. In the meantime, I will ask for some help out there to ensure your family are safe."

The maintenance men dressed in official overalls entered through the main entrance of the Whitehall building. They had been called to repair a leak in the rest room on the second floor and the woman on the reception desk had expected the visit and completed the security forms with them.

"Mr Shaun Walton and Mr David Shipley," she confirmed their identity, "could you please fill in these forms with your details and van registration." They silently completed the documentation and were escorted to the second floor to assess the task.

Looking at the work needed to complete the job, they estimated that it would take an hour, and as this was an hour too long for the hard working receptionist, she left them to it. As she returned to her post, she thought that it was fortunate that they had attended when the bulk of the staff had already left the building, and she had decided that there would be a minimum risk of any security breech as all doors were locked and the corridors were monitored by CCTV. The head of the operations room had long since gone home and apart from a bored looking security officer searching visitors, there was nobody else to request help from anyway. She returned to her desk and continued with her work.

A short time later, the lift on the ground floor pinged and David Shipley came back into the reception area and approached the desk.

"I just need to get some equipment from the van to finish the job. We may need to turn the power off up on the second floor for around twenty minutes while we isolate the hand dryers and extraction fan. Is that okay?" She glanced up at him and nodded.

"Yes, I am sure it will be fine, so long as it doesn't turn my system off. All other staff on that floor have left so no issues." He disappeared, returning five minutes later with a bag of tools and a new sink. He took the lift back up to the second floor.

Turning the fuse box for the entire floor off, David quickly made his way to room twelve whilst Shaun watched the corridor and lift for any signs of activity. Opening the office door, he photographed the room before he walked in and silently attached listening devices to a plug socket and one in the fire alarm panel. A bug was also fitted into the phone. It took no more than ten minutes before everything was installed and as he left, he looked at the series of pictures he had taken to ensure that everything was in the exact place it had been in before he entered.

Walking back into the corridor, he replaced the fuse in the box and the lights and CCTV came back to life. The two men stood in the washroom and activated the devices, two audio and one visual. They were perfectly concealed and picking up the signal well. David turned to Shaun.

"Right, get the instructions out for fitting a sink and let's get out of here." Twenty minutes later the lift pinged again as the workmen exited and booked themselves back out of the building.

James sat at his desk the following morning and having cleared thirty emails from his system, something niggled away inside his head. Something just didn't feel right and he couldn't put his finger on the cause. He was a stickler for detail and each item was removed from his desk top every evening and secured in a locked drawer, apart from the phone. He would never allow anyone to clean his desk and he would do this himself each Friday before leaving the office. That way, it ensured that nobody could enter the office without his authority.

Then the answer to his unease hit him in the face, the phone had been moved a fraction during the night with a thin dust-free strip on the desk just visible to the left-hand side, meaning the phone had been used between him leaving the office last night and now. He lifted it clear of the oak top, revealing a rectangle of dust-free wood signifying where it had sat for the past few days. It had been moved and replaced but whoever had been in the office had made a microscopic error, just the type of thing

James was trained to notice. He unscrewed the hand set, the screws sliding loose without resistance and he spotted a small listening device, recognising it as standard MI5 issue surveillance equipment. Quickly reassembling it, he put his jacket on and hurried down to reception.

"Did we have anyone in the building last night?" he asked.

"Yes sir, two workmen fixing the gents restroom on the second floor, they were only here for around half an hour." He left the building and was soon swallowed up by the swarms of tourists enjoying the London landmarks and taking endless photographs by the red phone boxes at the end of the street. Taking out his phone, he hurriedly made a call. It went directly to voicemail and he left a message.

"Lance, I am taking a break for a while. We need to talk, phone me in a couple of days." He headed home, firstly on foot, dodging in and out of shops, before taking a cab to Euston station. Here he headed directly to the tube and caught the train back to near his Chelsea apartment. As he travelled, he put together what must have happened. Someone who knew Stephen must have found him and secured his release from prison. The envelope would now, in all probability, be in the hands of the Security Services, hence the visit to his office last night.

Knowing MI5 were onto him was worrying, he only hoped that they were not in a position to have his home under surveillance just yet. If the devices were only fitted last night there was still a good chance that they would be assessing the evidence they already had on him so he needed to act quickly.

Opening his apartment door, he raced through to the safe hidden in the bedroom wall, and taking out the false documentation and passport, he also grabbed the envelope containing ten thousand New Zealand dollars in cash. He stood and looked around the apartment, if MI5 came calling, it was a treasure trove of evidence and he had no time to clear every piece of documentation, or the weapon and drugs hidden inside the safe, nor his dossier on Stephen Byfield. He had been sloppy in thinking that Byfield would be stuck in prison for another few weeks at least and he should have planned more thoroughly for exactly this scenario.

He placed the contents of the safe in the middle of the lounge on top of the oak coffee table which had cost so much money last month. Setting other fires around the apartment, he lit them and left without a care for the families living around him. He was already walking past the Chelsea Ram pub when he heard the first fire appliance rushing towards the housing development. He continued casually towards Fulham Broadway station before heading out to Heathrow. In his jacket pocket he had an open-ended flight ticket to Auckland, New Zealand in the name of Mr David Waterstone, complete with passport in the same name.

Stephen stood with a Police Officer outside the cordoned off area at the entrance to the blackened apartment. Firemen had finished their part in putting out the blaze and dazed neighbours looked on from the area below wondering how they had just lost everything that they had worked for.

"Any sign of anything?" Stephen asked the forensic officer.

"Arson, by the looks of it, the fire seems to have started in a number of areas. I can't be sure what evidence we can retrieve at the moment until we get it back to the office."

"No sign of a body?"

"No, the place was empty when we arrived but whoever did this was lucky that they didn't kill everyone else in the complex." Stephen doubted that James had even given it a thought. He knew that he had realised the game was up and this made him a dangerous enemy with nothing left to lose. The main question was, how far would he go?

"You may be interested in this one," the policeman held up a plastic evidence bag in which Stephen could see a charred document with the word 'Byfield' still visible on the cover. "When we have finished with it, I will call you over for a look," he was told. He smiled grimly,

"I can guess what it says, I have fucking lived it."

CHAPTER TWENTY-FIVE

Arriving at the security area in terminal two at Heathrow, James took a deep breath before confidently handing his passport over to the official. The sports bag on his shoulder was heavy and uncomfortable, and he began to feel awkward as he waited for the passport to be returned to him. Despite the training he had received and the many times he had flitted in and out of hostile countries, he couldn't seem to settle his nerves this time and his breathing became shallow as a bead of sweat ran down his temple. It was a red light to any decent airport official that something was different about Mr Waterstone, and it was with a certain amount of relief that the passport was handed back without a word, and he joined the queue waiting for the bag scan.

Taking off his belt and getting everything in order, he placed his items into the gray tray before passing through the body scanner. He held out his arms as the security official gave him the customary rub down search before returning to the conveyer belt to pick up the bag.

Standing and waiting for it to rumble back along to him, James noticed that his tray had been diverted to another belt, meaning they had questions about the contents of the bag. Maybe the ten thousand dollars had caught their attention but he could handle that detail. He approached the security official who now had his bag in front of them.

"Hello sir, we just need to verify an item showing up on the scan, do you have anything with a blade on it in your bag?" He racked his brain before remembering the shoe horn he had packed.

"Oh God, I am sorry, it's my shoehorn, I wasn't thinking."

"Can you show me sir?" He quickly unzipped the bag and held

the shoehorn aloft. "So sorry."

"No problem, have a good flight." He picked up the bag and turning to leave, almost bumped into the three security officers standing behind him.

"Mr Waterstone, we need you to come with us please, we would like to talk to you about your flight plans." Quickly assessing the situation, he realised that there was no point in not cooperating, he couldn't escape. If they intended to take him into custody for questioning, they had planned it brilliantly. With minimum fuss, they entered a restricted area and passed directly into a small, drab interview room, where they wasted no time in beginning. Curiously, he noticed that the digital recorder was not turned on.

"Mr Waterstone, where are you intending to travel today?"

"New Zealand, for a bit of a break. I have been working hard for the past few months."

"Where do you work?"

"I'm a self-employed security consultant."

"Where do you advertise your company?"

"I don't need too, it's word of mouth in the city. I provide a good service and clients like me."

"Enough to give you ten thousand dollars?"

"That's to buy a plot of land for a client, it's a down payment." They sat staring at him, giving him a period of silence that an untrained traveller would find irresistible to ignore before offering more information than they needed to give. The officers blinked first.

"Your name is not Mr Waterstone. Who are you?" James didn't flinch.

"Mr Waterstone, that's who I am."

"You are Mr James Childs. Why are you using false documentation?" He had his story ready.

"In that case you will know that I work for MI6. I am on my way to conduct an investigation into the recent terror attacks in New Zealand and I need to travel under an assumed name for reasons of security. You are putting the security of the nation in danger by stopping me travelling, you are also putting my life in danger by frog marching me across the airport. Extremist operatives could have been observing the flight and you may have compromised my mission." He sat back in his plastic chair, he had played his hand splendidly and now the ball was firmly in their court. The lead interviewer looked a little lost for a second until the noise of the door opening and closing again regained his focus. A woman's voice came from behind James.

"Hello Mr Childs, my name is Natasha Track, MI5. Can we stop this little charade now and get on with business?" Two uniformed police officer entered and helped James to his feet before forcing his hands behind his back and snapping shut the handcuffs. Natasha continued.

"Mr Childs, we are leaving by the back door as they say, you are under arrest but I will let the police officers deal with your rights. We need you to come in and answer a few questions."

"Can I phone my solicitor?"

"No, you gave up any of your rights when you betrayed your country Mr Childs. Help us sort out this mess and we can all get on with our lives. The Home Secretary is especially interested to know why you and your friends wanted her beheaded."

"I didn't, I was trying to protect the Government, trying to stop our country from imploding. I am not a traitor." His brain scrambling for a solution as they walked towards the black Range Rover parked in the secure car park, tinted windows stopping suspicious eyes from catching a glimpse of the occupants.

"Where are you taking me?"

"I am not at liberty to disclose that information, however it will not be a long journey."

Looking out through the tinted windows he recognised the landmarks as they passed and he knew instantly where they were heading. Sure enough, after fifteen minutes the vehicle turned into the gated area of R.A.F Northolt and he understood that he was in for no usual police questioning. The barrier was raised immediately and they sped through, quickly reaching a hanger at the end of the runway. They headed inside and drove to the far end before stopping suddenly. Caught by surprise, he lurched forward banging his face on the back of the passenger seat. The policeman sitting next to him said nothing, instead pulling him harshly back upright before jumping out and opening the door on his side.

"This way please Mr Childs." He took hold of the handcuffs and led him into a large, barren office.

The sound of the Range Rover driving away signalled the departure of the police and he knew that he was alone in the hands of MI5. The office measured around five metres across but ten metres in length, with a wooden desk positioned at the far end of the room. Sitting beside the door was a young man, early twenties and armed with a shoulder holstered pistol. It had been a carefully set trap that James had no hope of escaping from. A large, middle-aged man sat behind the desk that was three times the size it needed to be and held only one item, a small iPhone. A younger man positioned on his right, looking lean and professional, wasn't there to take notes of the meeting and gave the impression of an executioner. Again, as he was pushed into a chair in front of the desk, he noted that there were no recording devices to gain evidence. This all pointed towards a deniable intervention, classic MI5.

"Mr Childs," the older man began in a calm, steady tone. "We know that you are trying to protect the Foreign Secretary from prosecution, we also note that you and your associates have attempted to have a senior cabinet member murdered, not to mention your involvement in the murders of at least three other people." He stopped briefly, spinning the phone on the table as he considered his next words.

"By this association, you have made yourself responsible for an act of terror on the United Kingdom." He stopped again, looking James directly in the eye.

"Where is your brother hiding James? We need to talk with him."

"You're the man with all the answers, you find him."

"We will eventually James." He pushed the phone towards

him. Call him, tell him to come into the office. If you do, I will ensure a better result for you." James sat back in his chair crossing his legs.

"I don't think that there is a better result in store for me, you want me to go to prison for a long time, and all this on the information that a washed-up Prison Governor has managed to cobble together. Please, he's full of shit, a jury will never buy this fantasy." The man behind the desk leaned forwards slightly.

"Mr Byfield has been through enough thanks to you. You had him thrown into prison to be murdered you callous bastard. I think he has the right to reply, don't you?" James shrugged his shoulders and stared at the man for a few moments more before coming to a decision.

"Okay, I will phone Lance but I don't know what he will say so no promises."

"And nothing stupid from you Mr Childs," the man warned as he pushed the phone over to him, nodding to the man by the door to remove the handcuffs. James dialled the number and Lance answered instantly.

"Hi James, I have heard some rumours from London, what's going on?"

"Lance, I am with MI5 at the moment under detainment. They want you to hand yourself into the office in London." He looked up at the interviewer and nodded as though he had an agreed to surrender. "Are you still there Lance?"

"Yes."

"Go kill the bitch, Cape Town." The phone was snatched off him and a pistol was placed to his temple. The young man growled into his ear, "You stupid fucker," before punching him sharply in the side of his head. James fell to one side before regaining his balance as his arms were wrenched behind him and the cuffs reapplied. The sting of the needle entering his neck made him flinch, he tried to keep focused but darkness was beginning to encroach from all sides. A mumble of conversation rumbled in his outer consciousness as he was dragged to his feet before giving into the blackness filling his every sense.

A magnified beam of sunlight shone into his face as he regained consciousness. He was in a large tent, handcuffed to a metal bar concreted into the desert floor. His mouth was dry and head still fuzzy with the effects of the drug. It appeared that a Bedouin tribesman was standing guard at the door, an ageing AK47 slung over his shoulder. An English voice came from outside the tent before one of the young MI5 guys came through the flap.

"James, welcome back." He took a sip of water from an Evian bottle as he looked at him.

"Do you know where you are?"

"No, Africa somewhere obviously."

"You remember that tribal chief you had killed? We thought you might like to meet his family."

"You fucking bastards, hope you fucking rot in hell. You will meet your own sticky end, you wanker." James tried to get up as an older tribesman entered the tent, but with his hands still cuffed to the metal bar, he fell back on the ground.

"Your last chance to tell us everything," the MI5 guy suggested.

"Fuck you!"

"Thought you would say that. Got to go, I have a plane to catch." He tossed the handcuff keys to the guard, before opening an envelope containing photographs and handing them to the old tribesman. "This is the man who did this to your chief, enjoy your revenge." He turned and headed out through the flap, the sound of a vehicle pulling away ringing the death toll for James. Pulling desperately on the metal bar he tugged but nothing moved except for the skin on his wrists. The old man thumbed through the photos, shaking his head before looking blankly down at James. A frenzy could be heard, building up outside the tent.

"I will give you a million dollars if you take the handcuffs off," James tried in desperation. The old man continued to stare at him before speaking.

"We don't need your money, you ordered my brother to be

killed, and revenge is my payment."

The noise outside had built to a crescendo as the canvas front was theatrically pulled open by the guard, exposing the cause of the commotion. James saw that the entire village had gathered and glared in at him, hate filling their eyes. Two young men raced through the crowd and into the tent, swinging a wooden club into his rib cage before removing the handcuffs, and dragging him onto his knees and out into the village centre. The drag marks from his shoes formed a long line in the sand, a line which James had crossed weeks before in ordering the murder of their leader, the comfort of that Whitehall office from where he gave his order, long forgotten. Head forced down towards the ground and shirt hacked off by a rusted knife blade, silently praying for a fast clean ending, he waited. The smell of the people and the heat of the sun on his back magnified the hell that he had been dragged into, the broken ribs made catching every breath difficult as he decided that it was now or never. Springing to his feet, he threw sand into the eyes of the first guard, catching him unaware as he celebrated in the emotion of the gathered crowd.

Grabbing the assault rifle from the guard's hand, he crashed the butt into his blackened teeth, blood spouting out and onto the ground. He fired a three round burst into his chest before hitting the second guy with a straight head shot, seeing him collapse, crumpled onto the sand. Another two shot burst above the crowd caused chaos as bodies ran in all directions.

Sprinting past the corrugated iron demarking the edge of the village, with pain searing through his chest, James made it out into the surrounding desert landscape, bullets hissing past his body, head down, legs pumping and lungs ready to rip themselves from his chest as he pushed ahead. The sound of vehicle engines roaring made him spin round. Dust kicked up by the tyres four hundred metres behind spurred him onto a final burst. He knelt and fired a controlled round towards the lead 4x4, it stopped and the doors flew open as a lifeless body was pulled from the driver's seat. The thirty seconds of uncertainty was all that he needed to put another two hundred metres between them.

A cluster of rocks ahead offered some protection and throwing himself behind them and unclipping the magazine, James estimated that he had about twenty rounds left, not enough for a fire fight but enough to help him escape. Stopping to catch his breath, he took up a fire position and sent another three rounds into a silver Mercedes car that had ventured forward. Seeing the windscreen shatter as it came to a halt, he saw two men clamber out and run back the way they had come. It didn't appear that the locals had much stomach for a fight.

Taking off his shoes and socks, James quickly emptied the sand from them before putting them back on. If he could push forward, he would be able to get a couple of kilometres away before they could regroup. This could be just far enough to find a place to hole up and reorganise himself.

He kept running, leaving the rocks behind before finding dead ground, an old river bed providing the cover from sight he had prayed for. He ran for another hour before stopping again to listen. The rocks in which he had taken cover were now ten kilometres away, the faint crack of gun fire echoing around as the locals shot holes in shadows and hopefully themselves. A large boulder on the dry bed gave a good place to shelter from the sun as he sat in the shade and checked his rifle again. He needed to find his way to the coast and then down into Libya where hopefully he could arrange a boat out and back into Europe.

Voices closer to home heightened his senses, if this was a search party then the tone of the chat and the laughter was a surprise. He crawled to the top of the bank where he saw an old shack sitting between two large rocks, and relaxing at the base of the first rock, were two young men dressed in western clothing and sharing a cigarette as they waited for a pot of coffee to brew up on an open fire. At the side of the other rock stood a shiny black 4x4 which he could see was empty. Chances are that these two were on a road trip to somewhere and needed a break. Back tracking until he could exit the river bed without being spotted, James crept over the top, anxiously avoiding loose stones which would give his position away. Clicking back into Special Force mode, he traversed around before finding a spot fifty metres away. He lay and watched as they drank the coffee. Satisfied that there were only two of them, he moved closer, reaching the vehicle where he could see that the keys were still in the ignition.

Now he had two options, the first, to steal the car and hope that the owners didn't make too much noise, or option two, to kill them both and then steal the car. He quickly decided that the risk of these men raising the alarm was too great so he would need to kill them then hide the bodies. By the time they were discovered, he hoped to be out of the country.

Crawling forwards, he took aim. He was so close that he could now see that they were young men, maybe only eighteen years old and he could smell their expensive aftershave. They were not armed and laughed as they shared a story. He hesitated again, maybe they had stolen the car themselves and if that were the case, they wouldn't report him. He didn't see the rock that struck the back of his head, nor the old man who delivered the blow. The next thing he saw when he regained consciousness was the centre of the same village he had escaped from and this time he was tied up and going nowhere. The crowd had returned to the scene and the decibels had ramped up to a howling crescendo. The photos of the murdered leader were scattered in front of his face which by now was a couple of centimetres from the dusty ground. The same old man looked down at him.

"You killed my brother for no reason other than to protect yourself English man. By the laws of our people, justice will be given by his wife and children." Four men stepped forwards, one on each arm and one on each leg. Four stakes had been driven into the ground and he was tied to these like a starfish with the sun beating down on him mercilessly.

The first son stepped forwards, fifteen years old, slim and tall, holding a vicious looking sword in his hands. James begged for mercy but the excitement was building and his lone voice was drowned out. A single slice from the blade severed his left leg and he screamed before a man stepped forward and fastened a tight belt around the stump to stop the bleeding. They wanted him to live through the process, and when the shock and pain of the amputation caused him to pass out, water was thrown into his face to revive him before the next son stepped forward. The crowd roared as the blade slashed down across his right leg and again the blood was stemmed with a second belt.

Somehow the pain had vanished and life slid into slow motion as the wife stepped forward, waving the bloodied blade. His arms were cut free and his torso was placed on a table facing up. He was vaguely aware of the roar coming from a hundred distant mouths as the glint of the blade flashing in the sun was his last sight on earth, and vengeance was theirs.

CHAPTER TWENTY-SIX

Tanya sat in the drop-in clinic staring into a nearly empty coffee cup, lost deep in thought.

"Penny for them Tanya?" She lifted her head and noticed Sally standing at the door. It had been a busy morning and ever since the arrest of the police officers, it seemed that the staff were held in high regard by all. Such was their success that a large percentage of people dropping in just wanted to see what was going on and thank the staff for standing up for them. It was a nice feeling but added to the strain on consultation times.

"Just thinking about life Sally, you know, living out here in South Africa. It is all I have ever dreamed about, and now things seem to be changing. Stephen is making plans for a new beginning, Jack is on his way back to Australia and life is just a bit up in the air. I feel unsettled by everything."

"That's just life out here I'm afraid," Sally explained. "Doctors come and go, on gap years or career breaks and you know it takes a special person to want to come work here. I haven't had a bad one yet, men or women, all young and ambitious. It is what it is. Anyway, when you all get back together as a family, you may want to stay out here. Get your own bloody place though, I need my peace and quiet back," she laughed. Tanya looked thoughtful.

"I am going to chat with Stephen tonight, let's see where it takes us."

The privately charted plane touched down at Wonderboom National airport, Pretoria. The Iranian diplomatic delegation consisting of just one person had arrived, and he waited patiently to pass through passport control.

"Welcome to South Africa sir, will you be staying long?"

"Around two weeks hopefully."

"And are you on diplomatic business?"

"Yes, I have some research to conduct for the Iranian Government." The official stamped the passport. "Hope you have a good stay Mr Mitchell."

Lance Mitchell took his passport and slid it into his back pocket before walking through customs and into the arrival area where he quickly spotted his driver holding up a clip board with his name written on a piece of A4 paper. He was travelling light and just had a backpack with essential items in it. He planned on buying some new clothing at the Menlyn Park shopping centre as having passed through here before, Lance knew that he could pick up anything he needed at a fraction of the prices back in Iran.

Walking out into the heat of the sun, his eyes stung before he found his sun glasses in the side pouch of the bag. Looking around, he couldn't see any obvious signs of being followed, although acutely aware that CCTV at an airport had the ability to cover as much as ten agents could.

Opening the back door of the car, he tossed his pack onto the back seat and climbed in, instructing the driver to take him directly to the Embassy. After less than half an hour, the car pulled into a straight, tree lined road, where a modern brick building, resembling a prison, sat behind a black metal fence, with tall barred gates fronting the highly secure complex. It was a far cry from the gentile atmosphere of the British embassy in Tunis and Lance disliked the building, finding it cold and efficient but far from welcoming. The rooms for staff were basic but functional and he'd had his fill of that lifestyle over the past few months so had made no plans to stay.

Telling the driver to wait for him, he rang the bell by the guardroom and a young soldier smartly marched out and took his identification before unlocking the gate. Checking in with the on-duty official, Lance quickly made his way to the basement and found the armorer's room. He entered and signed out a PC-9ZOAF Semi-automatic pistol, a weapon he favoured, being a 9mm variant of the Swiss model. Slipping it into his shoulder holster, he left the embassy and got back into the cab heading for the coach station at Pretoria Central.

The next bus to Cape Town left at four fifteen that afternoon and arrived at the Cape Town Civic Centre just after midday the following day, a torturous twenty-one hour journey but he considered it the safest way to reach the city with a 9mm firearm stuck on his shoulder. The trip back would be different, the weapon discarded and a direct flight from Cape Town to anywhere in the world first class welcoming him.

Purchasing the coach ticket, he found a smart cafe a few hundred metres away from the station, and ordering a cold diet Pepsi, he pondered how the next few days would play out. Getting to Cape Town was the easy part of the deal, finding Tanya and then killing her was a different proposition. He didn't want to do it and he didn't agree with it, but this was business. One last job and he would head off into the sunset and do his best to spend the money.

Checking the time, he headed back to board the coach, finding the engine running as the last few people loaded their bags into the luggage storage in the belly of the vehicle. He kept his bag with him and pushed it into an overhead locker before taking his seat. The coach was only half full and as a result, Lance had no one sitting next to him as he leaned back into the seat and closed his eyes. This was going to be a long journey he thought as the doors hissed closed and the air conditioning buzzed into life, a welcome and unexpected addition. Heading out into the Pretoria traffic, Lance soon watched the last glimpse of civilisation pass as they pulled onto a long monotonous road heading through hundreds of miles of nondescript landscape.

Pulling the ring on the still cool can of Pepsi, he sipped, enjoying the feeling of the cold drink trickling down his throat. He had no real plan apart from arriving in Cape Town, and finding Tanya. She had to be staying in a safe area with friends and an earlier scan of her Facebook page had revealed one contact in the area, a nurse working in a local township. It never failed to surprise him how lapse people were with their online security, assuming the information was invisible to everyone other than themselves. He would book into a smart hotel in the city while he searched, he knew there were no hospitals in these townships but a few clinics so he reckoned it would take less than a week to find her. He closed his eyes as the rhythmic rocking sent him to sleep and when he next opened them, it was dark. Opening another now warm Pepsi, he took a quick sip before peeling a banana and eating it.

High above the coach, a British Airways flight cruised in the cold night sky at thirty thousand feet, and on board, Ernie stretched out his legs as he watched his second film. Business Class had been worth every penny and recent events in his life had provided plenty of cash for him to spend on such luxuries. He had been surprised to receive the call telling him James Childs was dead and that Lance Mitchell was in fact his brother. It just went to show you couldn't really trust anyone. He was then informed that his mission to eliminate Mitchell still stood.

Spinning the ice cubes around in his glass, Ernie sipped on the diet drink while he went through his plan again in his mind. His years in the Special Forces had led to a number of contacts with other S/F members and this gave him access to unlimited resources, firearms and information, and one of his guys was at this minute heading to the airport to collect him. He had a safe house arranged on the outskirts of the city for after Lance Mitchell was killed, and an escape plan to Paris before heading out to the Far East where he planned on living out his days.

If Mitchell killed him first, a full-scale rescue and evacuation of Tanya and the children would happen and they would be taken immediately to the safe house, before heading back to the UK on a military transport plane, not first class but very safe. He had an uneasy feeling in his stomach, Lance Mitchell was a formidable opponent and this was a fifty-fifty fight. Whoever got the first lead on the other would be the victor.

Lance's phone vibrated and lit up informing him he had a

text. It was from the Iranian Embassy in Pretoria and consisted of one sentence. *Your brother is dead and Ernie Stocken arrives at Cape Town airport this morning.* Staring at the screen his stomach flipped over as he reached under his jacket to feel for his gun. MI5 had killed his brother and now wanted him dead. The guy was good, nearly getting him twice in Morocco and Tunis but he had learnt a lesson from these encounters. Both times, Stocken had hesitated, the first time when he came onto the ship and gave him the chance to escape, and the second time in trusting others to do his dirty work. Lance just had to eliminate him swiftly.

He glanced at the time, he was still hours away from the city and Ernie would be away and hidden a long time before the coach rumbled into town. If only he had arrived a day earlier, he would have been waiting and taken him out on the way to his accommodation. Closing his eyes again and hoping to sleep the next twelve hours away, he fell into a restless slumber before jolting himself awake with a gasp. Ernie's face had been one inch in front of his, he could smell his breath and feel the spittle spraying into his dusty face until the vision receded with consciousness. He reached inside his jacket and touched the gun again before slumping back in his seat, trying to calm his heart beat down. He stood and took the last of his cans of drink from the overhead locker, the aircon had done its work and the liquid was chilled as he tipped his head back and swallowed. Fuck it, he thought, this job was pointless and if it wasn't for his brother asking him to do it before he died, he wouldn't be here at all. Now it was kill or be killed, and either way, it would never end. If he killed Ernie Stocken, another one would surely follow.

The driver made an announcement and five minutes later, they pulled into a service stop for refuelling and a driver change. Lance, taking the chance to get out and stretch his legs, grabbed a sandwich and another six pack of Pepsi from the shop. Looking back at the passengers mingling outside the coach, he could see that the majority were young and black while a stocky white guy dressed in safari shorts and shirt took a piss behind the bus, not seeming to care that a toilet was only twenty metres away. He gave the black driver a plastic bag containing a large number of empty beer cans.

"Put these in the bin boy," he ordered and the driver took the bag and keeping his head down, he dropped it into the bin. A large belch followed where a thank you should have been, and seeing Lance sitting on a bench taking in the cool early morning air and watching him, he wandered over towards him.

"Fucking blacks better know their place, what do you think son? This Government have given the kaffers too much. They are starting to feel that they are equal to us." He belched again and a stink of stale beer and tobacco invaded the fresh air before he continued. "There is one little bitch on there that has got it coming, she needs a real man." He nodded towards a young black girl no more than fifteen years old who was travelling alone and looked vulnerable. Lance kept his eyes down, not answering. This annoyed the man who poked him on the shoulder.

"You listening to me man? Oh, don't tell me you're a kaffer lover white boy?" Lance struck the man directly in the throat with a savage blow knocking him backwards into the shadow behind the bench. He quickly glanced up to ensure no one had seen him. Two men stood staring, the driver and his replacement and they smiled and nodded before turning their backs and heading towards the bus.

"Nothing to see here," he heard them laugh. The other passengers had boarded as Lance dragged the lifeless body behind the service stop and was surprised when the original driver appeared and took the man's feet.

"In here boss," he said, indicating the large green rubbish skip. "It gets dumped and crushed tomorrow. That guy was a monster, raped a young girl last month and beat me real bad so I kept silent. He deserves to be dead." Climbing back onto the coach, the new driver smiled at him before the doors swished shut and the aircon kicked in. "All Aboard, next stop Cape Town," he told his passengers.

The plane wheels squealed as they touched down on the tarmac and grabbing his black rucksack from the overhead locker, Ernie made his way through to passport control. A multitude of faces waited on the other side, and he scanned the crowd before seeing his South African Special Force counterpart.

"Hey Jan, how are you doing?"

"Better than you man, you look like shit!" Laughing they hugged each other, before Jan pulled back.

"You smell worse than you look Ernie, let's get you back and cleaned up. I'm parked just out front, V.I.P. all the way." The temperature was heating up as they got into the rear seats of the Range Rover, another guy behind the wheel who Ernie guessed was part of the S/F Recce team as well. Younger than both of them, he still looked as though he were on active service. Jan introduced him.

"This is Joe, a good mate of mine. He is still involved in Recce and can give us any help we need." Joe smiled in the rear-view mirror while he spoke to Ernie. "I have a selection of weapons you may be interested in, they are all stored back where we're heading so whatever you need is yours." Ernie nodded back before catching up with more abuse from Jan.

"We've done a bit of research on your guy, he is on the way here by road poor bastard. I have a couple of guys waiting at the coach stop and he'll be dead before his foot hits the street."

"Saves me a lot of work Jan," Ernie laughed, "this guy has more lives than a fucking cat." Jan smiled.

"My guys hunt big cats for breakfast."

Two blond haired, stocky men sat watching the coaches coming in. The Pretoria bus was running late and as it slowly pulled into its parking bay, they stood as if greeting a friend. The doors hissed open for the last time that day and the stream of passengers filed off. The men scanned every face, easy to do as there was not a white man amongst them. The last person came off as the cargo doors at the side opened up. Still no sign of their man.

One of the men entered the coach crouching as he made his way along the tight space between the seats as the other covered him, weapons drawn. There was no point in concealment when the danger could be imminent. Empty. Pistols back in their holsters, the men approached the driver.

"Where is this white guy?" They held out a photograph. The driver hardly threw it a glance.

"No white guy today, this is all I have." Four hundred metres away, Lance sat in a coffee shop watching the drama unfold, thinking that they must have thought they were dealing with a novice.

Back in the airconditioned safe house, thirty minutes from the bustle of the city centre, the phone rang. Joe answered and listened before placing the receiver back down. "He wasn't on the coach. The driver said that he had never seen the guy before." Ernie nodded.

"This man is good and this can only be settled between me and him. One of us will die in the African dust my friends." Joe and Jan raised a glass to Ernie. "Here's hoping it's not you."

Three days had passed and Lance had already found his prey. A simple check of township clinics and a small amount of cash had led him to Tanya. Sitting inside a corrugated iron shack overlooking the clinic car park, he watched as Tanya said her goodbyes before climbing into her car. Lance was relieved to see her leave as the smell from the two dead bodies of the previous occupants of the home was beginning to bother him, the blood from the gaping wounds to their throats had long since congealed and had become a meeting place for every fly in the area. Quickly leaving the sweltering shack, he made his way on foot to the main road where his battered van sat and climbing inside, he peered into the dusty wing mirror as Tanya drove slowly past him, not giving a second glance to another wreck of a vehicle. Carefully, he followed her keeping a good distance behind. He had no need to get closer, the traffic was light and he could guess where she was heading. Cruising past her as she pulled into the secure gate area of the compound, he didn't glance once at her car, there was no need, she was his.

CHAPTER TWENTY-SEVEN

Tanya jogged around the lake in the compound with her running friend Kate. Their children both attended the local school and they quickly found that they shared a love for fitness. The Cape Town 10k fun run was approaching and both had agreed that it would be a good incentive to get fitter and lose a couple of pounds, not that either needed to do so. Stephen had sent two running tops out to Tanya when he heard of the plan, he'd had their names printed on the front and back so that the crowds watching the race could cheer them on and encourage them to finish.

"When is the court case for the two cops going to end Tanya?" Kate had this annoying habit of never seemingly running out of breath or energy regardless of the distance they ran or the sun's burning heat.

"They have been found guilty already and sentencing is in two days' time. I may go along to support little Bandile, he hasn't got much going for him," Tanya panted as they turned onto the last section of their run. They ended soon after back at Kate's house at the far end of the compound. Her husband was away in Saudi working for a few weeks, so Tanya came in to keep her company for a couple of hours while they had some lunch. She had brought a change of clothing with her and they both quickly showered before preparing their meal. As she put her running kit back in her bag, she called out to her friend.

"I'm putting my sports stuff in the wash Kate, shall I throw yours in as well? It always seems such a waste to run the machine with just my running clothes in. I can drop it off in a couple of days or you can change at mine before the next run?" Kate came out of her room with her kit.

"Brilliant, thanks. I will come over to yours to save on the messing around."

"Make it around three, the court case should be done in the morning so I'm free after that until we pick the kids up."

The two defendants stood in the dock as the judge took her seat. All eyes were on them, the fear on their faces evident with one sporting a large bruise to his right cheek. It seems that the locals in the prison didn't like bullying policemen either.

"Your Honour," the legal representative for one of the men stood to address the judge. "While my client has pleaded guilty to the charges placed against him, may I point out the violence that he is facing on a daily basis due to the high profile of this case. If imprisoned, he faces a very uncertain future." The judge asked him to proceed.

"The Prison system is unable to protect my client from danger and his life is at risk should he return to custody. May I suggest that his period on remand within this prison has sent him a very clear message. He has lost his job, his ability to pay his rent on the family home and he has lost his good name within the community. It could be argued that he has already served his punishment for the crime." The second solicitor stood and echoed these feelings, finishing with a plea that both men should be released and allowed to rebuild their lives. The judge looked at both barristers.

"Thank you for your thoughts regarding sentencing. I have thought through the same argument myself. Prison is a last resort, and certainly not an option I take lightly for two serving Police Officers.

I also understand the great strain that is placed upon them in the policing of some very difficult areas." Tanya leaned over and whispered to Bandile, "I don't like the sound of this."

"I am adjourning for thirty minutes to consider the sentence given the obvious wounds presented to me by the accused and the passionate defence against imprisonment. We will reconvene at 10.45."

Sitting in the legal interview area outside the courtroom, the defence solicitor approached Tanya and Bandile. "Not sure how this is going to end, the judge seemed to listen to that utter nonsense and I don't know her. If this doesn't go our way I can only apologise." He'd barely uttered the words when a court usher came in to summon them.

"The judge wants us all back in, she doesn't need thirty minutes apparently."

Gathering their documents, they made their way into the court where the two policemen were back in the dock and both smirked at Bandile seemingly knowing the outcome already.

"This is going to get bad for me Tanya, these guys will hunt me down," he whispered, panic in his voice. Tanya took his hand and squeezed it. "I am here for you Bandile," she muttered but she didn't sound convincing. The judge came back into the court room, taking her seat and looking down at her prepared statement.

"I apologise for bringing you all back here at such short notice but I have considered everything in depth for the past few days and hearing today's speeches reinforced my initial feelings." The policemen looked at each other and smiled as she continued.

"We employ only the very best people to represent the law and order of our nation. The vast majority of the time over the past few years you have acted as a service with integrity. The Chief of Police has made massive strides in irradicating crime and corrupt practices from our city, and as this case points out, is not afraid to put the Police Service fully in the spot light of publicity to give transparency for all. You have both fallen a long way short of what is expected and you have behaved like the thugs you attempt to prosecute. You are both a cancer to the system we try to uphold and therefore I sentence you both to imprisonment for eight years."

A gasp was heard from the families in the room as the two condemned men stood in shock. As her words sunk in, tears flowed as the impact of what they now both faced hit them. One looked over at Bandile his red eyes showing his devastation. Bandile looked away, he knew not to respond as there was sure to be someone watching. The Judge then addressed him.

"Bandile, I wish to apologise on behalf of Cape Town for your treatment. Your bravery in coming forward has been appreciated and I understand that the city Police Department wish to compensate you for the damage caused. I will leave these details to you and your legal team." She looked once again at the crying men, her face expressionless.

"Take them down to the cells." Then they were gone, never to trouble the townships again, and Tanya and Bandile hugged in the court room, bonded by the brutality of township life. She looked down at her watch, it was already 2.45pm and she would be late for her afternoon run. Taking out her phone, she sent a text to Kate pushing the run back an hour.

Lance sat in his car near the compound gates, watching the guards checking vehicles in and out. Armed with holstered pistols, they seemed competent enough although delivery vans appeared to go through without a detailed search of the cargo. He was now pretty clear on their routine, the guards rotated each hour, the guy on the barrier would go into the office area, the two patrolling the wall would park up the truck and go onto the barrier while the ones from the office got into the truck.

He waiting until the changeover at three o'clock and drove straight up to the barrier, his reasoning being that the guard would not yet be settled into their routine and may still be a little disorientated. Winding down the window, he passed over his ID to the young black man dressed in combats and shades, looking every inch a bad ass except that he was only in his teens.

"Hi, I'm from the BBC, United Kingdom and I am here to do a short interview with Tanya Byfield about the brutality of white police against black people," he told the boy.

"Why are you interested in that sir?"

"The British public support the black people of South Africa and when we heard about the current court case against the two policemen here in Cape Town, we wanted to report on the story.

If it is possible, I would like to interview you too after you have finished work, the public would love to hear your opinions." The boy's eyes grew wide. "The BBC want to interview me?"

"Of course, I just need to meet with Mrs Byfield first. Can I book an hour with you? I will pay 100 rand."

"Six o'clock at the bar just down the road, 100 rand," the boy agreed, unable to hide his excitement.

"In cash," Lance confirmed.

"She lives at number 12 just up that road on the right," he pointed out Sally's house. The barrier shot up and Lance was in.

Kate and Sally were sitting chatting in the garden, Ellie was playing in the bedroom as Harry was at school practicing his part in the school play and Hector had stayed in the nursery while Tanya was at the court. They wouldn't be home for ages. She knocked on her window pointing at Kate who was sitting with her back to the window, and laughed.

"What are you laughing at monkey?" Sally called over.

"You've got Mummy's running shirt on Kate." Sally looked behind Kate's back, "So you have Kate, never mind, they will both be in the wash again tonight." Kate smiled and shrugged her shoulders. "Maybe I will run as fast as Mummy now," she called back to Ellie. Ellie sat back on the floor and carried on playing, oblivious to the sudden breeze caused as the front door slowly opened.

Lance moved quickly down the hallway and into the kitchen, he could hear two people talking in the garden and through the glass door, he could see the back of one of the women, Tanya. He took a glass and crashed it onto the floor hoping that they would hear the noise and come in to investigate. He crouched watching but there was no reaction at all as they continued, engrossed in their conversation.

Ellie heard the smash and standing back up at her window, she saw Sally and Kate still sitting chatting in the garden. Mystified, she looked out of her bedroom door and down the hallway to the kitchen as Lance took a large knife from the work top, a twelve-inch carving knife glistening as the sun reflected on its cruel blade. This wasn't right and she slowly made her way back into her room silently praying, in the faint hope of reaching the window in time and calling to Sally to run. Memories flooded back into her mind about the men who had taken her and Harry back in England and she didn't want this man to take Sally.

It was too late and as she watched helplessly, she saw that Lance was standing over Sally, slicing down into her chest, the force so great that the tip of the knife broke against the bone, He raised his arm again and plunged down, this time the blade sticking firmly into Sally's shoulder. He tried to pull it out two or three times before pushing her away in anger. Kate ran, grasping for the kitchen door handle in the vain hope of escaping but reaching her in two strides, Lance punched her unconscious with a savage blow to the back of her head. She fell face down onto the patio, nose and forehead broken open with the impact of the fall, blood oozing out onto the gray slabs. Ellie saw her twitch twice before lying still. Lance stepped over her and came back into the kitchen where he searched for another knife.

Slowly Kate climbed back onto her knees and feeling the blood seeping down her face, she tried to wipe it clean with the t shirt as Ellie watched in silent horror. She stood up on unsteady feet, her one thought to stop this man before they all died, and steadying herself, she hurtled into the kitchen. Ellie wanted to help Kate, but remembered the last time bad men had come to her home, she had hidden and stayed safe. Daddy had told her afterwards that this was the best thing to do so climbing into her toy cupboard, she slithered into the large box of soft toys, hardly daring to breath. There was another crash in the kitchen and what seemed like two people fighting. She could hear Kate screaming and grunting before crying out in pain. Then silence, silence interrupted by the sound of footsteps approaching her room and walking around the bed. Ellie's toys were still scattered around and one hit the cupboard door as Lance kicked it out of the way. He scanned quickly around, sure that he had heard someone else in the house, and certain he could smell fear in the room. One of the children must be here.

A knock on the front door made him freeze, and a female voice called out as someone entered the hallway. There was a sharp intake of breath as the woman saw the bodies, follow by a horrified shriek.

"Tanya! Sally! Oh my God!" The woman fumbled for her phone as Lance appeared behind her and grasping the side of her head, he swiftly broke her neck, her body slumping down into the pool of blood oozing from the gash across Kate's throat.

He looked down at the bodies and pulling Kate's head back by her hair, he stared for a few seconds at her bloodied face, before releasing his grip allowing her head to crack back down onto the floor tiles.

He studied himself in the full-length mirror in Sally's bedroom. Covered in the blood of the two women, he was in no hurry as he looked himself in the eyes. They were vacant, no longer caring for anyone or anything, his conscience having long since stopped trying to make sense of this day. Ellie could hear the sound of cupboard doors opening in the other bedroom and a shower being run. Ten minutes later, Lance walked out of the house dressed in an old pair of men's shorts and t-shirt that he had found in a bottom drawer, the rest of his clothing thrown on the bathroom floor. He couldn't give a damn about leaving DNA, he was a dead man already.

Striding back out into the sunshine, he looked as though he belonged there, confident, smiling and without a care in the world, his wet hair tight across his head. Getting in the car, he drove back through the barrier, shouting out to the guard, "See you in the bar later," before gunning the engine and heading back to the hotel.

Ellie crept out of her hiding place, she knew what was waiting for her in the house but she had no wish to see any more pain and death. She reached up for the front door handle and ran out into the street, not knowing where she was heading, just that it was a lot safer than inside. The security guard's 4x4 came to a halt beside her and she looked up at the kind face staring back at her before collapsing on to the path and crying hysterically.

Five minutes later, armed police entered Sally's house, where they found the body of Ellie's teacher blocking the hallway, her neck almost broken in half. A young woman lay on the kitchen floor, her running shirt telling the police that this was Tanya Byfield, her face a mask of congealed blood. Sally's body lying in the garden, painted a further grotesque image. She had lost almost all of her blood onto the patio slabs, the knife still sticking up from her clavicle area. Her eyes were wide open and staring quizzically at the intrusion into her home. She had been dead for maybe an hour already, and the flies were swarming around her body. The police moved back and put a cordon around the front door.

"Where are the other children?" the sergeant asked one of the neighbours who was craning her neck to see the action."

"They are at the school with my son and should be home in twenty minutes. Is everything okay? We heard a scream."

"Stay inside for the minute please Ma'am, we will need to take a statement." He turned to his colleague, "Someone better tell Mr Byfield that he needs to get here."

CHAPTER TWENTY-EIGHT

Stephen sat in court number one at The Old Bailey. It was a room where a thousand court dramas had been played out, grand theatre of the highest scale where beautiful old oak wood walls surrounded the key players decked out in their theatrical costumes. He had presented his evidence to a packed court room as journalists scribed every hushed word uttered.

The evidence was damning against the accused, Mr Uden, Mr Sadiq and Mr Khan. Although they had pleaded guilty to corruption and the large scale dealing of drugs while serving in a public office, they had firmly denied the act of terrorism. However, photographic evidence along with MI5 and MI6 surveillance footage, proved without a doubt that each of the three men had conspired to smuggle firearms and ammunition into the hands of terror groups, alongside the training of Muslim prisoners in committing acts of terror both in the United Kingdom and abroad, and conspiring to murder the Home Secretary. The prosecuting barrister had made mincemeat of the flimsy defence provided in order to confuse the jury and place doubt in their minds.

The preposterous story of the recently retired Foreign Secretary becoming embroiled within the scheme was dismissed in total, with the Prime Minister interjecting, and in an unprecedented move, giving a written testimony which completely cleared his name from any wrong doing. His diagnosis of Motor Neurone disease shortly before the arrest of the three senior prison service managers, had provided them with a smoke screen, and the thought that this fine man who had served the government for his entire working life could be blamed for greedy corrupt officials, was just a sick and twisted version of events, aimed at manipulating a jury who they hoped had long lost confidence in politicians. The lie didn't work and in a clear show of support of defiance against the terrorists, every major news network broadcast the Prime Minister's words. Stephen accepted this statement uncomplainingly although he knew different.

The jury were dismissed to consider a verdict, the judge had asked them to consider all facts and to return to the court in the morning. Leaving the court room, Stephen turned his phone on, and found a voicemail from the Cape Town Police.

'Mr Byfield, could you please phone me on this number immediately, I am afraid that there has been an incident.' Scribbling down the number as it was slowly read out to him, he dialled, sweat dripping from his forehead as his fingers fumbled over the numbers. What did they mean by the word incident? He could scarcely breath as the voice at the other end answered in a gentle voice.

"Mr Byfield, do you have anyone with you at the moment?"

"No, why? What is going on?"

"There has been an incident at Sally Cowan's house, we believe your wife was staying with Ms Cowan?"

"Yes, along with my children."

"Your children are safe Mr Byfield." These words bounced around in his head, if they are safe, what about Tanya?

"Where is my wife?"

"We believe that she has been killed Mr Byfield, along with Ms Cowan and a local teacher."

"Believe, what does that mean?" Stephen asked, clutching at straws.

"The lady was wearing your wife's clothes and fits her description but we haven't formally identified her yet. We think it is Tanya, Mr Byfield. When do you think you might be able to fly over?"

"Oh my God! Fuck, fuck, fuck! Tomorrow, I will get there tomorrow." He hung up and sat staring at the wooden ceiling. He had brought this hell to his family and now it had caused the death of his beautiful wife. Tears flowed down his cheeks as the public walked past ignoring him. The phone rang again, it was an unknown number and he thought that maybe it was the South African police again with more information.

"Stephen Byfield," he answered.

"I need you here Stephen, I am so scared." It was Tanya. Stephen gave a sob.

"The police told me you were dead, just five minutes ago. I thought you were dead," he cried and laughed simultaneously. "What the hell is going on?"

"I'm not sure what is going on anymore either," Tanya replied, sobbing too. "I'm fine but it's not good Stephen. Sally, my friend Kate and a school teacher were murdered in the house this afternoon but apparently the killer was looking for me. I'm on the way to the Police Station in Cape Town as we speak. I was at the court supporting a lad from the township and the security at the compound stopped me at the gate when I came home. They are taking me there now. Ellie, Harry and Hector are already there safe, waiting for me but poor little Ellie saw the whole thing." She sobbed even harder, the pain of losing her friends overwhelming her.

"But who did this?" Stephen asked, still trying to get his head around the fact that his dead wife was in fact alive.

"Lance Mitchell, Stephen, who apparently is the brother of your former boss. He left a stack of evidence in the house and it looks like he wants to destroy us all." They sobbed together for a few more moments before Stephen promised he would get on the first plane available, and Tanya arrived at the police station to be reunited with her children.

CHAPTER TWENTY-NINE

The tale of two prisoners

The prison van pulled up at Pollsmoor Admission Centre. The two men looked anxiously at each other as they were led out of the secure vehicle and into the sunshine. They had sat in the prison on remand for some time but had been kept separate from the overcrowded population. The Prison managers had shown some sympathy for two white policemen accused of brutality against a popular boy from the township. They had argued that they were not guilty until the court said otherwise, and now the notorious Numbers Gang who ran the general population without mercy, were after them. The gang were broken up into three factions, the 26's, 27's and 28's and were to be feared by all other inmates. If they noticed you, it spelt bad news.

The 26's secured money through gambling and smuggling, the 27's served as gang enforcers and the 28's were the soldiers for all three groups. They also dealt with procuring and keeping sexual partners or 'wifies.' They maintained power through physical and sexual violence and paid willing volunteers to do the dirty work.

The minute the gang learned that the two policemen were coming into the main population of Pollsmoor, a hit had been arranged on both men by the 28's and it would be honoured, if not today, then tomorrow, or next month or even next year. There would be no escape from the retribution planned.

The men arrived at the reception desk where normally they had been greeted in a friendly manner, seen by the staff as one of their own before disappearing into the comfort of their own secure cells. This time the mood was very different. Pushed into a large holding room, they sat with thirty other mainly black prisoners where the mood was hostile and barbed threats were shouted across the room.

"White boys, you are fucked tonight. Two new wifies for the 28's." The rest of the room laughed. A large white correctional officer opened the door and gestured towards the men to follow him, they didn't hesitate, leaving the room quickly without a backwards glance.

"Thank God for that man, we thought we were finished back there," Hicks said to the officer. He didn't reply as they walked through the prison corridors, along a route they hadn't taken before. They reached a large single room, where perhaps forty other men were lying on beds, playing cards or standing quietly talking and glancing at the barred gate. It went silent as the men reached the entrance. Hicks turned to the officer in confusion.

"What's going on man? This isn't where we stay, we have rooms in the other part of the prison, you know that. You have taken us there before, you filthy bastard." The officer unlocked the gate.

"This is all yours now boys, eight years' worth so enjoy the stay." He pushed them through the gate where they stood with a small roll of bedding in their hands and forty sets of eyes staring at them. They felt like rats about to be fed alive to venomous snakes, walking around the cage helplessly, waiting for one to strike. And strike it would, hard, fast and deadly.

A small, older man stood and walked over towards them, he had no upper teeth and was covered in gang tattoos. He pointed at two broken beds at the back of the room and walked away to join the others. The correctional officer had long gone and there was no sign of anyone else to control the prisoners. They dropped their few possessions and sat on the beds before the man came towards them again.

"You have been called to attention," he informed them.

"What the fuck does that mean? I am not standing to attention for anyone," Hicks replied, still playing the big man.

"It means, white boy, that one of our leaders is going to tell you something."

"You can't tell me shit." The man laughed as some others approached and they were pulled up from the beds and dragged to a makeshift office area hidden from the gate by bunk beds. A large guy stood leaning against the wall, he had a bandana around his closely cropped hair and a wicked looking scar across his bare chest. Although only in his twenties, he appeared every inch a warlord gangster as he sneered at the men before him, their fate already decided. Four of his soldiers stood alongside him and they were clearly high on something.

"You," he pointed at Andy Hicks. "You are the white man who beat my friend Bandile," his eyes glowing with hate. Andy didn't respond, he knew it was futile. The man turned to his soldiers. "Give the motherfucker a passion gap so he can suck man's dick." They grabbed him and pushed him down onto the floor, his face looking up towards his friend in a silent plea. In the police force, they had always backed each other up but this was different and the shaking Thomas Eaten was far too scared to move a muscle.

Held down while his top lip was roughly pulled back exposing his top teeth, they smashed each one in turn until they had all been torn out. The pain was excruciating as blood poured onto the floor and down his throat. He twisted his body in pain as he tried to break free but it was futile and the man laughed as he kicked the teeth under a bunk.

"Get him out of here so he can earn his money, fucking white bitch."

"Fat Man!" He bellowed. Before the words had left the gate, the officer returned as though he had been waiting for his cue to reappear. "Take this little whore to where she belongs," and he opened the gate and pulled Hicks back out into the corridor.

"And don't forget my little parcel in the morning white boy."

"I'll have it, don't worry man," the officer called back as they both disappeared into the heart of the prison, pain ripping through Hick's body with every step. He knew what was coming and through numbing lips he hissed, "I heard what was said, if you take me to the isolation unit I will keep quiet." The officer stopped and looked at him.

"If I take you there, what do you think that they will do to me? Sorry man, you are literally fucked."

Dragging him on, they reached the high security area where Hicks could tell that the staff and prisoners knew a new game was in town, but it also seemed that nobody cared enough to do anything about it. They drew to a halt outside a large, dark, gated cell where he noticed four names were written on cell cards on the wall beside it and next to each name, the word 'Life'.

The door slid open with a mechanical clunk before the officer pushed him forwards towards the entrance. Hicks hesitated, fear overcoming his pain. Standing outside the pitch black cell, he could hear breathing coming from the unseen beds, he could smell the body odour of four other men and could feel their eyes staring at him as he stood in the light of the corridor. He could sense the anticipation of what was going to happen to him as a distant laugh could be heard before an office door banged shut.

The gate closed as Hicks stood motionless and very alone until he heard the creak of the men climbing from their beds. Facing his worst nightmare, he was dragged into the darkness of the hell that he was going to have to endure indefinitely, while the staff stayed in the safety of the office, door shut, and carried on with their work.

That night his screams could be heard throughout the prison. Eaten tried to drown out the noise by covering his head with a pillow knowing that life was not going to be so simple for him either. Dragged from his bed in the early hours of the morning he was called to attention again.

"Your friend is busy paying back his debt, now we have to deal with you. My men here haven't seen a girl for a long time so you will satisfy their needs every night." He was dragged onto a table top where his trousers were pulled from him, boxers ripped down by unseen hands as the men took turns in raping him. Falling unconscious through pain, he came to, lying on the floor of the large cell, every inch of his body throbbing and stinging. He tried to sit up but the blood flooded from his anus over the floor, so staggering to his feet, he fell face down onto his bed, pulling a sheet over himself to cover his exposed body. The cell leader pulled the sheet back and took his arm, wrapping a lace around his bicep and exposing a vein. Gently finding its target, he pushed the needle into him and introduced Eaten to another mistress. Heroin.

"Sleep, you have a busy time coming, I think my boys like you." And so the pattern continued night after night, screams and heroin, until the drug kept the screams away, and then it was all about heroin and nothing else mattered.

Thomas Eaten lay on his filthy bed out of sight of the guards, looking for his leader. He needed the drug. "White boy, you are being called to attention, better be quick bitch," he was told by another cell inhabitant. He pulled on a stained pair of tracksuit bottoms and walked to the make shift office.

"You want your medicine boy?"

"Yes."

"Well, you need to work for it. We are fed up with your stinking arse and we don't need you anymore. If you want drugs, you have to do something for us."

"Anything," he promised as the craving for heroin crawled across every inch of his skin. He was passed a large handmade knife. "Go kill your boy on the yard right now. My friends want him dead, he is of no use any more." He didn't hesitate. "Drugs first, then I kill him." The men laughed, "No man, he is there now, kill him and we fix you up all week." He looked at the knife and stuck it into the waistband of his tracksuit bottoms, pulling a stained green t-shirt over his top to conceal the weapon. The leader called the guard.

"Guard, this man has forgotten to go out on exercise, he stinks and he needs fresh air." The fat young officer appeared with the keys in his hand. He wrinkled his nose as he unlocked the gate.

"What the fuck is wrong with you? You fucking stink man." He took him to the exercise area and pushed him through the door.

"Take a shower when you are done, you fucking animal."

Hicks was sitting with his back to the wall, his face still swollen from having his teeth ripped out. His backside torn and bleeding from another night of rape, he desperately wanted to get out of the prison. Looking up, he spotted his colleague.

"Fuck me Thomas you look as bad as I feel. Fucking bastards, we need to get out of this place. We need H.I.V. testing as well, these animals have fucked me every night, swear to God I am going to kill every one of them if I get a chance." Eaten stumbled closer to him, almost in a zombie state.

"What the fuck have they done to you Thomas? Your eyes man, you are fucked up." Hicks reached out and grabbed his arm exposing the needle marks.

"You idiot, the only thing we have left in this world is our brain and you are giving yours away to that shit." He pushed the bruised arm back down.

"Get yourself sorted out man, we need clear heads to get out of here and into a better prison. You are pissing away any chance we have of release." Eaten had a moment of clarity as he listened to the words.

"Hicks, I am here in this shithole because you couldn't let a little black kid beat you. If you had used your fucking brain we wouldn't be stuck here, my arse wouldn't be split and I wouldn't be taking this shit to get through my day. You are the fucker who started this." He bent down and pulled out the blade, "And I am the fucker who is going to finish it." He lunged forward with the blade but missed by a mile, a drug induced fog impeding his judgement. Spinning back, he tried to strike again as a rifle shot from the watchtower took off the front of his head. He lurched backwards briefly staring at Andy before closing his eyes and dying on the prison yard. The alarm sounded and all prisoners fell to the ground afraid of further shooting.

"You fucking idiot, we only had to put up with this shit for another few days and we would have been transferred," Hicks yelled at the lifeless body.

"You ain't going nowhere white boy." A young black man with

wild eyes had taken the knife.

"Easy man, you will get us both shot," Hicks begged, holding his hands in the air. Shooting his thin arm forward like a Black Mamba biting a rat, the boy plunged the rusty blade into Hicks' chest. Bubbles of blood shot out of his mouth before dripping down onto his shirt as a misty fountain erupted from his chest. He knelt forwards, looking at the knife handle sticking from his body, briefly wondering what to do, until another shot blew the attacker off his feet, his lifeless body lurching over the back of Thomas Eaten as if he were being raped again in death. Hicks felt a cold chill throughout his body as his blood leaked out over the yard, so tired, he needed to close his eyes. The shuffle of boots and taste of the dust kicked up by the correctional officers as they emptied the yard, made him open them briefly. One stopped and felt for a pulse as Hicks weakly pleaded for help.

"Sorry man, you are not making it, you have bled out." He closed his eyes again and stopped breathing for the last time. He had escaped the hell.

CHAPTER THIRTY

The familiar crack of the 9mm pistol had died away as Ernie made the weapon safe and slid it back into the leg holster before walking down the twenty-five metre range to inspect the grouping of his shots. Taking in the beautiful mountain backdrop, he admired the scenery as his boots crunched onto the shingle surrounding the soldier shaped target. Five shots centre chest all within a few centimetres, followed by five shots in the centre of the forehead. Pleased with his shooting, he shared a joke with the range worker as he patched up the holes. The harsh sound of the loud speaker interrupted the punch line.

"Ernie, phone call for you, the guy can't wait." Jogging back, he took the stairs two at a time into the Range Marshal's office where he took the proffered phone.

"Hi, it's Ernie, how can I help?"

"Stephen Byfield here, we have a problem."

Ernie's car raced up into the driveway where Jan and Joe were standing by the door as he walked up to the house. "We need to move quickly guys, he has had a go at Tanya already, he killed three but missed her. It was definitely Lance Mitchell, he has left his calling card all over the house. It's worrying because he doesn't give a shit anymore about covert operations and he's out in the open, killing at will."

He went into his room and packed a rucksack. Slinging it on his back, he grabbed a South African Denel R4 assault rifle, its short barrel making it perfect for the job in hand, and walking back through the house, he filled his friends in with the details as he hurried back out to the car.

"She's with the kids in the SAPS Cape Town Central, they want a safe place for her. Can we bring them all here?" Jan rushed out after him and climbed into the driver's seat of the car.

"I think that they will be safe with us Ernie. Let me drive, I can beat the city traffic in no time." Checking his pistol and magazine he called over to Joe.

"We'll be back in a couple of hours, turn the dining room into a defendable area. We are bringing the family back here and we'll need to be able to withstand an attack from possibly two to four people. Call in some favours mate, we need this place to be secure." Joe nodded and got straight on the phone as Jan and Ernie pulled out onto the empty road.

Ernie phoned ahead and spoke to the Security Manager at the building, they were coming in armed and expected to pick up the family quickly. Stephen had also phoned the officer in charge and had spoken to him and Tanya, Ernie had given him specific instructions about what to disclose. Lance was at large somewhere in the city and it could be very possible that he had contacts inside the Police Management team. The least the police knew, the better the chances of survival.

The black Range Rover pulled up directly outside the doors to the building. A blue sign on the wall stated 'South African Police Service. Community Service Centre' and this was the agreed meeting point. Two police officers stood outside scanning the street while Ernie walked inside with his pistol holstered on his leg. Jan stood at the door with the automatic rifle butt sat in his shoulder, ready to unleash hell in a split second. Less than a minute later, Ernie reappeared with Tanya and the three children and ten seconds after that, they were back on the road, driving. From parking to leaving had taken less than seventy seconds. He got back on the phone to Stephen.

"Everything is okay and we're on the way back home," before handing the phone into the back seat for Tanya. When Tanya had reassured Stephen that they were all safe, they hung up, and immediately the phone rang again. This time it was the security manager.

"Ernie, you are not going to believe this. A guy professing to be from the British Embassy has just tried to get into the building to see Tanya and the children. Can I send his photo over for verification?" It came up a second later. It was a clear picture of a well-built white man, heavily scarred face, very smartly dressed and with Embassy identification. Lance Mitchell had missed the family by five minutes, confirmation that he indeed had friends in high places. Ernie confirmed his identity.

"Yes, that's the man we are worried about. Listen no word about us please mate, obviously walls have ears in your building."

"No dangers Ernie, stay safe mate." Ernie turned round to talk to Tanya.

"Tanya, I know that you hate this situation and so do we, but we need to get you home safely. The only way that I can do that is to remove the man chasing you. Do you understand what I am saying?"

She nodded.

"It's not going to take very long I am glad to say, but he is going to come looking for us. That is going to happen in probably three or four days depending on the information he pays for, maybe even a little faster and we need to be ready." She nodded again.

"How are you doing in the back there?" Ernie looked at the children. Ellie was the only one who answered and she had a haunted look in her eyes, a look Ernie had seen many times in people who had seen too much.

"Are you going to kill that bad man?" she asked him. It was pointless lying to her.

"Yes I am sweetheart, you won't see it happen though, I promise."

"I want to see it happen, he killed my friend Sally." She shrugged and then looked back out of the window at the passing shops.

They pulled back into the driveway of the house, a beautiful single-story property sat in an acre of its own land. The nearest place was two hundred metres away so they had a lot of privacy. The back of the house had a small plunge pool and a wide view of vineyards and mountains, it would make a wonderful holiday home which is what Jan intended to do with it one day. As they climbed out of the car, they noticed the newly installed bullet proof door and the hundreds of empty sandbags by the side of the house. Joe had a beaming smile.

"You wanted it safe, come in and let me know what you think. We had thirty mates turn up and sort this shit out in an hour or so." Every interior wall was sand bagged and the smell of hessian was everywhere. The external doors were bullet proofed and the dining area resembled something from Camp Bastian in Afghanistan.

"Bloody hell Joe, I am glad I didn't leave you for three hours, we would have had a helipad in the back yard," Jan quipped.

"Funny you say that Jan, it is arranged." They all laughed but mainly because they knew it was true.

"If the shit hits the fan, we can have seven guys flown in at ten minute's notice, only for the next week though. It's all in hand."

"Is there any room left to sleep," Ernie asked?

"Fuck, I hadn't thought of the kids and Tanya," he laughed again. "Course, we have four beds for them in the safe room, us three can just move around between stagging on."

"Good work Joe. Hope it's for nothing though. Let's see how it pans out over the next couple of days, we might need to find him if he can't find us."

The quick flash from the binocular lens from the mountains behind the house went unnoticed. It hadn't taken four days for Lance Mitchell to find them, it had taken four hours and a quick call from the helpful Police Sergeant on the front desk who had a wife with expensive tastes and a liking for spending a lot of money. He slipped back into the rocks and waited for darkness to fall.

Tanya finished her last mouthful of the curry Joe had prepared. Made entirely from fresh ingredients, it had been mouthwatering and even the children had eaten every last morsel.

"That was so yummy Joe, who on earth taught you to cook

like that?" she asked, sitting back in her chair, full to bursting.

"My father, he was fighting the Russians in Afghanistan with the mujahedeen. They taught him so many things other than how to kill foreign soldiers. When he eventually returned home, he opened up a small restaurant serving food from Afgan. He died in 2006 and my brother sold the business but I think it is still there in Paris. Cheeky bastard kept all the money and buggered off to the UK somewhere. Good riddance to him."

"Well at least he left you with great cookery skills. Let me wash up and then I need to hit the sack with these three." The children sat on the sofa almost in a coma after the long day and the big meal.

"Ellie, Harry, Hector, come on, teeth and bed," she chivied them along. After a few seconds of moaning about the smell of the sandbags in the bedroom, they trooped through and got ready and within ten minutes they were fast asleep.

Jan joined Tanya at the sink and dried the dishes as she washed them. "How is this going to finish Jan? We're frightened," she told him.

"Do you want an honest answer?"

"Of course."

"He will come to kill you, either here or elsewhere. He has nothing left to lose and wants revenge on his brother's death. Either we kill him or he kills us all."

"What will he be doing now?"

"If he has found us, he will be watching us, probably from the mountains during daylight and then work out our routines and attack us. That is what I would do." Tanya glanced out at the blackness through the kitchen window and shivered.

"On his own?"

"No, he will hire some guys, he has seen that there are three of us here ready to fight to protect you and he will think he needs at least ten people to beat us. I think he will need more than that, but ten is a lot of people to organize and the quality of the fighters may be questionable. What he doesn't realise is that we can have air support quickly and that will be a game changer."

"Bloody hell, I am not going to sleep knowing that," she said with a small laugh which did nothing to mask her fear.

"I would rather have a good sleep before I die, nothing worse than getting shot at when you are knackered" he laughed. "Go on, we have this place nice and safe, get some sleep." Tanya looked at the kitchen clock, it was 10.43 and dark as hell outside.

Ernie, Jan and Joe sat in the kitchen, talking arcs of fire and contingency plans should the house get hit and they take casualties. Joe had a few surprises up his sleeve. If the enemy attacked from the rear of the house during the night time, it would be easy for them to melt into the darkness, climb onto the roof and smash their way in. If they got into the house, the only defendable room would be the dining area where the kid's beds had been set up. Should they be unable to get past the defences, they would just burn the place down forcing everyone out into the open. They might try this tactic anyway and the only defence would be to spot them and stop them, as far away as possible. For this reason, a series of night vision cameras had been set up around the land surrounding the house and any movement would trigger the sensors and activate the camera. Whoever was awake in the house would see them coming. He had also planted a number of mines designed to explode at leg and groin height - one mine could take out a number of attackers and he had five set out.

Joe and Jan lay on the sofas grabbing some sleep, Ernie had the first stag. He sat thinking about Lance for an hour before a screen burst into life. Camera two, three hundred metres away had been activated and he watched, waiting for a sign to detonate the first mine. Nothing happened until a small deer walked past carefully eating the grass from the field. The screen then went dark indicating no further movement. He was just breathing a sigh of relief when screens three and four then flashed up and as he squinted at the images, he saw five or more people approaching, possibly two hundred metres away. They were armed and then, as screen one and two spat into life, he saw another four armed people approaching. Ernie woke up the other two while still watching the screen, and could see that the men were not trained, with a number smoking and chatting, and two of them having what looked like an argument. Joe learnt over Ernie's shoulder.

"Strap yourselves in," he muttered. The first two mines detonated and he could see five men fall, legs blown to pieces as three other men took to the ground and sprayed a burst of gunfire at the house.

Tanya called through from the dining room, "What do we do?"

"Stay where you are, heads down, and don't move," Ernie shouted back.

The next burst of fire thumped into the sandbags at the rear of the house and the cameras showed four men moving cautiously forward, still two hundred metres away. Mines three and four then erupted leaving two of them dead.

Ernie looked at the screens seeing only three left alive, moving forward, one hundred and fifty from the house. The last mine took care of a squat man holding a radio, obviously in contact with Lance. Joe and Jan took their chance and climbed through a small window at the front of the house, disappearing into the darkness with their night vision goggles. Creeping forward, they got to within fifty metres of the remaining two men, who seemed both confused and afraid. Jan took the first one down with a single shot and the last man stood up with his hands held above his head.

Jan bounded forward, his gun aimed at the man's head.

"Who fucking sent you?"

"A white guy with a lot of money, he said we could kill the men and rape the woman and the girl. He told us you were bad people." Jan pulled the trigger and fired into the man's forehead dropping him on the spot. He then found the radio and sent a message.

"If you want us, come down and get us yourself big guy." There was no answer, just static. The roar of the helicopter drowned out any further contact and touching down in the back yard, soldiers spilled out across the field before returning.

"Eleven dead, look like local people, no whites amongst them," they reported back. Jan went back into the house and into the dining room.

"Tanya, get the kids, we are going on another adventure. How do you like flying?"

CHAPTER THIRTY-ONE

Stephen took his seat back in court number one. His flight to South Africa was later that afternoon and he just had time to witness the punishment handed down to his former colleagues. The jury had returned to give their verdict and the three former prison managers sat silently in the dock, exchanging no words and staring down at their feet. The judge entered the court and everyone stood, the atmosphere around the room electric. Court clerks scurried between desks until the judge began to speak. Clarifying that the jury had reached a verdict, he asked what it was. The jury foreman stood facing the judge.
On count one, guilty.
On count two, guilty.
On count three, attempted murder, guilty. There was a ripple of applause from the public gallery. The judge regained the order of the room, his final speech ripping any hope of leniency from the men. He concluded with, "You will all go to prison for a minimum of thirty-five years. Take them down please." The rustle of the men's feet leaving the dock and descending the wooden stairs into the waiting cells was the only noise in a hushed room. The rats had been caught and would face a miserable life behind the bars they once helped keep unsecure.

Later that afternoon, Stephen sat in the departure lounge at Heathrow, his plane was due to leave in an hour and the passengers were being called through to the gate. Unaware of the firefight his wife and children had survived, he had tried to phone Tanya a number of times that morning but had found both hers and Ernie's phones unobtainable. He decided to try one last call before boarding and this time Tanya answered but the noise from the bad line was drowning out most of the chat.

"What do you mean you were in a helicopter with the children, why were you in a helicopter Tanya?"

"We are safe Stephen, I will tell you when you get here, a man named Jan is picking....." The call was lost and Stephen tried again but couldn't get through. *What the fuck is going on?* he mumbled to himself as he headed through the last passport check. Sitting in his seat on the plane, he sent a last text before losing all communication for the next few hours. *'Tanya, I love you sweetheart, stay safe and I'll see you in the morning.'*

The helicopter had touched down in a bone dry, tented army camp in the middle of the bush. She had no idea where they were other than it was only a short flight from the house, maybe ten minutes at most. Ernie slid the door open and escorted them all into a large green tent somewhere in the middle of the base. "This is possibly the safest place in South Africa at the moment," he told her as the children bounced on the camp beds set up under the canvas.

"Where have I heard that before?" Tanya replied, not even having the energy to smile.

"Tomorrow morning we will pick Stephen up from the airport and get a plan together. This guy Lance is going to die sometime this week."

"How can you be so sure?"

"Because I am going to find him and kill him personally."

The wheels of the plane bumped down and briefly screamed as they held onto the Cape Town runway.

"Ladies and Gentlemen, it looks like a lovely morning here in Cape Town, the temperature is around twenty five degrees and the local time is 11.43. Sorry for the slight delay in our arrival but we hope that you have a pleasant stay in the country." Stephen wasn't sure that anything was going to be remotely pleasant about this next few days, in fact he was sure that by the end of the week there would be a high body count somewhere, and it was all as a result of him.

Clearing customs, he scoured the faces waiting in the arrival area, hoping to see Tanya and the children. Instead, he was greeted by a man in his thirties, six feet tall and with zero fat on his toned body. He was dressed in combat style trousers and a short sleeved green t-shirt, with cropped black hair. A dark stubble highlighting him as a man who'd had little sleep for the past few nights. He didn't need to hold up a greeting card, he knew who he was looking for and touched Stephen gently on the right shoulder.

"Stephen, my name is Jan, you need to come with me quickly, we will talk in the car." Jan walked so fast that Stephen needed to jog every third step, noticing as he did so, that Jan's eyes were scanning everywhere as they raced out of the airport terminal and into the Range Rover waiting outside in an authorised parking area. An airport security guard was standing by the bonnet as if on a close protection duty as Jan opened the back door and tossed Stephen's case onto the seat before telling him to get in the passenger seat quickly. The engine roared and they were gone.

It was five minutes before Jan held out his hand, "Welcome to Cape Town Stephen, I guess we have a lot to catch up on. Let's wait until we get back to your family and we can fill in each other's blanks." A traffic light turned red a few metres in front of them, and as they slowed down to a stop, a young black man stepped into the road directly in front of the car and moved around to the driver's window. He looked spaced out on the local drugs and seemed a little erratic in his mannerisms, so, without taking his eyes off him, Jan reached down and in one movement pushed the barrel of a pistol square into the man's forehead.

"Not today man, bad timing," he told him as the man backed away cursing as Jan sped forwards. He turned towards a somewhat shocked Stephen.

"Sorry mate, we can't take too many risks today, it's a dangerous place at the best of times and with your friend Lance Mitchell running around, it's fucking deadly," he laughed as he put the gun back down beside his seat.

Leaving the tarmac road behind, they pushed onto a bumpy track leading into the bush until they reached a single barrier manned by two white soldiers. Stopping the car, they grinned and waved the car straight through and after a small bend in the track, they were at the gates of the army base. Stephen sat staring around in amazement, feeling that he was in the middle of a Hollywood movie set for a war-based drama. Pulling up by a large green tent, Tanya and the children ran out to greet him. It was wonderful to hold each other again after so long and it was a while before the two of them released each other long enough for Stephen to hug the children. He looked up at Tanya.

"I will never put you through this again, I promise."

"I don't think we could cope with anymore," she replied, "the kids are spent and Ellie has seen the worst horrors imaginable." He nodded and stroked Ellie's hair as they spoke. "Sorry darling," he smiled down at his daughter. She nodded and walked back into the shade of the tent where Harry and Hector had returned to play with the toy cars one of the soldiers had provided from somewhere. Tanya and Stephen followed them and sat in the shade recapping their stories for each other. Tanya finished telling Stephen how they had ended up in the camp, but then continued.

"It's not over though Stephen, we need to kill Lance Mitchell. This can never end while he is breathing. He wants vengeance for James' death and won't rest until he has it."

"We kill him? What does that mean?" Stephen asked, wondering if their lives could get any more screwed up.

"Not us Stephen, Ernie is going to do it." As if hearing his name, Ernie walked into the tent and shook Stephen's hand. "The last time I saw you, you were in the ship in Tunis just before I kicked your arse into the embassy. A lot has happened since then," he laughed. Stephen looked at him in consternation.

"I don't get it, why are you helping us? You were with the Brood gang on the other side last year, and you wanted us dead."

Ernie returned his look, now serious.

"I was in the wrong place at the wrong time, what more can I say? This time, luckily for you, I am in the right place at the right time. It is also in my interest." Stephen knew exactly what that meant.

"MI5 made you a deal you mean, to keep you away from a thirty-year sentence."

"Call it what you like, I am here to make things right and hopefully I live to tell the tale." Stephen gave a small nod.

"Well, after this, here's hoping we never have to meet again Ernie."

CHAPTER THIRTY-TWO

Lance sat in his hotel room in Cape Town, pistol stripped down for cleaning on his bedside table. Still seething from the fact that he thought he had killed Tanya, he had hoped to be on the next plane out of Africa until he found out differently. Then he had trusted a section of former Nigerian soldiers, who he had paid to mount the attack on the house and they had let him down badly. If whoever was guarding the Byfield's hadn't killed them all, he would have done it himself. Watching from the mountainside, he saw how their skills were akin to the boy scouts and they had deserved to die. Next time he would do the job himself and trust no one.

He had also seen the helicopter evacuation, and watched the chopper land a few miles away. He thought it must be a special force's training camp out in the bush and knew that he could never get close to the place. It needed a fresh approach and thinking carefully of his next options, he decided that the necessary funeral of her friends would be his one and only chance as Tanya would be bound to attend.

He put the weapon back together and checked online for forthcoming funerals in the area to find nothing listed. Picking up the phone he dialled the local mortuary. "Good morning, we have a number of flowers that need to go on top of the coffin for Sally Cowan, could you let me know when the funeral is due to take place please?" He heard the rustling of pages turning before the answer came.

"Ms Cowan is Wednesday at 4.30pm. If you would like to drop them off no later than midday on Wednesday, we can take care of that for you." He threw the phone onto the bed, "Wednesday pm, Tanya dies," he muttered to himself. He picked up his laptop and quickly found the page he needed. One first class ticket to Tehran flying out at 22.00 on Wednesday night.

Tanya stepped into Ernie's tent where he was sitting talking to Jan and he looked up in surprise as she wasted no time in making her request.

"I have a problem, my friend Sally is due to be buried on Wednesday and I would of course like to attend." Ernie looked at Jan before replying.

"I can guarantee that Mitchell will be there waiting for you and he will try to kill you." Tanya nodded.

"My thoughts too Ernie but what if you are there also? Maybe he will break cover to get me and you will have an opportunity to get him." Ernie puffed his cheeks out, releasing his breath slowly.

"That's a high cost strategy, what if he pays someone else to do his dirty work like last time?" Tanya had her answer ready, she had thought about this long and hard.

"It went tits up last time Ernie, would he really take that chance again?" Jan, who had been sitting listening added his thoughts.

"She has a good point Ernie, what if we set a trap for him? He will literally have around an hour time slot to strike, and after that, Tanya goes to ground again. He won't miss the chance."

"Let me think about it, I don't want you dead Tanya." She looked at him, "Please Ernie, we need this over, one way or another. I am sick to death of living in fear." Ernie made a decision.

"Fuck it, I would gamble on me getting him before he gets you so we need a plan. Jan, you and Tanya know the area and she's a township expert, so between you, you can find out the details of route and security planned. Tanya, let's go for it but not a word, even to Stephen. Jan and I will drive the route tomorrow." They all slept on it and Tanya was first on the scene at breakfast, having made a few calls.

"The funeral cortege starts at the clinic. There will be no police presence as the leaders have agreed a no police zone in the area. They think that they can ensure that it runs smoothly as

Sally was so well loved in the township, but they don't know what we know." Jan took out a map, prodding a stubby finger along the township roads.

"The rest of the route will be heavily guarded, the murderer is still out there and the police know he wants you. Unless he takes a shot from a sniper hide, the route through the township is his only chance. He doesn't care about an escape plan, a plane ticket has been purchased for Iran on Wednesday night so this is going to happen for sure. He then thinks that he will be able to stroll out of town without a hitch, the guy is deluded." Before he could say any more, Tanya stopped him.

"Okay, listen you two. I don't want to know the plan as I'll worry that he will see it in my eyes and body language. You do what you need to do and I will just be there, following the crowd."

At the same time that they were putting their plans in place, Lance Mitchell slowly drove the route himself, taking in every detail, every building, each rat run he could use. It would be impossible for him to disappear, a white man in the township was not a good hiding place, although creating havoc and fear could give him a head start. Killing her silently without anyone noticing was another option, with either a lethal injection, or a broken neck being possibilities.

Decision made, covering all bases, he devised a fluid plan depending on circumstances. He knew he would be walking into a trap without a doubt, he just needed to act first. Hit hard, run fast, and what would be would be, so long as she was dead. As he drove back to the hotel to prepare, he realised that to kill Tanya, he would need to kill Ernie first. He was cut from the same piece of stone as Lance, and would put duty first, stepping in front of the bullet, or whatever it took to succeed. They were two heavyweights slugging it out to the death. Ernie had nearly killed him twice but failed. Lance needed one opportunity and here it was.

He pulled up outside his hotel while gathering his plan together, he would not emerge from his room until the last minute as he could not afford to be compromised at this late stage. Police would be checking hotels and facial recognition and as he was booked under a false name, a different name to the flight booking, if they found him it would be pure luck. Shutting his door, he started to prepare his weapons.

Jan and Ernie drove the same streets, not knowing that Lance Mitchell had left less than an hour before. Their mission was different however, it was a defensive plan with a quick brutal counter-attack once Mitchell broke cover. Unknowingly, they chose the same attack location as Lance, a crossroads in the tracks which would produce a bottleneck of people with congestion and chaos, an ideal ambush location. The million dollar question for them would be how would they recognise the threat and eliminate it quickly before it became reality.

CHAPTER THIRTY-THREE

Wednesday

Tanya woke up with a knot in her stomach and she cuddled into Stephen in the small makeshift bed under the canvas roof. He pulled her close, his arm around her.

"Morning darling, you've had a restless night, I guess thoughts of the funeral today kept you awake?"

"Couldn't shake the thought that it could have been me. If I hadn't been in court with Bandile that afternoon he would have got me and Ellie."

"What did Ernie say about today, will it be safe?" Stephen asked, worried that she could be in more danger going to the funeral but understanding her need to be there.

"They are going to be with me all the way, it is starting at the clinic and moving through to the church. There will be thousands of township people there too as they all loved Sally."

"Just keep safe, I know that you are in good hands, but I would rather be there myself to protect you."

"I know you would but we agreed that the children couldn't be left alone after all they've been through, they need one of us with them," Tanya reminded him, glancing over to where they were all still asleep in their camp beds. "After today, I think we will have some closure, I can't see Mitchell hanging around waiting to be arrested and sent to court over here. They would kill him in prison, he's everything the black people hate about colonialism."

The children were still dozing in their beds as Tanya took an improvised shower in an adjoining tent. She walked back in drying her hair, to find Ellie lying in bed playing a game on her phone.

"Hey you, Mummy didn't say that you could play games on her phone, I need a battery for today. Be good for Daddy while I am gone this afternoon." She nodded and carried on playing while Tanya got dressed. Looking at her watch, she kissed Stephen before slipping out of the tent to meet Ernie and Jan. Entering their tent, she saw them both sitting hunched over a street map of the route, a number of yellow post-it notes were stuck around the table and a small marker board had a detailed plan drawn out on it. She took it all in before speaking to them.

"I am not going to lie, I am so scared. Promise me that you will keep me safe."

"We'll do our best," Ernie told her, "do you want the plan? Yesterday you didn't want to know but have you changed your mind?"

"No, just the fact there is a plan is comforting."

"We have given it our best assessment and I'm confident you will be fine. Go have breakfast with the family and come back here at two o'clock." Once she had left, the two men studied the map again, Ernie voicing a concern.

"There will hardly be any white faces on the street, so if we get into the parade we will be spotted straight away. He could take us out and kill Tanya at his leisure." Jan had thought of this.

"I have a guy from the township on my team, he will walk to the side of Tanya all the way. He will be in constant comms with me, and at any sign of danger will alert us and act. Mitchell will probably use some type of disguise to infiltrate the parade and I would guess that he will use the chaos of the crossroads to make his move. Any white guy must be treated as hostile during this phase." Ernie nodded.

"Yeah, I agree Jan. What's the plan for if he takes her hostage and goes on the move?"

"We follow and kill him, no negotiations."

"And Tanya?" Jan cocked his head to one side, "Shoot straight man, only when he's dead is the mission over, we can't risk him breaking away again."

Lance lay on his hotel bed with a grin on his face, it had been a long night but he had finally found the chink in the armour that would deliver Tanya to him and her death.

Stephen and the children sat around the small table in their tent, Tanya had tried her best to look reasonable for the funeral but she only had the clothes she had worn to court a few days before.

A white shirt, black knee length skirt and flat black shoes - higher heels were impractical on the roads in this area - completed the look as she faced them all.

"Okay you lot, I will be back as quick as I can, don't do anything stupid." Even as the words left her mouth, she felt the full irony of the statement. 'Don't do anything stupid,' like walking onto a street unarmed waiting for a murderer you wouldn't recognise to kill you. That was pretty dumb.

Getting into the car, she was surprised to see a younger black man sitting in the back seat and introduced herself. Jan turned around in the front seat.

"This is Zac, he will be walking near you at all times today. He is armed but will not communicate with you in any way unless he feels that he needs to do so. You will ignore him until that time. Do you understand?"

"Got it." Tanya gave him a nervous smile.

"We will stop half a mile from the clinic and you will get into a taxi driven by another of my men, acting as though he is your driver. Understand?"

"Yep." She took a sip from her water bottle.

"Once you are at the clinic leave everything to us."

"One question, what do I do if you all start shooting?"

"Get onto the ground and crawl for the cover of a shop. Do not leave the area."

"Okay."

"One last thing, check that you have Ernie's number in your phone, if anything happens and you become lost or confused phone Ernie." She opened her bag and rummaged around.

"Fuck it, my daughter took it this morning and hasn't put it back. Sorry." Jan opened the glove box.

"We have a spare, use this, the only number on it is Ernie's," and he passed a battered old phone back to her."

The car rumbled into a lay-by just outside the township where a large white minibus was waiting with the engine idling gently to keep the aircon flowing. Blue lettering at the front spelled out EXCITE, and Tanya guessed it was the name of the taxi company. She got out of the car and climbed through the sliding doors of the van, she was in character and didn't look back at Ernie who admired her confidence.

"HealthCare clinic in the township please," she said as she took a seat two rows back from the driver.

Lance was sitting in a shack watching the clinic when he saw the taxi pull up and noticed that Tanya was alone. He continued to watch the driver wondering if he would show too much caution to Tanya, giving himself up as a policeman or would he just drive away cursing the traffic on his way to another job. He took her money and didn't give her a second glance before pulling out and blasting the horn at a wayward motorbike. It seemed as though she was alone as Bandile came out from the clinic and hugged her, she smothering him as though one of her own before moving into the reception area out of the glare of the people beginning to mass outside.

Lance checked his clothing, all in black with a name badge spelling impressively on his chest.

Mark Adams. Senior Manager. Peninsula Funerals. His dark rimmed hat would go some way in covering his scar, particularly from a distance.

A large white van pulled up outside the parking area and the crowd grew silent, respecting the coffin in the back, as it sat motionless before turning and driving away at a slow walking pace. Hundreds followed, at first in silence and then breaking into song, songs from the Zulu tribes from across the ages. Soon they were all gone, Tanya in the middle of the swaying snake of people. They knew her, recognised her grief and consoled her while still singing the haunting rhythms. Bandile was locking the secure car park gate as one of the funeral directors walked towards him.

"I am really sorry, I need to place the book of condolence inside the reception area, will you allow me to do that please?" Bandile glanced at his name badge.

"Man, I'm trying to join my friends, be quick Mr Adams." He was enjoying his moment of power as he led the man across the carpark towards the clinic door and making a big deal of finding the key, he deactivated the alarm and swung the metal door open before flicking the foyer lights on. Stepping inside, a crushing blow knocked him onto the floor, Lance powering down upon him before dragging Bandile into an open treatment room and taking a roll of thick tape, strapping him securely into a chair. He tried to struggle but found he couldn't move in inch.

"There aren't any drugs or money here man, there is nothing to steal," he pleaded with him.

"I don't need to steal anything," Lance replied as he set up a gopro facing Bandile.

"I am not interested in hurting you my friend and I don't want money or drugs so stay here quietly and you will be safe. Don't do anything stupid because I will be watching you at all times." He tested the tape had done its job tightly binding his hands and feet before gagging him. Taking the pistol from his pocket, he put the end of the muzzle to the boy's chest." Don't die a hero son, it's not all it's made out to be," he warned him.

Holding up his phone, he took a last photo of a terrified Bandile and then leaving the clinic, he pulled the door closed before ensuring it would still open without a key. He wanted Tanya inside before he killed her, he wanted to see her face as she tried to rescue the boy, the look of terror as he killed her little friend first and then the end, one swift shot to her head and he would be free.

The funeral procession was winding its way through the streets approaching the crossroads, Zac half walking and half dancing with the throng but keeping an eagle eye out for all dangers, and seeing no white faces in the street at all. Ernie and

Jan worked their way unseen from door to door as they scanned the crowd, noticing the three white funeral workers at the head of the column which Ernie estimated to be a thousand strong. Tanya walked in the middle, so overcome with the sentiment from the people that she had lost concern for her own safety, and one funeral director walked at the rear, consoling people as they needed it. Zac listened to his ear piece as Ernie gave a commentary, ten metres before they reached the crossroads. "Another fifty waiting to join, no sign of Mitchell."

Hiding in plain sight at the rear, Lance Mitchell had seen Ernie and he took his phone out of his pocket and pushed send, waiting for Tanya to see his work. In the confusion that would follow, he would be the winner.

Ellie sat at the table playing a game on the phone when a message flashed onto the screen and she dropped it in horror. "Daddy, there is a boy in trouble on Mummy's phone," she cried out and Stephen picked it up, looking into the eyes of a frightened Bandile. The message read *'Come find me.'* Stephen could see the notices on the wall behind him, HIV, Drug abuse and Alcohol warnings and knew he was in the clinic. He looked up at Ellie.

"I need you three to stay here, I will ask Joe to look after you, I am just going to help Mummy and Bandile." Harry and Hector said nothing, too engrossed in their car game but Ellie said, "Be quick Daddy, that boy needs you to help him."

Rushing into Ernie's tent, he found Joe listening into the conversations between Jan, Zac and Ernie.

"So far so good Stephen," he said glancing up.

"I don't think so, look what has just arrived on Tanya's phone. He's trying to draw her out."

"Fucking lucky she didn't see it then, that's his plan A up shit creek," Joe said, about to warn his friends of the danger.

"I need to get over there and rescue him," Stephen said, snatching Joe's car keys from the table.

"Stephen, wait,", he yelled, "you could fuck up the operation." It was too late, Stephen was gone, unarmed and without a thought to his own safety. Joe got straight on the radio.

"Ernie, Jan, Stephen is on route to the clinic, Mitchell has a kid tied up there."

"Holy fuck, stop him or this could all go tits up."

"Sorry bud, he is halfway there."

Mitchell checked his phone to ensure the message had been sent, it had and it had been read. Why wasn't she moving? Why didn't she tell the people who were protecting her and why did she just keep on following the coffin? This didn't make sense. He checked the gopro footage, Bandile was still sitting on the chair, the tracks in the dust on his cheeks evidence that he had been crying. He pushed forward in the crowd to get closer to Tanya, willing her to move and return to the clinic. Ernie spotted him and spoke quietly into the radio. "There he is Jan he's the funeral director at the back, fifty metres behind Tanya, he is watching her. Eyes open Zac, something is going to happen.

Stephen pulled up outside the secure parking by the compound as a young guy came over.

"Bandile ain't around boss, I can look after your car out here if you want?"

"Can you get a gun?" Stephen asked him.

"I don't need a gun man, I just tell them to fuck off."

"No, I need a gun, Bandile is in trouble inside the clinic," Stephen explained urgently.

"Wait man." One minute later he reappeared, taking a gun from his waistband.

"This is going to cost you two hundred rand for two minutes okay?"

"Just give me the gun," Stephen ordered, "I will pay you when it's over." The man produced a massive machete from his tracksuit bottoms. "Fuck the money man, let's get him out of there."

The car park gates pushed open and there was a deafening silence around the area as everyone else was a mile away. "Let me go in first," suggested Stephen.

"You're the fucker with the gun, I ain't gunna go anywhere first, any blood spilt will be white, no offence man." They both pushed the clinic door and it swung open slowly, revealing the empty waiting area. They could hear the rustle of someone in the treatment room and Stephen kicked the door open revealing Bandile strapped to the chair. He turned to his accomplice.

"Use that knife to cut him free, let's get out of here quickly." He pulled the tape from Bandile's mouth.

"The white guy has gone to kill Tanya, get the boys out to protect her," Bandile yelled as he struggled free from the tape. The other man rushed out in a second.

"What do you mean, kill Tanya?" Stephen asked in panic.

"I ain't got time to explain, get out of the way man," he pushed past Stephen and ran out of the clinic.

Lance's phone vibrated, alerting him to activity back at the clinic. He checked again for Tanya and seeing that she was still there, he checked the screen and saw Stephen walking past the camera.

"Jan, Zak," Ernie's voice came over the radio, "something's happening, a large township gang are running towards the crowd. Stand by, stand by."

"Wait Ernie, don't engage," Zac instructed. The group of thirty black boys aging between fifteen and twenty joined the procession and surrounded Tanya. Bandile was at the head of the gang and approached her.

"Tanya, meet my friends, we are going to make sure that white bastard doesn't hurt you," he had a beaming smile on his face.

Lance saw the development and stepped towards the side of the street, not wanting these boys seeing and stabbing him, while Ernie walked to the other side, ensuring a good view of his target. Their eyes met through the crowd, now twenty deep and which had swelled to five thousand strong. Both men drew their guns, and angled for the best shot but it was impossible. Ernie tried to force his way through but the volume of people traffic made him lose sight of Mitchell.

"Ernie, he has gone ahead of you, get out of the crowd before he outflanks you," the radio barked.

There was a single shot and a body fell onto the path in front of him. It was Zac, one clean shot through his forehead, his gun falling gracefully onto the dirt as he collapsed. Seeing this, the gang tightened their perimeter around Tanya as people began to panic thinking that a gang attack was inevitable. Bandile jumped onto the hearse roof, he held out his arms as if in church, and people listened and stopped running. He had exerted the power than Tanya always believed he possessed. He had turned into a leader. "Calm, everyone calm," he called to them. They listened and continued with the procession, picking up and continuing the singing in one united voice. Tanya looked around hoping to see Ernie or Jan but it was too hectic to catch sight of anyone.

Suddenly Ernie caught sight of Lance again and pushing through the crowd, he got to within five metres before pulling out his gun. Before he could shoot, a large man saw him and smashed the gun out of his hand, yelling at him. "What the fuck are you doing man, my family are here, no weapons man." Lance spun around and seeing what was happening, he sprang towards Ernie and they grappled for a second before Ernie punched him in the temple sending him spinning to the floor. His pistol fell from his pocket and disappeared under the feet of thousands of marchers.

A gap appeared in the crowd and the two men squared off again, Lance throwing a brutal left hook before grabbing Ernie and smashing his face into the pavement. Blood spurted out from a three-inch gash which had opened up across his forehead. He kicked Ernie three more times in the face almost knocking him unconscious and as stars filled Ernie's head, he couldn't shift the confused feeling that the concussion had given him. He got slowly to one knee before another hard punch knocked him down again, and he lay there, his groggy senses considering his options. If he stayed down, he was dead, Jan couldn't see him and he probably didn't know what was going on.

"Jan, Jan," he tried calling but there was no reply, the radio broken during the struggle. Mitchell grabbed him from behind and put him into a strangle hold, his forearm cutting off Ernie's wind pipe.

Ernie smashed his head back and connected with Mitchell's nose splitting it almost in two. He let go and staggered backwards into a doorway. Ernie followed and punched him onto the floor. He looked around quickly, they were in an illegal drinking bar where soft African music filled the room as the punters watched on still drinking and smoking as though this were an everyday occurrence. Ernie thought how surreal this was but it was a second that he should have been more focused.

Grabbing a small knife from his waistband, Mitchell plunged it with all his energy into Ernie's stomach. It sank in effortlessly before Mitchell twisted the blade to give added venom to the blow.

He fell back looking almost disbelievingly at the small black handle that protruded from his abdomen. He felt no pain other than the thumping headache developing following his encounter with the pavement. Blood spurted out as he fought to stop the bleeding by clasping his blood-soaked hands around the hilt of the blade.

Mitchell had fallen too, his body exhausted and broken. Climbing onto his knees, he looked at Ernie where the pool of blood spilling onto the floor of the bar spelt its own story. Lance had thrown the winning punch. Managing a smile, he spat blood from his mouth onto the floor before rearranging his bloody clothing. He had all the time in the world to end this fight. It was over for Ernie, there would be more MI5 and MI6 to follow, but this battle belonged to Lance Mitchell.

Just as he was revelling in his victory, the bar door flew open with a crash and two small black children walked in, no more than twelve years old, dressed in Manchester United shirts and dirty blue jeans. They looked down at Ernie and without a word pulled out a gun and shot Mitchell twice in the chest. He died instantly, eyes glaring at the audacity of their actions. Heroin filled eyes glared back at him. The guys in the bar carried on drinking unmoved. What was another dead guy in the bar to this town? It was an everyday event.

Quickly and professionally, the kids emptied Mitchell's pockets of any valuables and taking off his watch, dragged his dead, bloody body into the street, the crowd now two hundred metres away and Tanya unaware of the battle behind her. As they passed him, Ernie heard one speak. "Normally white man, we would have killed you too but Bandile says that you must live," then they were gone, back out onto the street fist bumping with an expensive watch and five thousand rand in their pockets.

Drifting in and out of consciousness, he could hear the sounds of the ambulance approaching, louder and louder until the dust from its wheels kicked up into the bar room. Opening his eyes for one last time, he saw Jan talking to the paramedics as they fought to prevent him bleeding out. He had gone cold all over, he wanted to sleep and death was gathering pace. They were looking frantic, he could see their mouths moving but couldn't understand the words. Voices echoed around inside his head as he started to shut down but he wasn't afraid, he had done his duty. Tanya was alive and Mitchell lay dead in the street. Ernie had dealt with these injuries before on the battlefield and he knew that his chances were slim. He was slipping into the twilight zone and every second was critical. The ambulance crew put him on the stretcher and pushed him out through the door as the music started again and the door was pushed shut. Just another day in the Cape Town townships.

Still surrounded by Bandile and his gang, Tanya reached the small chapel where the crowd continued to chant as the coffin was carried through the door. They then fell silent in respect of one of the kindest people to have worked amongst them. Tanya made her way to the front row of chairs where Stephen and Jan joined her.

Jan leaned over and whispered in her ear. "It's done," before walking back out and into the street. It was bitter sweet for him. Lance was dead, but so was Zac and Ernie was fighting for his life in intensive care.

Later that evening, they all gathered back in Ernie's tent, the street map still lying on the table and Joe busy packing up his belongings, unsure if Ernie would survive the operation he was undergoing in the hope of repairing his stomach wounds.

"Where is Ernie?" Tanya asked. The look on Joe's face told her all she needed to know.

"Oh God, please tell me he is okay."

"We don't know, he is on the operating table now. He was stabbed in the stomach by Mitchell, we will know more later tonight. They are doing all they can."

"And Zac?"

"He died at the scene, Mitchell killed him."

"And what happened to that bastard?" Tanya asked in tears.

"He was killed by the local gang after a fight with Ernie. His body has been taken away and disposed of so no word of what happened Tanya. No word about Ernie or Zac either, it's how we operate."

She nodded, "What hospital is he in?"

"Tanya, I can't tell you where he is but I will give you an update when I know anything. Jan is there now. Anyway, we need to get you all sorted out, life in our camp isn't for you. I have arranged for you to move into a hotel while you plan your trip back to the UK. A cab will take you there in an hour, so you need to get your stuff together." Stephen and Tanya nodded in unison, both still in shock over what had happened.

"And listen you two, you did okay today, thank you," Joe told them as he stood up to leave. Tanya stood and hugged him, "Is there anything we can do for you?" He laughed, "No, I have your number if I am ever stuck in the UK."

CHAPTER THIRTY-FOUR

The Taxi pulled out of the camp and headed towards the city. As they sped past the township area which Tanya had grown to love, a distant flicker of smoke crept over the corrugated iron roofs, and groups gathered on the periphery of the roads discussing today's events in a matter of fact manner. She wondered if Bandile would be waiting at the clinic for her to return, and then her thoughts drifted to Ernie, Zac and Lance Mitchell and how so many families had been affected. The past years had taken their toll on the family with massive unseen scars forced upon Harry, Ellie and Hector but hopefully, being so young, they would heal with time. She reflected how Stephen's job had been the catalyst for so many deaths, the dirty businesses he had been involved in sucking them in before blowing out the bones.

Two weeks of sorting out Sally's belongings and tying up the details after the funeral passed by quickly, there had been no word from Jan and any efforts made by Tanya to contact him about Ernie came to nothing. The phone line was no longer working. She felt a little sad about walking away from everyone and everything but she knew that she would never again see the people who had helped shape her limited experience of Cape Town.

Making their way to the airport, it was impossible not to let her mind drift back to the feelings she'd had during the drive to Sally's on the day she arrived, not knowing if her marriage would survive.

They had all been on such a horrific journey, yet here they were, stronger than ever. What would the next phase of their life offer? She had liked Africa and despite the massive problems the country was facing, there had to be recovery. It needed brave people to stay and fight for these changes, maybe people like the Byfields and the idea bumped around inside her head.

The children sat colouring in the departure area, Stephen was reading a trashy novel he had picked up in the hotel foyer and Tanya was people watching, wondering how to pursuade Stephen to return to this bonkers country and work for virtually nothing as a charity worker. She heard a familiar voice ordering a coffee from the counter beside her seat and turning, she saw it was Jan. He ordered two cups and took them to a table behind where they were sitting. He hadn't seen her and seemed preoccupied as she slowly glanced over and saw where they were seated. Jan pushed the other cup across the table where Ernie picked it up and took a quick drink before looking directly at Tanya. Their eyes locked for a few seconds before he shook Jan's hand and left.

The flight to Bangkok had been called, he walked alone towards the gate, just carrying a small backpack and walking with a slight limp. Jan headed to another gate, the two never exchanging a backward glance. As Jan had said, this was just the life they lived. Tanya turned back to their table.

"Stephen, what if we didn't stay in the UK but came back here to live and work?"

"What about the children's education?"

"They loved the school they were in."

"What about work?"

"I found the work in the Townships both rewarding and interesting, you would love it Stephen."

"What do the children think?" They were all looking at him.

"Well, I did mention something to them back at the hotel and they seemed excited that we might come back." Stephen laughed. "Toss a coin on it, heads we stay, tails we don't." They gathered around his chair. He flicked the coin in the air, it spun up a few inches before he caught it and slapping it onto the back of his hand, he briefly studied the coin before looking at the family.

BOOKS IN THIS SERIES

The Byfield Trilogy

As a young prison governor, Stephen Byfield has seen just about every type of criminal there is. What he doesn't bank on is the personal vendettas some of them have towards him and his family. Throughout the trilogy, serial killers, notorious gangs and even his own government attempt to end the lives of himself and those closest to him....will good always prevail over evil?

High Risk

Can prison stop this serial killer?

When Stephen Byfield takes on the challenge of becoming the youngest governor of a high security prison, he fails to realise the depth of devious behaviour plotted amongst his own staff. He also faces the murderous intent from the psychopathic serial killer Martin Heard.

Stephen Byfield's loyal Deputy Governor, Terry Davies, a battle hardened former soldier, once again stands in the cross hairs of the enemy's sights, without realising the consequences to his own family. The true cost for adopting a cold blooded killers baby son years before will be paid in full as Heard's murderous rage will remain unsoothed until he can take back what is his.

Will Stephen Byfield keep this figure from all our worst nightmares locked inside his cell? Can Martin Heard's calculated mind plot a way out? If he does, don't dare blink as he may be coming for you!

Resolution

How far would you go to save your children?

As a hardened Prison Governor, Stephen Byfield thought that he had seen everything that life could throw his way. The moment he dismantled the Brood family's drug trafficking business into Her Majesty's Prisons, he saw a level of vengeance waged against him that he could never have foretold. Not in his worst nightmares, could he envisage what his children would face in the name of revenge.

No horrors are out of bounds for The Broods as the gang attack anything and everything that stands in their way. Can the Byfields ride the storm, or will this hurricane of violence destroy them for good? One thing is for sure, Stephen Byfield will die trying.

Between The Shadows

Does your family always come first?

Beaten and bloody in the depths of a cargo ship in a Tunisian port, Stephen Byfield wracks his brain to answer the questions fired at him from a murderous, mysterious English interrogator. "Where is the parcel?"

If Stephen had known, he would have spat the words out along with his broken teeth. If British Security forces knew its whereabouts they would have let his murder happen, if an early morning phone call from Whitehall to a waiting vehicle hidden in the dock yard hadn't ordered an intervention, you would be reading an obituary.

With breathtaking action swinging from the dusty, lawless roads and alleyways of a Cape Town township in South Africa, to the oak lined offices in government in London, England, revenge and menace are relentless and indiscriminate. Byfield is on the cusp of understanding this.

Selected by Whitehall to investigate corruption amongst high ranking officials takes Stephen into a world of murder and betrayal. A world in which the most senior Government officials are legitimate targets and collateral damage is nothing but dust on the polished wooden office floor.

What is contained within that sealed paper envelope that is so good people would die to own it? Stephen is about to find the answer, and with that secret will come misery as MI6 systematically try destroy him for the contents.

Framed and falsely imprisoned within a bleak Scottish prison, can Stephen save his family from the stalking assassin sent to kill them all, and blow the lid off the corruption happening at the highest levels?

BOOKS BY THIS AUTHOR

High Risk

Resolution

Between The Shadows

Coming In 2021, Vengeance

ACKNOWLEDGEMENT

The Byfields have been discussed so much within our household that they feel like part of our own family, and for this reason, I feel a sense of sadness that I have come to the end of writing this trilogy. Thanks go, as always, to my wife Jo, who as well as reading through the manuscript countless times, also spends hours listening to my thoughts on plots and characters.

Thanks also to Melissa who gives me her honest opinion for each book, along with constructive criticism on improving the flow and grammar, and a big thank you to Jacky who has lent us a laptop for the last year so that we can write and edit simultaneously.

Finally a big thank you to all of you who have bought my books, I hope you have enjoyed them, and if so, I would really appreciate a review on Amazon.

PRAISE FOR AUTHOR

'Utterly BRILLIANT!! I couldn't put it down. It's an absolute page turner from dusk till dawn (you won't go to sleep early, be warned, you'll be reading till the early hours). Not only is that a sign of a fantastic book, but also the feeling of bereavement you will experience when you have finished it.'

'This book is a real page turner, gritty and charged with some clever sub-plots. It definitely keeps you hooked and I will be very interested to see what the author writes next.'

'I discovered it was one of those 'ignore the dirty dishes in the sink' books. I was riveted to my Kindle and turned the pages as fast as I could. It's easy to tell the author worked in the prison system and he found that delicate balance between realism and excitement without overstepping the boundaries.'

- HIGH RISK

'This is the second book in the series. The first is brutal but sets the scene brilliantly for this one. A really great read that will keep you wanting turning the pages. A real insight into the life of a prison officer, prisoner and criminal.'

'Great follow up for first book in this series (High Risk). Lotsa sus-

pense, but a definite 'Resolution' — until the third book of the series comes out! Can't wait too long...'

- RESOLUTION

Printed in Poland
by Amazon Fulfillment
Poland Sp. z o.o., Wrocław